BOTH can be TRUE

BOTH
can be
TRUE

Jules Machias

Quill Tree Books
An Imprint of HarperCollins Publishers

Quill Tree Books is an imprint of HarperCollins Publishers.

Both Can Be True
Copyright © 2021 by Jules Machias
All rights reserved. Printed in the United States of America.
No part of this book may be used or reproduced in any manner
whatsoever without written permission except in the case of
brief quotations embodied in critical articles and reviews. For
information address HarperCollins Children's Books, a division of
HarperCollins Publishers, 195 Broadway, New York, NY 10007.
www.harpercollinschildrens.com

Library of Congress Control Number: 2021934341
ISBN 978-0-06-305389-2

21 22 23 24 25   PC/LSCH   10 9 8 7 6 5 4 3 2 1

First Edition

To my animal-loving, creative, funny, musical,
label-defying wild child: I love you with my whole
entire heart, plus my auxiliary heart.

1

Normcore

Ash

I can't put it off any longer: It's pick a gender or pee myself.

My best friend, Griffey, crashes out of the end-of-day crowd and bumps into me so hard I nearly pop. "Oof! Didn't see you there torturing yourself over a toilet choice!" He adjusts his wire-frame glasses and grins at me. "It's just peeing. It doesn't have to be an existential crisis."

"For you it doesn't." He's 100 percent dude at all times. Lucky him.

"Isn't that bathroom the main reason you moved to this district? Just use it, for Pete's sake." He nods at the pictureless door with the word NEUTRAL between the bathroom entrance with the girl symbol and the one with the guy symbol.

I shift my stance like it will help. "My *mom* moved us to this district. She doesn't have to worry about getting called a freak when she takes a leak." Or about being misgendered forever for using the "wrong" bathroom or peeing in the "wrong" position or—

"You need moral support? I'll go in the neutral too."

"That'd be weird. I think it's a single."

Griffey huffs a sigh, but he hasn't thought this through as obsessively as I have. If I go in GIRLS, I'll be "Ashley" forever to everyone in this jam-packed hallway who sees me, and if I go in BOYS, I'll be "Asher" forever. Either one means I can never go in the other one no matter what. I made two resolutions when I started at this school two weeks ago: I'd avoid the whole dumb conundrum of feeling weird about bathrooms by never peeing at school, and I'd always let people assume I'm an Ashley. People think it's cute for a girl to be a tomboy. But an Asher in a dress is a freak. So it's safer to let people guess *Ash* is short for *Ashley*.

But the girl mode I've been in for a couple months has started to shift back toward guy. This morning on the bus, I was trying to write down a melody I heard in a dream last night, and the light, airy feeling of it kept wiggling away. My awake mind ran off with the dream-sounds, changing them to a song with power and energy and a fast beat, and I realized I'm headed for that in-between state I hate. I've been tied up in knots over it all day and now I'm about to pop, so I gotta *pick* and picking is the *worst*—

"Ash, your eyes are turning yellow. You're gonna burst if you don't let it out."

I lean forward against the building pressure. "Why are bathrooms split by boys and girls? It makes way more sense to do pee versus poop—"

"Oh my god, *go*." Griffey shoves me toward the bathrooms.

I stumble toward NEUTRAL because it's closest, but then of course, of *course*, Daniel Sanders steps out of the middle-school herd of hormonally hijacked humans and stops at the fountain. I freeze in the river of kids and stare, distracted from my bladder by the spectacle of him: sad, dreamy Daniel. Daniel with the Hair and Eyes. Daniel who in our photography class on Friday shared a smile with me when our teacher made a Led Zeppelin joke no one else got. Daniel who probably thinks I'm Ashley-as-in-girl, not Asher-as-in-boy, definitely one or the other but not both or neither. Daniel

3

who'll be surprised if I pick the wrong bathroom or go in the NEUTRAL. Daniel who Griffey says kissed smart-gorgeous-graceful Fiona Jones at a party in June, so he's definitely, probably only into feminine girls like her—

Daniel who's making eye contact and smiling at me.

Something takes over—instinct, pointless crush, the threat of total humiliation if I don't make it to a toilet in two seconds. I veer away from NEUTRAL and duck into GIRLS, trip into a stall, undo my belt, pee and weep in frustration and relief.

Griffey makes a *ba-gawk* sound when I come out of the bathroom. Daniel's gone, thank the lord/dang it, and the hallway is leaking kids like my ancient beagle, Booper, oozes smells. "How about let's not make a thing of it," I tell Griff.

"I'm not *making a thing*. I'm just glad we won't be late to Rainbow Alliance because of your pee crisis."

I follow him down the hall. It sucks that I was just forced by my full bladder into declaring to Daniel that a part-time truth is a full-time one. I've been wearing boot-cut jeans and band T-shirts and Converse every day, trying to look as neutral as possible. The kids in my overstuffed classes are wrapped up in their own dramas

4

and seem too busy to notice me, which I am 100 percent fine with. We're all in the same boat, paddling through the chaos of seventh grade. Except everyone else's oar is pink or blue and mine's purple with glittery flecks of angsty confusion on it. "I just don't want to make a declaration by peeing," I say. "Why can't I be plain Ash?"

"*Plain* Ash? Please." Griff dodges a frantic boy careening toward the front doors. "I hoped when you said you were moving here that you'd be you out loud." He plucks at my Imagine Dragons T-shirt. "Instead you're boring me to death with this normcore Walmart crap."

"Did you get the spiky haircut you've wanted for six months? Have you worked up the guts to wear that hot pink jacket you bought? Did you ask Jacob to the fall dance yet?"

He laughs as if my barbs don't sting, and just like that, just like always, I forgive him. He's been my best friend since we met in kindergarten at Bailey Elementary. We were together constantly until he moved here to Oakmont during my first trip through sixth grade. Which is part of the reason I had to do sixth grade round two, 'cause Griffey left at the same time my appendix went kablooey and I missed a month of school and my parents split. It's hard to focus on fractions and adverbs when your whole life comes apart all at once.

Lately it feels like that's happening again. New apartment, new school, a chance to be Ash 2.0 after Ash 1.0 crashed and burned at Bailey Middle. It's all so intimidating, and now I have to go to this Rainbow Alliance meeting with Griff and I'm having second (and third and fourth and fifty-seventh) thoughts because I don't want to stand out. At all. In any way.

"Ash. Breathe." Griffey pulls me into a side hug as we walk. "If any of the big scary gays try to eat you, I'll go mama bear on them."

I take a deep breath and try to refocus. To be grateful for what's good in my life, like Mom says I should do when I'm stressed. I'm lucky to have Griffey. I'm so glad we're at the same school again, even though he's in eighth grade and I'm in seventh since I flunked sixth. But I'm dependent on him to fill the entire friendship hole in my life. Sucking up my fears and going to Rainbow Alliance with him is the perfect chance to make more friends. Like Mom's said eleventy billion times since Griff "casually" mentioned it in front of her, because he knew if *she* knew about it, I wouldn't be able to weasel out.

It's just that Griffey's safe. He likes the music I write and listen to. We share a sense of humor. He *gets* me, no matter what gender I am on a given day. When people don't get me . . . well, I'm gun-shy for a reason. It's not like there's a guarantee that just because it's called Rainbow Alliance, they'll be cool. One of the worst bullies at my old school was a super-girly lesbian who insisted that trans women aren't real women and that trans guys are just girls cross-dressing to smash the patriarchy from the inside. Which, *no.*

Griffey makes a quick pit stop to tie his shoe. While he's hunched over, for a flash of a second, I'm back at Bailey Middle: Jackson Burgess twisting my Avicii shirt and blocking my locker, hissing *No flip-flop freaks allowed.* Hallway kids laughing. Alana Meyers sneering, *Look, it's so embarrassed. It's turning purple like its hair.* Madison Blevins saying, *It should be embarrassed. That haircut is trash.*

Griffey grabs my hand and plows through the mass of kids like he thinks I'm gonna bolt. It feels like we're swimming upstream. I keep my eyes on the back of his strawberry-blond head and apologize to everyone we bump. When we finally make it to the classroom, my palm is so sweaty Griff has to wipe his hand on his plaid button-down.

Someone is taping a poster to the door with their back to us. The poster has a bunch of colorful flags surrounding *WELCOME/BIENVENIDO* written in big rainbow letters.

"See?" Griffey points at a pink-white-purple-black-blue flag. "There's one for you."

I don't even know what those colors mean. The kid taping the poster turns around.

"Hey, Sam," Griffey says. "This is my best friend, Ash."

"¿Cómo estás?" Sam holds the poster against the door with an elbow and reaches to shake my hand. "Thanks for coming."

"Hola. I mean you're welcome. I mean thanks for—um, having me." Great, off to a graceful start. I search Sam's smiling face for signs of makeup or a hint of facial hair, but find neither. Just friendliness and purple-framed glasses and a curious expression.

"Come on." Griffey tugs me into the room. There are twelve or so kids clustered in groups. Griffey bee-lines for the back corner where a tall, skinny Black guy is talking to a short white girl with a high ponytail and a lip piercing. "Ta-da!" Griffey says, "You each owe me five bucks." He holds his hands out like he's presenting me.

The guy pulls me into a hug I'm unprepared for. "You exist! We were starting to wonder." He pushes me back, holding both my shoulders, and spins me in a circle. "Griffey, you were right. I can't tell either."

Alarm rises in me. "Can't tell what?" Did Griff tell them I switch genders? I'm gonna straight-up strangle him if he did—

"If 'cute' or 'adorable' is a better word for you," he says. "Alyssa, what do you think?"

Alyssa tears the top off a box of jawbreakers and gives me a casual once-over. "Cute. Not my type, though." She pops a jawbreaker in her mouth.

I must look crushed, because she laughs. "Don't sweat it. I got a thing for girls built like tanks." She shows me her phone background, a photo of her hugging a blonde girl who is, in fact, built like a tank. "Trish. She'll be here later."

I sit at a desk and cross my legs one way, then the other. *Cute* and *adorable* make me feel like I'm five years old. "Um, what's your name?" I ask the guy.

"Henry. And this is Alyssa, and the Filipino chick in the pink shirt is Esme . . ." He points around the room and names everyone, but my eyes keep snapping back to Sam in the front corner, talking in a mix of Spanish and English to a curvy red-haired girl wearing purple jeans and a black blazer. More kids keep coming in. I start to think the *Rainbow* in *Rainbow Alliance* means more

9

than just people on the LGBTQIA+ spectrum. Oakmont's way more diverse than Bailey Middle, and RA seems to contain a sampling of everyone. It's refreshing after mostly white Bailey.

Mr. Lockhart, the guy who runs the club, is a tall, skinny white dude with unruly Einstein hair, a nose like an eagle's beak, and a wide, friendly smile. He starts by saying there are some new folks and we should introduce ourselves with our name, grade, the pronouns we want to use in this room today if pronouns are important to us, and anything we'd like to share.

While everyone's moving desks into a circle, I quietly freak out. No one but Griff, Mom, and my former friend Camille asks what pronouns I prefer. They just assume, or call me "it." And here's this guy asking our preference. And "in this room," which means he gets that some spaces are safe and some aren't. And "today," which means he gets that . . . it can change.

He understands that.

I trip over the desk I'm shoving. I look across the room at Sam sliding into a desk next to the girl in the purple jeans.

We get situated and start. Henry and Alyssa go first (Henry's a he, Alyssa is a she, they're both eighth graders), then Griffey, then I tell everyone I'm Ash and in seventh, since I'm too intimidated to say anything else. The girl Henry pointed out introduces herself as Esme and says she goes by she/her at school and is pre-HRT MTF, but I'm not sure what that means. Sam is an eighth grader like Griff and claims not to care about pronouns. Sam's friend's name is Mara, in seventh, and is going by he/him today. The rest of the kids use the pronouns I expect from their appearances.

"Great," Mr. Lockhart says when we're finished. "Last time I asked you to think about ideas for decorating our booth in the gym for the fall dance in a few weeks, so let's start with those." He uncaps a marker. "Just shout stuff out."

"A rainbow balloon arch for photos," Henry says.

Alyssa says they should give away rainbow light sticks. Griffey suggests a punch bowl full of Sprite with rainbow ice cubes. Sam says the dance is the same day as National Coming Out Day and it could be a great chance for anyone who wants to come out publicly to do it, maybe with a premade poster they could hold up under the rainbow-balloon photo arch.

Griffey wiggles his eyebrows at me. "How's *that* for an opportunity?"

I ignore him and play imaginary piano scales on my legs under the desk, trying to settle my nerves.

There's so much conversation, and I'm missing most of it, because I can't stop staring at the kids around me. Trying to figure out Sam. How Mara can so casually proclaim to go by he/him with those curves. What the heck all those letters Esme said might mean.

Griffey jabs me. "Stop staring."

I snap my eyes to Mr. Lockhart, my face burning. I'm doing the exact thing I hate when people do it to me. All the arguments I imagined yelling at kids at my old school about not assuming my gender crowd my mind. But now they're aimed at me.

It does not feel comfortable.

I doodle the shape of Mr. Lockhart's croaky vocal fry to distract myself. Then I draw the triangular scuff-shuffle of my shoe scraping the tile floor. Then I draw Griffey's explosive sneeze that looks like a bomb going off, and then I'm nowhere, lost in sounds and lines, far away from bathrooms and genders and uncertainty.

Griffey squeezes my arm and I blink back. It looks like we're finished. I've filled the bottom of my notebook page with a sketch of the dream-song I was trying to write down this morning. Stick figures are breakdancing on top of it. It's so thick and angled and *guy* I can barely look at it.

I rip out the page and crumple it. My eyes drift again to Sam. Their voice is in that middle range where mine is, with a texture and color like sun-faded purple construction paper. Their black shirt, black jeans, black canvas shoes, and wire-frame glasses could go either way. Like the carefully neutral outfits I've been wearing.

It's an itch in my brain I can't scratch. A box I can't check off. Next to a box labeled *Mara* that keeps changing from pink to blue and back again, and two boxes labeled *Yes* and *No* under a question Mom asked me a while ago: *Does your soul have a gender?*

When the meeting is over, I follow Griff to the front of the school where the activity buses line up. "You okay?" Griffey asks. "You're quiet."

"Fine. Um, do you know what . . ." I bite back the question. I can't ask if he knows what Sam really is. It's the wrongest thing I can ask. It's fully disrespectful. Not to mention "what Sam really is" is a flawed concept to start with, which I *totally freaking know*, despite my dad telling me that gender fluid and nonbinary aren't real identities.

So why can't I stop thinking about it? What if puberty hits me like a freight train and I don't look androgynous anymore, like Mara doesn't? What if I still feel undecided after that? How can Mara be so casual, like this stuff isn't terrifying?

"Do I know what?" Griffey asks.

I blink back to the line of buses. "Um, Esme said a bunch of letters. Pre . . . something."

"Pre-HRT MTF. That's pre–hormone replacement therapy male to female. She's trans. Hasn't started physically transitioning yet."

"Oh. Right."

"Which doesn't make her any less of a girl."

"I know." I say it so fast it sounds defensive. As if I don't know.

But I do.

"I'm glad you came with me." Griffey wraps me in one of his rib-cracker hugs, then punches my arm. "Ladies first," he smirks. He gestures for me to get on the bus before him.

We slide into a seat at the back. Griff sticks his left earbud in my left ear and the right one in his right ear. He opens TikTok and we laugh at stupid videos the whole ride while my brain does its acrobatic best to figure out where I fit with my gender that never holds still.

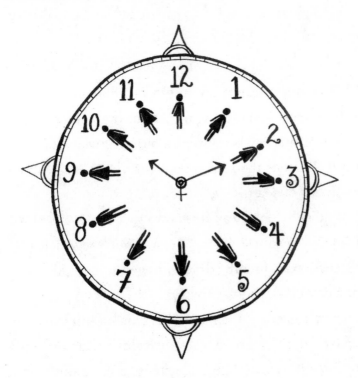

2

Dog Smuggler

Daniel

Tuesday afternoon, I'm coaxing a Siamese cat out of a dryer and kicking myself for the millionth time for forgetting my best friend's birthday when Tina the vet tech opens the kennel door carrying a black plastic trash bag of death.

I quickly look away from the bag. "Here, Houdini," I say in my softest voice. "Tuna flavor, mega delish." I extend a treat into the dryer's dinged-up innards where he's crouched, spooked by Roxy the husky's loud barking ten feet away. "Come out, little kit-kat. I'll make sure you're safe." I keep up a steady, calm stream of words, trying not to hear Tina's footsteps as she walks toward the Freezer of Doom to put in the euthanized pet she's carrying. When I started volunteering at the kennel a month ago, seeing anyone open the death freezer sent me to the bathroom in tears. Now whenever one of the vet techs brings down a bag from Dr. Snyder's office upstairs, I go find the most sad or scared kennel resident and give them a hug or a snuggle to distract myself.

I guess today Houdini's my snuggle buddy, if I can get the scaredy-cat out of the dryer. I'm so focused on him that it takes a minute to realize Tina has passed the freezer and her footsteps have stopped at room C, the cages we only use when the rest of the kennel is full. I crane my neck to try to see what she's doing.

Houdini finally takes the treat from my hand and jumps out of the dryer. I scoop him up and return him to the relative silence of the cat room he escaped. "Guess we know why your name's Houdini," I tell him. "Bit off more than you could chew out here, didn't you? All those doggos doing big, loud borks."

Houdini puts his paws on my chest and rubs his head on my jaw, all affection now that he feels safe again. I scratch his chin, then carefully peel him off me and put him back in his cage, double-checking that the latch is fastened all the way.

I leave the cat room and glance down the hall. The door

to room C is closed. I tiptoe over and lean my head against it. It's hard to hear over Roxy, but between the barks, Tina is making the quiet murmuring sound she uses to calm an upset dog. I knock softly and the murmur stops. There's silence for a moment, and then the door opens.

Tina's lips are pressed together. I wait for her to explain, but she leans to look around me. I turn to see what she's looking at. There's nothing. "Uh . . . what are you doing?" I ask.

She studies my face like she's trying to decide if she can trust an eighth-grade kid. Her dark eyes are bright like always in her warm brown face, as if they've sucked in specks of sunlight. But surrounding that, in the smile lines at the corners of her eyes and mouth, is worry and sadness. "You good at keeping your mouth shut?" she asks in her gravelly smoker's voice.

"I'm good at forgetting important stuff." Like Cole's birthday. Like the fact that guys who are almost fourteen should never cry in public.

"Guess that'll do." Tina steps aside to let me in. When she pulls the door shut behind us, Roxy's barking drops by thirty decibels. In the last cage, a ball of orange fur with tiny black feet twitches on a towel. "Chewbarka. Spared from death by a botched euth and lucky timing."

I walk over and touch the sleeping Pomeranian's fur. "Dr. Snyder used the wrong drug?"

"Nope. He gave her the Telazol, the injection that makes them fall asleep. Then he got called to sew up a mutt who'd been mauled by a dalmatian. He told me to do the second injection. The lethal one." A muscle in her jaw moves like she's grinding her teeth. "I didn't."

I've never seen Tina mad, but I guess this is what it looks like. "Won't you get in trouble?"

"Who kills their little dog just 'cause she's going senile?" Tina touches her mouth like she's smoking, then realizes she's not holding a cigarette. She kneels and runs her hands through Chewbarka's fur. The dog twitches again and opens her cloudy black eyes halfway. "You're okay, girly," Tina croons. "You're just a little loopy. Gonna be real thirsty soon."

"Why thirsty?" My voice cracks and I clear my throat.

"From the Telazol. The guy who brought her in left when Doc Snyder did, soon as she was asleep." She rubs Chewbarka's ears. "I've wanted to stop so many euths. People put their pets to sleep for the worst reasons. A dog's getting old and needs meds, or is peeing in the house because they're incontinent, or a kid turns out to be allergic." Her eyes are all anger and sadness. "Doc's in charge, though. I'm just the assistant. But today, for the first time, *I* was in charge. So I skipped the barbiturate, stuck her in the death sack, and brought her down."

I cover my mouth to keep in the giddy laugh. I've liked Tina since I started coming here, and now I know exactly why: She's like me. Her heart's too big. It's impractical and causes problems. As my twin brother, Mitchell, would sneer, it makes you an *overly emotional train wreck who cares too much about dumb stuff.* "You just walked past Doc Snyder with her like no big deal?" I love the thought of her fooling him. He's so crotchety and intimidating that the idea of sneaking anything past him is very, very satisfying.

"Yep. That's the part where you keep your mouth shut. Case it ain't obvious."

"Yeah, I've got it." Dr. Snyder was surprised when I stopped here on my way home from school last month to ask if I could volunteer to walk the dogs at the kennel. *You want to work for free?* he'd asked. *Why the blazes would you do that?*

I just shrugged and told him I liked dogs. Which is the understatement of the year, and left out the sob story about my border collie, Frankie, getting sick and dying in July and my mom refusing to get another dog because she's already *stretched too thin* and *can't take on one more thing*. Not to mention the part where I needed something to do after school since I'd always hung out with Cole before, and if I spent one more afternoon alone in my room avoiding Mitchell and looking at my dad's old Nikon and feeling wrecked, I was going to lose my noodle for good.

Chewbarka makes a feeble coughing sound. Tina leans down and touches her forehead to the dog's. "You're okay, little one." She kneads the back of Chewbarka's neck, which must feel good because Chewbarka nestles into Tina's palm even though her eyes are still mostly closed.

"What are you going to do with her? Just take her home after your shift?" I ask.

"Yep. My house has been dog-free for too long. It's getting lonely."

"I know that feel." My house has been dog-free since Frankie died, and it makes everything seem empty. But I can't imagine what Mom or Mitchell would say if I tried to rescue a dog like Tina's doing. They already think I'm the world's biggest softie, and they constantly tell me in big and small ways to stop being so sensitive. Last week Mom said that everyone has feelings and I need to get better at managing mine. Which, thanks, I know.

21

"Tina . . . would it be weird if I said you're my hero?"

She smiles as she braces her hands on her thighs and stands up, both knees cracking. "I gotta go upstairs to help with that dog that got attacked. You gonna be here awhile?"

"Till six." That's when the office closes and I'm supposed to leave, since I'm not on the payroll and don't have a key to lock up behind me.

"You mind checking her every ten minutes or so?"

A fizzy bubble of joy fills me. I couldn't save Frankie, but I can help Tina save this dog. And Mom doesn't even need to know. "Of course."

"Give her as much water as she'll drink. And keep the room C door shut in case anybody else comes down." Tina heads for the door that leads to the outside stairs she came down with Chewbarka in the bag. The building's old and it's the only way to get between the office upstairs and the kennel down here. "I'll get her soon as Doc leaves at six."

I nod to show I've got it, just like a real employee instead of a thirteen-year-old volunteer.

I'm usually focused on the dogs while they're outside in the gravel yard, offering different toys till I find one they like and playing until they get bored, but today, all

I can think about is that little Pomeranian waking up confused and thirsty in a strange place, abandoned by someone she probably loves. Every time I check on her, she seems a little more awake, but she won't drink water, just lays on the towel blinking and turning her head like she's looking for something.

After I finish with the last of the boarders, I sit in room C, pull Chewbarka into my lap, and curl up with her, rubbing her soft ears as she blinks and works her tongue around in her mouth. Her heartbeat is a warm flutter against my stomach. "Good girl," I murmur in her ear. I touch my forehead to hers like Tina did, telling her with my thoughts that she's wanted, she's loved, even if it's not by the man who brought her in. "Tina will be a good mom for you," I say. "Yes, she will. You're a lucky pup to get to live with Tina."

Chewbarka relaxes in my arms. After a while, I stand her in front of the water dish. She takes a big drink, wobbling on her feet. I keep my hands at her sides in case she starts to fall. She pees while she's drinking like she's not aware she's doing it. When she's finished, I settle her back on the towel and clean up the pee. I try to brush her orange hairs off my black T-shirt, but they're stuck good. In my photography class the other day, the new kid, Ash, was doing the same thing with the three colors of fur on her shirt. I asked how many pets she has. She said just one, a beagle, but that his epic farts counted for at least three dogs. Then she blushed and pretended to be interested in her phone.

I don't know why I keep thinking about her hazel eyes and pale skin and sandy hair with purple streaks. She was wearing a Pink Floyd shirt today. I used to listen to Pink Floyd with Dad.

I finish picking the hair off my shirt and stand up. I've walked all the dogs, but I should keep an eye on Chewbarka till Tina's shift is over in half an hour. I take Roxy the husky back outside and we play with a tennis ball. Then I walk a couple other dogs again, then I cuddle with a tired black Lab with a gray muzzle for a while, and then it's 6:02.

I hang out in the kennel office and read the logbook while I wait. It's full of feeding notes for the boarders, which I don't have to worry about since I don't feed the dogs. I check my phone: 6:07.

I tap my fingers on the logbook. I flip its pages and set it neatly in the center of the desk. At 6:15, it occurs to me that maybe it's taking longer than anticipated to fix up the dog who was attacked. I bite my knuckles, nervous that Dr. Snyder will ask why I'm here so late and I won't have an answer. Maybe I could tell him I'm waiting for Tina to come down and lock the door after I leave. I don't usually wait, though, so that might be weird.

I finally drum up some guts and climb the outside steps. The late-September air is still warm and humid. The overgrown field beyond the kennel's gravel parking lot is backlit by the low evening sun, glowing and lovely.

Mitchell complains Ohio is boring, but he never stops to really *look* at it.

The office lights are off and the surgery room is dark. Gavin, the college freshman who answers the phones in the afternoons, is the only one around, putting a file away. He spots me and jumps. "Jeebus, kid! Make some noise or something."

"I'm sorry. Just looking for Tina. Is she still here?"

"Left early. Her daughter was in a bad car wreck in Iowa or Illinois or someplace."

Uh-oh. "That's awful."

Gavin glances at Dr. Snyder's closed door. "Doc was cold as ice. Soon as she left, crying, he was grumbling that getting someone to cover her shifts will be a huge pain in his butt." Gavin shakes his head. "Some people have no sympathy. It's gross."

"Yeah," I say, my mind churning. "I guess not." My phone pings with a text.

"You need something, or what? I'm getting ready to leave."

"Oh. Uh, no. I just wanted to ask Tina—um, about one of the dogs."

Gavin's eyes brighten. "Anything I can help with?" Tina told me last week he wants to be a vet, that he's always super interested in the animals who visit Dr. Snyder.

"No, it was just about, um, whether she fed one." The lie feels flimsy. "It's no big deal. I'll go back down and make sure everything's good."

"Cool, then I'll lock this door behind you." He gestures at the back door I just came in. "Not trying to be rude, just, you know. I forgot once and the night-shift lady found it unlocked and told the doc. He almost fired me."

"Oh. Right. Sure." I go out the door and he locks it behind me. I turn and look through the window. He gives me a wave, then heads toward the front door through the dark office.

I walk down the steps, glad Gavin was only worried about his door-locking task and not Tina's. I check my phone. The text was from Mom. **Home soon? I've got dinner going.**

Sorry, kennel is packed, I write. I hate lying, but

26

sometimes . . . it's necessary. **A cat escaped and every-thing turned into chaos. Still trying to help settle things down.**

I'll cover your plate, Mom writes. **Let me know when you're on your way home. I'll come get you if you're there after dark.**

At the sound of the opening kennel door, Roxy starts barking again, which sets off the schnauzer next to her and the mutt next to the schnauzer and a poodle a few cages over. I slip into room C and pick Chewbarka up. She smells like pee. I hug her and bury my nose in the back of her neck.

I can't just leave her. The night worker will find her here with no tags or info, and she'll ask what's up and the vet will find out Tina lied and he'll fire Tina and put Chewbarka to sleep.

I can't let that happen.

But I can't take her home. Mom was telling me all summer to stop moping, to get up and do something productive. I hoped volunteering at the kennel would fix that, but now she says I come home all sad because I want a dog. She's not wrong, but still. Bringing a dog home would *not* improve relations. And Mitchell would give me no end of grief for being a sucker for a hopeless case like Chewbarka. Cole doesn't talk to me anymore, but if he found out, he'd roll his eyes and sigh.

Last year, when things were still good between us, he would've wanted to help. But since the spring, when his voice dropped and he grew three inches and started hanging around Erin Rogers, he's become . . . different. Tougher. Better at hiding how he feels, unless it's anger at me. For forgetting his birthday. For kissing Fiona Jones, the girl he and Mitchell both liked, at a spin-the-bottle game at his end-of-the-year party in June.

I pace in the tiny room, holding Chewbarka to my chest. "It's okay," I tell her, or maybe I'm saying it to myself. "You're okay. You're okay." Even if I take her home and lie that I found her as a stray, Mom's been insistent that we are *not* getting another dog under *any* circumstances. She'd take Chewbarka to the pound, and Chewbarka's so old that no one would adopt her and they'd put her to sleep within a week. Dad's a dog lover like me, but I can't plead my case with him because he moved out in August so his commute would be shorter. Me and Mitchell know that's a lie, though, since he only moved twelve miles away and he's supposed to come home on the weekends but mostly hasn't and this is really a trial separation with Mom. I can't ask Mitchell to help because he's also mad that I kissed Fiona. I can't ask Cole because . . . well.

There's got to be a solution. One I can implement alone.

Maybe . . . maybe the tent's still in the garage from when we were a happy family and went on camping trips. I could keep her in the tent.

But where?

My mind roves over our neighborhood: the gas station at its entrance, then the condo complex, then the houses. There's a scraggly patch of woods between the back of the gas station and the start of the condos. It's not big, maybe the size of a block, and it's mostly honeysuckle so thick you can't easily walk through it. But maybe there's room to hide a tent. If I can sneak home and get the tent, I could put it up in the woods and keep Chewbarka there till Tina comes back. Or at least till I can get Tina's number and call her to ask what I should do.

It's almost October, but not cold out yet, so I won't have to worry about that. But the other logistics . . . I'd have to lie to Mom, which is a big risk because I suck at lying and sometimes cry and give myself away. I'd have to hide Chewbarka in the shed tonight when I get home and hope she stays quiet till I can sneak out after Mom goes to bed and attempt to put up the tent in the woods in the dark. Then if all *that* worked out, I'd have to sneak out every morning before Mom gets up and let Chewbarka out of the tent to pee. I'd have to go straight to the tent after school and sneak there again after bedtime, and probably spend some time playing with her because she'd be bored from being alone all day. And how will I even get her home tonight? Two miles is a long way to walk a bike while carrying a Pomeranian. I don't have a leash or collar for her. And if I did take her and keep her in the tent, I'd have to find a way to feed her. I could maybe scoop some chow out of the kennel's bin, but that's stealing. . . .

There's no way. Mom would be furious if she found out what I was trying to do. I'd never hear the end of it from Mitchell. I should put Chewbarka back in the cage. Walk away. Forget I saw anything.

I'm setting her back on her towel with a heavy heart when I hear tires on the gravel parking lot. The night kennel worker must be here. I'm always gone long before now, so I've never met her. I don't know if she's nice, if she'd understand about this, if she'd rat Tina out.

Chewbarka licks my wrist. Her tongue is rough and dry like she's thirsty again. I look at her graying face and cloudy eyes.

She'll be killed if I leave her here.

The kennel door opens. I pull room C's door closed and turn off the light. I listen as the night worker plods down the hall to the office. The chair creaks when she sits in it.

Ten agonizing minutes later, she finally gets up and fills the mop bucket in the laundry room. I listen to her take it to room A, then put the first dog into an empty cage so she can clean the floor in there.

I tuck Chewbarka under my arm and grab a leash off the hook by the door. There's an empty cloth shopping bag that held a kennel resident's toys. I take the bag and slip outside. I'll return it tomorrow.

As quickly as I can, which is not quickly because I'm holding a loopy Pomeranian, I unlock my bike from the tall fence around the dog-walking yard. I slide my arm through the short handles of the shopping bag, give it a yank to make sure it's sturdy enough to hold Chewbarka, and slip her in.

This is going to be a disaster. I don't know why I'm doing this. Why am I doing this? Mom will lose her mind if she finds out.

I text her, my fingers shaking with adrenaline: **On my way**. I get the bike free and push it clumsily across the gravel parking lot with one hand. Just as I go around the corner of the building, I hear the night worker open the kennel door to let a dog outside.

We're safe. Barely.

But the real trouble is about to begin.

3

Klutzy Nincompoop

Ash

In photography class on Friday, which has kids from all three grades since it's an elective, Daniel seems exhausted. He's looked more and more wiped out all week. Like something's really wearing on him. He takes out his folder and notebook at the table he and I share with Fiona Jones, the tall Black eighth-grade girl Griff said Daniel kissed, and Braden, an obnoxious sixth grader with a non-ironic blond mullet who likes to talk like he's an announcer at a monster truck show. Fiona asks Daniel if he stayed up too late playing *Super Smash* with Mitchell again.

"Yep, I dominated," he says unconvincingly. He

knocks his folder to the floor with his elbow. When he leans down to get it, he bumps his head on the table.

Fiona laughs her perfect, dainty laugh girl-me would die to have. Her cheekbones are so defined when she's smiling. "You're a hot mess. You good?"

"I'll let you know when I figure it out." Daniel rubs his eyes and starts to yawn, then notices me watching. He cuts it off and clears his throat.

I quickly look down at the Billie Eilish song measures I've been doodling to try to hang on to my fading femininity. I hate it when people stare at me too. I'm always worried they're trying to figure out if I'm a boy or a girl. Even though Mom tells me all the time the puberty blockers I'm on till I "figure things out" are working just fine. That no one can tell what's under my clothes, and even if they could it's none of their ding-dang business.

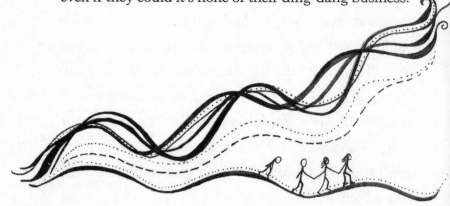

Our teacher, Ms. Bernstein, is an older white lady with pin-straight dark hair and unfortunate bangs. She tells us we have two tasks today: to learn about an assignment due next week and to use the darkroom to load photo paper into the oatmeal-box pinhole cameras we made yesterday. "The rule of thirds is a way of composing a photo so the most interesting parts align with the intersections of four lines." She flips on the projector, which displays a rectangular grid. "It's easiest to see in landscape photography. The horizon falls along one of the two horizontal lines. A point of interest, like a tree or a mountain or a rock formation, falls along one of the two vertical lines." She shows us photos cropped with the horizon line and point of interest in the center, and cropped with them along the lines. The rule-of-thirds photos look so much more interesting, even though they're of the exact same thing.

I glance at Daniel, who's looking at the screen like he already gets it. Ms. Bernstein tells us to take out our phones.

"That's a first," Braden laughs. "Y'all always tell us to put them away."

"For this assignment, you'll use your phone camera. I want you to experiment with composition without worrying yet about the mechanics of the single-lens reflex cameras we'll use later on." Ms. Bernstein shows a slide with instructions for getting to the camera settings on iPhones and Androids. "Almost all phones have the option to overlay grid lines. Follow these instructions to turn them on."

Everyone does except Daniel. Fiona peeks over his shoulder. "Of course you already had them on, photo geek."

"My dad turned them on," Daniel mumbles around a suppressed yawn.

"Your assignment, due next Friday, is to make a photo that has two subjects placed at the intersections created by your grid lines. Experiment with placement. See what feels right. As for the content, choose two objects that are personally significant to you and place them on a plain background. That could be a towel, a stretch of pavement, a poster board, whatever. As long as it's all the same color and texture and it fills the frame."

Braden snickers under his breath. "How about a couple hundred-dollar bills on my left butt cheek?"

Fiona shoots him a look like *you're disgusting*.

"Any questions?" Ms. Bernstein asks.

A kid at table four raises her hand. "Why'd you say

'make a photo' instead of 'take a photo'?"

Fiona pokes Daniel. "You know."

"Daniel, what do you think?" Ms. Bernstein says.

"Um. You make a photo when you choose what goes in the frame and like . . . compose it. I mean put the subject there on purpose. Instead of taking a photo, where you see something interesting and snap a shot of it."

Ms. Bernstein smiles. "Correct. When you use your pinhole cameras next week, you'll *take* a photo. When you do your rule-of-thirds assignment, you'll *make* a photo. Each of you will present your rule-of-thirds photo to the class next Friday." She claps her hands. "On to loading the pinhole cameras. Make *sure* when you put the paper in, the shiny side is *toward* the hole you poked in the box." She says it like a thousand students over the years have done it wrong. "Table one, go on into the darkroom. Table two, when someone comes out, one of you can go in. We'll go around the room that way. Four kids max in there at a time. The rest of you, please take out your lens worksheets from yesterday."

Daniel yawns about fifty times while Ms. Bernstein walks us through the worksheet. His dark wavy hair keeps falling over his forehead and he keeps pushing it away. Braden is sneaking popcorn out of his drawstring bag, eating most of it but occasionally flicking pieces at us when Ms. Bernstein isn't looking. Fiona notices me watching Daniel and one sculpted eyebrow goes up. She hides a smile with her hand.

I focus on my worksheet, a blush spreading over my face. I always feel like a klutzy nincompoop around eighth graders, which makes no sense 'cause I'm the same age as them since I flunked sixth grade. They're just so . . . I don't know. Like they know something I don't. Like they're about to spread their wings and take flight while the rest of us are pushing out pinfeathers.

Especially Fiona. How she can make a navy-blue Avengers T-shirt look elegant is beyond me. Maybe it's her thin gold charm bracelet with all the tiny Avengers charms. Or her gold Squirrel Girl earrings. Or the way she's built all willowy and strong like a ballet dancer.

Two kids from table three come out and Daniel and Fiona go in the darkroom. It's hard to focus on the worksheet with Braden chewing like a cow next to me. When the guy I have a minor crush on is in a darkroom with a girl he kissed. I switch to sketching my beagle, Booper, doing the cute little *awoo* sound he makes when I get home from school and hug him. It's one of my favorite parts of the day.

When another kid comes out of the darkroom, I grab my oatmeal box and photo paper off the shelf and open the door to the vestibule, the coffin-sized pitch-black room that's there so no classroom light gets into the darkroom. I wait till the classroom door is closed and then reach for the darkroom door just as I hear it start to open. The darkroom's dim red safelight isn't bright enough to show the person's face. They collide with me and make an *oof* sound.

"Daniel?" I ask.

"Yeah, who's—I mean sorry, I just—oh god." A peal of laughter comes out of him, bright and contagious in the cramped, dark space. "This dog thing's got me so tired I don't know what year it is." He giggles again like a rippling purple ribbon, and then there's a fuzzy curved thump like he's slumped against the wall.

"Dog thing?" I giggle too. "Like, a mutant zebra-platypus-shepherd mix?"

He laughs like that mental image is sending him over the edge. "No, no. Forget I said that." He tries to stifle the laugh and fails. "Sorry, I'm just tired because—because—"

"*Super Smash?*" I suggest.

"Yes!" Something hits my arm like he just gestured. "Oh crap, sorry, it's dark!" His laugh flattens and thins as it edges toward hysteria. "I can't see you because it's *dark!*"

I'm worried the boy is gonna blow a gasket. A sharp knock sounds at the classroom door. "What's going on in there?" Ms. Bernstein asks.

"Nothing," Daniel gasps. "Sorry. Oh my god." He sucks in a breath and holds it, then lets it out. "Okay. Wow." He clears his throat and pulls open the classroom door. Light spills in as he steps out. He wipes away a tear streaking down his face before the door falls shut and I'm closed in the darkness.

4

Nothing to Lose

Daniel

The classroom is painfully bright after the pitch-black vestibule with Ashley. Or at least I think it was her. I squint as my eyes adjust and my brain shifts out of that embarrassing giggle fit. Ash isn't at our table.

Okay. Cool. Just made an idiot of myself in front of a cute girl.

At least it was too dark for her to see me laugh-crying.

Ms. Bernstein gives me a suspicious look as I go back to my seat. Braden clips my shoulder as he heads to the darkroom because he's that kind of guy. I trip into the corner of table three. The kids sitting there laugh. I make it to my seat and collapse onto it. If this growth spurt doesn't end soon so I can figure out what shape I am, I'm going to wind up breaking a bone.

I blink blearily at my worksheet. It made sense before I went in the darkroom, or as much sense as anything can make when you've had a total of six hours of sleep in three days because you're hiding a—what, stolen? borrowed? rescued?—tiny dog in a tent in the woods. A dog whose tongue doesn't quite stay in her mouth. Whose eyes go in two different directions sometimes. Who limps when she walks. Who pees all over herself constantly, which is probably the real reason that guy tried to have her killed. A dog I've fallen stupidly in love with despite my life totally upending because of her.

". . . eleven, Daniel?"

"What?" I check my paper. "Um, I didn't get that one yet. But I got f/4 for number ten."

"Number ten is f/5.6. As we just said. Please try to pay attention."

"Oh. Sorry." I write $f/5.6$ for number eleven—or wait, she said it was for ten. I try to erase what I wrote but I'm using a pen. I scribble it out and the paper rips.

My eyes sting with incoming tears. I swallow hard and cover the mess on my worksheet. It doesn't matter. It's not a test or anything.

But it's *photography*, the thing I shared with Dad that

was just ours. Before he moved out in August, I took so many photos with his old Nikon D80 DSLR that the shutter button started to stick. Now I haven't picked up the camera in two months and I can't even do a worksheet right and I'm regretting choosing this class for my art elective because it feels like jabbing a bruise for forty-three minutes a day.

I rub my eyes and try to figure out question twelve. But thinking is impossible. When I was volunteering yesterday, Gavin said Tina's daughter broke her back and that Tina will be gone for a month. I couldn't think of a non-weird way to ask him to look up her number. I've been biking the three blocks to the woods to check on Chewbarka after school every day, and after dinner if I can think of an excuse to go outside, and after Mom goes to bed at eleven, and in the morning before her alarm goes off at 6:03. Last night I was so stressed I didn't even go home between the late-night check and the early-morning one. I just lay on the stinky tent floor staring at the dark roof with Chewbarka asleep on my stomach, my mind a riot of all the things that could wind up with her getting killed. When I went home to get ready for school, I stuffed my hoodie behind the shed. I didn't want to put it in the laundry smelling like pee and prompt awkward questions from Mom.

Who totally suspects something is going on because I bombed two quizzes this week.

I can't let her find out what I'm doing. She'll tell me I'm too tenderhearted, then she'll demand I tell Dr. Snyder the truth, and then Tina will be fired and Chewbarka will be killed.

I grit my teeth. I don't care how hard this is. I'm *not* letting them kill her.

Ashley sits down and gives me a shy smile. A thought pops into my head that I could tell her. Just tell her everything. When we were talking about her beagle the other day, she said she loves dogs. She made that joke about her dog's farts and then got embarrassed.

Maybe she'd understand. And what do I have to lose? She already thinks I'm a screwup after that vestibule mess. And she's basically a stranger, so she's not going to rat me out to Mitchell or Mom.

I could tell her. I really could. It would feel so good to not be alone with this.

When class is over, I get behind Ash as everyone is leaving. I tap her shoulder in the hall. "I can explain about the dog," I blurt. "I mean, if you want to hear it. It's a funny story." I don't know why I said that. And I'm suddenly less sure this is a good idea.

She smiles. "The mutant platypus-zebra mix?"

"Yeah. I mean she's a Pomeranian." Did I already say that? I can't remember. "This lady Tina at the vet office where I walk dogs . . . um, had to go out of town all of a sudden. She—" Ah, shoot. "Where's your locker? I'll walk you to your locker."

"In the 700 hallway." She looks perplexed.

"Oh, right. I forgot you're in seventh." The grade levels aren't supposed to go in each other's wings, but no one keeps track. We set off through the swarm of kids. "So, Tina brought Chewbarka to work with her that day because Chewbarka, um, needed shots." Yes, that could happen. "And then Tina got a call that her daughter was in a car wreck, in like Indiana or Iowa or someplace. She was rushing out the door crying, and I was like, 'What about Chewbarka?' and she asked if I could take her till she got back and I sort of said yes." My armpits are going sweaty. I hate lying. "And my mom is all, 'No dogs allowed, ever!' and I can't tell her about it. So I'm watching Chewbarka till Tina gets back."

"Isn't there someone else who can help?" Ashley asks. "Did you call her and see if one of her friends could take her dog?"

"I don't have her number." Not a lie.

"Can you ask someone who works at the vet office to give it to you?"

"Well, I mean, I did tell Tina I could watch her dog." *Ick*, lying. "Apparently her daughter's wreck was really bad and she's going to be gone for like a month." I stumble through explaining how I'm staying up super late and getting up before the sun, and it's made me kind of loony and that I'm sorry about my vestibule hysterics.

"Your hysterics were cute." She looks away like she knows I'm noticing her blush. "So you're taking care of Chewbarka till like November?"

"Yeah. I just, I mean, I'm sure it'll be fine. A person can't die from lack of sleep, right? Like you'd just fall asleep instead of dying. I think."

"Maybe don't run that experiment to find out." We reach her locker and she spins the combination lock. She tucks a strand of purple hair behind her ear and I notice that her pastel pink nail polish is chipped. "So, my mom's a dog lover too. She might be cool with us keeping Chewbarka till Tina gets back. If that would help."

A spark of hope darts through me. "Really?"

"We already have a dog, so it wouldn't be a big deal. As long as you think Tina would be cool with it." She pops her locker open. "Maybe you could come by this afternoon with her? My mom gets home at four thirty."

My knees go rubbery at the thought of relief. But then I tense. Oakmont's a huge district that serves seven suburbs. Ashley could live ten miles from me. "Where's your house?"

"We live at the Glenview Apartments. Is that close to you?"

Relief again. "I'm in Green Oaks. Not far." I take out my phone and check the distance from my place to hers. "It's two point four miles. I can bike that easy." Unless I run into a tree or a car because I'm seeing double from a gnarly case of the tireds.

Ash closes her locker and hikes her bag onto her shoulder. "If you're gonna hit your locker before the buses leave, you better hurry." She points up at the clock.

"Oh, right. I'll text you when I'm leaving the . . . wait, what's your number?"

"It's 555-3265. Last four digits spell 'DANK.' Easy to remember."

I laugh as I put her number in my phone. "How'd you figure that out?"

"My friend Griffey did like two seconds after I got my own phone. He was jealous 'cause his only spells 'LAMP.' See you in a while?"

"Definitely. Thank you times a million. You're the best." I start down the hallway, then turn and nearly collide with her. "Sorry. Um, I just wanted to say thanks. Again."

"Duh, of course." She gives me another one-dimple smile.

My brain goes a little goofy at the lopsided cuteness of her grin. She steps around me and is swallowed by the crowd.

Mitch has swim practice three days a week, so we only ride the bus together sometimes. On Wednesday when we got off at our stop and he went left and I went right, he didn't say anything. But today he's nosy. "What are you doing?"

"Nowhere. I mean nothing. I just feel like walking."

"With all your crap?" He whacks my bag with his trumpet case. "You suck at lying."

"You suck at trumpet."

"Not as much as you sucked at saxophone, dropout."

I reverse course and head for home. He follows, pestering me to tell him where I was going. He finally gets bored of me ignoring him and takes out his phone. He opens Insta and the first meme that shows up in his feed is one of Fiona's, because he likes and comments on everything she does on there like that's not creepy or weird. On the surface, it looks like they're friends, but he nearly lost his mind in June at Cole's party when we played spin the bottle and I was supposed to kiss

Fiona. I thought Fiona would be mad if I didn't kiss her because it would look like I was rejecting her in front of everyone. But I knew Mitch and Cole would be mad if I did it, since they both liked her. Which is so far beyond awkward it needs a new word invented to describe it.

I kissed her, hoping they'd both get over it. But Cole can't forgive me for breaking the bro code, and soon after that party Fiona started dating a jerk named Ryan, who's two years older than us, and somehow Mitchell blames *me* for that. He says it's because I sucked at kissing, so now Fiona won't date guys our age, but really, he's been mad at me forever because I'm closer to Dad than he is, and the Fiona fiasco is just a new excuse to treat me like crap. So even though she has a boyfriend, even though I've told Mitch a hundred times I don't like her *that* way, even though he joked around her once that she'd friendzoned him and she gave him an earful about why that's a sexist concept that needs to die—he still acts like he's mad at me for kissing her. When really, he's mad that Dad and I did photography together and liked the same bands and Dad didn't shout huzzahs at Mitchell's sportsball games enough (which, hello, is because Dad's an artist guy, not a sportsball guy).

I don't know why Mitchell's brain works that way, where he transfers all his mad about one thing onto something else. But we'll never talk about it because Mitch isn't a "feelings" dude. I don't think he's aware he *has* feelings. He just acts on them while pretending he's made of logic.

Cole's not like that. He's wicked talented at oil painting, and he's funny and smart and good at making people feel better when they're down. It made him a great friend. One time last fall, before everything changed, I had a nightmare that my mom died. I couldn't shake off the grief all day, even though I knew it wasn't real. Cole sat with me at lunch and listened to me describe the dream in detail, and then he said, "I can see why you're upset. That sounds really hard to forget."

It was exactly what I needed to hear. He did that sort of thing all the time. I didn't know how much I relied on him to prop me up until he ran out of patience and stopped doing it. I don't just miss having a friend, even though that's huge. I miss *him*.

I wish I knew how to fix it. *I'm sorry* wasn't enough. Now he's besties with Erin and they ignore my existence, which is awkward since we all have first-period chemistry together, and Erin and I have English together, and we see each other in the halls and all of us eat during the same lunch period. Which means I eat by myself.

In the house, I drop my bag in my room and go to the

kitchen for a protein bar. I'm itching to head for the tent, but Mitchell's sticking annoyingly close, and of course he wants to complain about our parents. Again. "How long do you think it'll be before they officially split?" he asks as he peels a banana. "Seeing as Dad didn't bother to come home the last three weekends. And when he came home four weekends ago, he slept in the basement."

I unwrap the protein bar. "He's had work stuff. A client moved up a deadline."

"He could've come home at night. It's not like he moved to Texas."

I take a bite, but I can't chew the tough chocolate. My tired brain is grinding through all the stuff over the last few months that's left me sobbing in my bedroom like a Disney princess: my dog, Frankie, dying. Fighting with Mitchell. Getting ditched by Cole. Dad leaving. Mom saying I'm too emotional and need to grow out of it.

I swallow the lump of protein bar. It hurts going down, but I won't cry in front of Mitch. It's not like I'm going to ask him to take it easy on me because Ow I Have a Sad About Dad. He does too, big-time. I put the rest of the bar in a plastic bag and go to my room.

Fortunately, he doesn't follow. I sit on my bed and try to find Tina on Facebook. Her last name is Martin, and there are thousands of Tina Martins. I filter it by city and the number drops to a few hundred. I scroll the list, searching for anyone who looks even remotely like the Tina I know. Some have pets as the profile photo, so I check those people's other photos. None of them are her.

Maybe I could call the vet office and ask for her number. But I *hate* talking on the phone. Mom had me call a restaurant once to ask what time they stopped seating and I had a minor panic attack, which Mitchell found hysterical. And anyway, what would I say to the vet office? *Hi, I'm a random kid who volunteers downstairs, can I have Tina's number?* Ten to one I'd sound like a jibbering dingbat and accidentally draw attention to the situation, which, yikes.

I search the Tina Martins on Facebook for ten more minutes. Twelve minutes. Fifteen. Finally, at 4:22, Mitchell leaves the kitchen and goes to the bathroom. I empty my backpack, slip out the back door, and pull my bike out of the shed.

When I get to the woods, I shove my bike behind a honeysuckle bush so it's out of sight, then fight my way through the brush to the tent. As I'm coming up on it, I hear Chewbarka whimpering and turning in circles like she does when she's excited.

I unzip the door a few inches and her little nose pokes

out. She pushes her way through and bounds into my arms reeking of pee, her whole back end wet.

"Aw, baby, I'm sorry! I know, you were in there for *so* long! I'm so sorry." My eyes sting as I clean her up the best I can with the paper towels and water bottles I've stashed in the tent with her. She needs to be brushed. Mats are forming in her long, thick fur. I pull out the old blanket from our basement that's now her bed. The corner of it is wet with pee and the rest of it smells like dried pee. "Little doggo, what are we going to do with you?" I spread the towel over some honeysuckle branches, then pour some kennel food I've been stealing into Frankie's old bowl. Chewbarka sniffs at it and then digs in. It suddenly occurs to me that I forgot to tell Ashley Chewbarka is sort of leaky.

Well . . . maybe it won't matter. Maybe they can let her out more often than I can. Or maybe their kitchen has a tile floor and they can shut her in there during the day. They probably have a doggy gate already, since they have a beagle.

When Chewbarka's finished eating, I put my backpack on my front and carefully tuck her into it, leaving the top unzipped so she can breathe. I tighten the straps and carry her out to my bike. I'm not sure if this is going to work.

I wheel the bike out to the sidewalk and give it a try. We're wobbly at first, and I have to sit at an uncomfortable angle with my back ramrod-straight. But it works, and Chewy settles down right away.

We set off for Ash's apartment, my foolish heart an equal mix of fear and hope.

5

Crossed Fingers

Ash

I'm arguing with Mom about cross-country at quarter to five when I finally get a text from Daniel: **Almost there!**

I shove my phone in my pocket. "You're not getting this," I tell Mom. "You're confusing 'This school has a gender-neutral bathroom' with 'Ash will have no problems with sports at this school.' Those are two totally different concepts."

"Kid, we didn't move to the whole other side of the city so you could go back in the closet. How can you know sports will be a problem here if you won't even try?" She's still wearing her blue work shirt and it has a big smear of truck grease on the shoulder. She slices a lime and drops a couple wedges into a cocktail glass with some ice. "I'm sure they'd be fine with a gender-fluid kid running as whatever—"

"Ugh, 'gender fluid' sounds like some goopy crap you gotta dump in a car when it's making a weird noise." Plus Dad says it's a made-up label for people who haven't figured out what they are yet.

Mom gives me that look like *I know you better than you know yourself.* "I'm sure Oakmont would let you run as whatever gender you want if you joined. The whole mentality at your new school is different. They have a Rainbow Alliance, for example."

She's freaking obsessed with RA. And anyway, maybe at cross-country they'd let me run in the group I want at practices, but competition races are divided into boys and girls and they'd definitely want to know the deal then, just like they did at Bailey Middle. "Why can't 'I don't want to' be enough? Why are you pushing me to do this?" The guy feeling that started to creep in earlier this week has gotten stronger over the past couple days, and I'm afraid it's starting to show. My voice wants to drop low and come out of my chest instead of my throat. My hands feel awkward and too big when I play my keyboard.

Mom dumps cherry juice concentrate over the limes. "Honey, you loved cross-country at Bailey. I just want you to be happy here. This and Rainbow Alliance seem like a way to make that happen."

"I liked practicing, not competing." At practices, it's just plain running. Not worrying if you look like the correct gender while everyone watches you race against other kids in a gendered group. I get the 7UP out and hand it to Mom. Booper sits by my foot with his Nylabone, making his funny *nyar-nyar-nyar* sound as he chews it.

"You were friends with everyone on the team. Joining would be a great chance to make more new friends at Oakmont." She pops open the can and pours 7UP over the juice and limes.

"I was friendly with them, not friends. Anyway I already have a friend here. His name's Griffey. Pretty sure you've met him six thousand times."

Mom rummages in the fridge and comes out with a pint of blackberries. "You hung out with the cross-country kids. You went to Ethan Schmidt's preseason party in August." She pops a blackberry in her mouth and gives me a handful of them.

I bite into one. It's super sour, just how I like them. "I spent the whole time playing with the dog. I couldn't wait for you to come get me."

Mom gives an exasperated sigh as she smashes black-berries against the inside of her glass with a spoon. "Sometimes I think we're from two different planets, kiddo."

"Yeah, you're from Planet Extrovert. I'm from Planet Introvert." We have to stop arguing. I need her to be in a good mood when Daniel gets here, not cranky 'cause I'm ruining her Friday post-work mocktail. "So. Speaking of friends. Someone from school is gonna come by."

She smiles. "Yeah? Someone from Rainbow Alliance? What's her name?"

"*His* name is Daniel. From photo class."

"Oooh, a boy!" She chugs her drink. "Friend or crush?"

"Oh my god, Mom." I take my water bottle out of the

fridge. When I close the door, I grab the flowery cross-stitch magnet she made that says *I stab fabric so I don't stab people* and shove it in a drawer because it's embarrassing. "I'm going outside to wait. Don't be weird when I bring him up here. And don't drink your weird drink in front of him."

Mom holds up both hands. "I'm the paragon of normal. I'm exceptionally ordinary."

"You have green hair and ear gauges and a porcupine tattoo on your butt cheek that you always bring up within like three minutes of meeting someone. You fix trucks for a living and your hobby is cross-stitching profanity."

"Says the 'normal' kid who sees sounds and has purple hair." She tugs a curl.

"*Partly* purple, and I'm thirteen, not thirty-six. It's normal for me to 'experiment with my look.'" I do air quotes to mock the words from the book she bought me when I turned eleven, *Puberty: Weird but Normal*.

"I'm not experimenting. I've settled on porcupines and green hair." She sticks out her pierced tongue. "But about cross-country—"

"Okay, I'm out." I take my water bottle and leave.

The apartment complex's playground is swarming

with kids burning off the school day's pent-up energy. I sit on the only unoccupied swing. I wish I hadn't left Booper upstairs. Our last apartment was on the first floor and we'd clip him to a tie-out so he could sniff all he wanted. Now we're on the third floor, and every time he has to poop or pee, one of us has to take him outside. The stairs are rough for him since he's getting so old. I usually carry him and wind up with fur all over my clothes.

I'll walk him after Daniel gets here with Chewbarka. We can take them around the complex together.

My stomach does that roller-coaster dip thing. I can't believe Daniel's *coming to my apartment*. I didn't quite follow the story of why he has the dog—it seems like someone else could take her, if Tina just left her at the vet by mistake. But I guess if he doesn't have her number, and he told Tina he would help, it makes sense. And now he's coming over and I'm sixty-two kinds of nervous. I can't believe I actually *like* someone again after what happened with Tyler, the last guy I was into. The reason we moved. It feels dangerous.

But Daniel's nothing like Tyler. This won't turn out like that.

I look down at my outfit: red Converse with one of the laces coming untied, sorta fashionably ripped jeans I got at Goodwill, a purple T-shirt with a stegosaurus surfing on the back of a shark. An outfit that could go either way.

I brush fur off my stegosaurus. There's so much more to me than my gender. But people interact with me differently if they think I'm a girl than if they think I'm a boy. And if they read me as a girl during a boy time, or a boy during a girl time, nothing past that feels right.

I really want Daniel to read me as a girl.

Maybe I'll get lucky and the boy feeling will fade without taking root. This has been my longest stretch yet as a girl, all the way since the end of last school year. But these past few days, it's like the feeling I have when I hit a wrong note on my keyboard. There's this nagging discomfort with my clothes, with how my shoulders curl forward when I'm relaxed, with the way I walk. Think. Breathe. My makeup has started to feel garish, not girly and understated. My stride is lengthening. I'm eating more, sleeping less. The music I'm listening to is changing from light and airy to heavy and loud. If things keep on like this, after an uncomfortable, in-between week or so, boom: I'll be 100 percent dude. Sarcastic and overconfident. I'll feel stronger, I'll play *Fortnite* and listen to punk and metal and use basic dude wash in the shower instead of Mom's girly products. I'll stop daydreaming. I'll slack on my homework.

Maybe I can hide it this time if it doesn't fade. Duck my head and hold my breath till it's over. Hurry along the days until I catch myself listening to Schubert again and admiring the graceful shape of the kitchen faucet, or thinking about how good a silky skirt feels on freshly shaved legs. Then I'll paint my nails, smear on a little eyeliner, blink mascara onto my lashes. I'll braid my hair, smile more, pay attention to how people interact and stop taking what they say at face value. Soon, with luck, I'll be flying fully girl-style again, doodling vines and flowers and the elegant curves of harp notes in my notebook margins, instead of scribbling the craggy-jaggy shapes of dubstep or thrash guitar.

Dad would sure be happy if I stuck with the same jam he's seen me in the last five or six times we got together for lunch. Which, ugh, I have to do *that* tomorrow. Last time, when we met for Chinese food right before Mom and I moved, he told me that labels like *enby* and *gender fluid* and *nonbinary* are the equivalent of deciding your identity is *airport*: somewhere you go to get from one place to another. Not somewhere you *live*. Not somewhere you feel settled, or at home. He said it's for my own good that he "encourages" me to pick-and-stick. That he doesn't want me to be uneasy or unhappy forever.

I guess there's a kernel of parental love in it. He wants his kid to be happy, or whatever.

He just totally disregards that I'm truly happy when I'm with people who see *me* instead of my gender. People who roll with it. People like Mom and Griff. Like my friend Camille from Bailey did. They never act like I'm a pain in their keisters when I shift.

But boy howdy, it sure gets under Dad's skin.

I finger-comb the tangles out of my hair as I watch a kid climb up the slide and get totally creamed by another kid coming down. I'm laughing at the cuss words they're slinging at each other in their little-kid voices when someone says "Hey" right in my ear.

I jump up from the swing and turn. Daniel's looking uncertain, holding a small orangish-brown dog in a backpack he's wearing on his front. "Oh, hi!" I say too enthusiastically. I catch a strong whiff of pee.

"Meet Chewbarka." Daniel lifts her out of the backpack and sets her on the ground.

I squat and scratch her chin. "Hey, Chewbarka. Hey, little girl." Chewbarka looks up at me with cloudy eyes like she's confused. Her face is gray and her back end is damp. "Did you walk through a puddle on the way here?" I ask Daniel.

"No, I biked here with her. I mean, um, she had an accident in the tent." He moves the empty bag to his back. "I have to be out of there by five forty in the morning to get home before my mom's alarm goes off, and then I can't get to her after school till like three fifty. It's too long for her."

"Aw, poor thing. Maybe we can give her a bath."

"I did already, sort of. With water bottles. She's just not all-the-way dry yet."

I pick Chewbarka up and tuck her under my arm. "My mom's gonna love her." I say it with more conviction than I feel. Chewbarka is cute-ish, but definitely smelly and past her prime. Plus her breath is a little fishy. I guess I was hoping she'd be a little more . . . I dunno, Bambi-eyed. And less stinky. It'd be easier to make my case.

When we walk into the apartment, Booper immediately charges Daniel, his tail going like a helicopter. Daniel's whole face lights up. He kneels and rubs Booper's soft, floppy ears. "You didn't tell me he was old!

64

Old dogs are my favorite. Yes, you are, you *are!*" He scratches under Booper's chin and Booper rams his head into Daniel's stomach. Daniel wraps his arms around him and they hug like they've been best buds for life.

Mom laughs as she comes in from the kitchen. "He only rams people he's known a long time or really, really likes. Consider that an honor."

Daniel does a double take at Mom's appearance. "Um, hi, I'm Daniel." He stands up, brushes dog hair off his shirt, and offers his hand.

"Kate." Mom shakes his hand, clearly amused at his formality. "What's your dog's name? She looks pretty old too."

"Oh, she's not—um, it's Chewbarka."

"Fellow *Star Wars* fan!" She points at the framed cross-stitch on the wall with a picture of Princess Leia over *A woman's place is leading the resistance.* "Which movie's your favorite?"

"Um . . ." Daniel glances at me helplessly. Chewbarka sniffs the air, trembling in my arms like she's afraid of Booper. Mom tries to scratch her head but she ducks away.

"Oh, she likes to be scratched under the chin instead of on top of her head," Daniel says. "I mean, don't take it personally."

Mom grins at him. "My hide's tougher than that, kiddo. Takes more than a snub from a dog to rile me up."

I cringe, bracing for her to bring up the porcupine on her "hide" or to mention Rainbow Alliance. I set Chewbarka on the floor. Booper sniffs at her. She scrambles back into my arms, trying to climb me, then turns and snaps at him. I'm so surprised that I drop her. She snaps at Booper again and Booper growls, and then suddenly they lunge at each other and they're fighting, mouths open, god-awful snarls and barking and teeth flashing and spit flying everywhere—

"Whoa!" Mom grabs Booper's collar. "Booper, get back!"

Booper struggles to reach Chewbarka, who Daniel's trying to pick up without getting bit. Mom wrangles Booper back to my bedroom while I try to block Chewbarka from chasing them. Daniel keeps saying, "I'm sorry, oh my gosh, I'm sorry!" He manages to scoop Chewbarka up, but then she pops out of his arms like a squeezed bar of soap and tears down the hall. I lunge and catch her leg as she's snapping at Mom's ankle while Mom yanks a barking Booper into my room.

"I'm so sorry," Daniel says. "I had no idea she was fear-aggressive, I'm so sorry!"

I stand up with the dog, my heart pounding like mad. Chewbarka is struggling and barking in my arms and I'm pretty sure she's peeing on me.

Daniel takes her. "God, I'm so sorry, I really am." He sounds like he's about to cry. "I just—I didn't know, I didn't know she'd do that—"

"Dude, it's okay." My whole body is shaking. I glance at Mom trying to shut the door to my room without shutting Booper's nose in it.

Mom finally gets the door shut and says "O-*kay!*" She turns to me and Daniel. "So your dog's not socialized, then."

"She's not really my—" Daniel starts. "I mean she's sort of—"

"She's not his dog," I say. "He's just taking care of her for a month while her owner's out of town. But he can't keep Chewbarka at his house because—" Wait, I shouldn't make it sound like he's doing something he's not allowed to do. "Because his mom's allergic." I bite my lip and mentally beam the crossed-fingers emoji into the universe. "Can we keep her until—"

"Absolutely not." Mom has her no-arguments face on. "Dogfights are no joke, even if the dogs are small. You saw how they went after each other like—"

"But it's just for—"

"I said no. Daniel, did you check her over? Make sure she's okay?"

Daniel crumples. He kneels and starts pushing Chewbarka's fur around with shaking hands, trying to see if there's any damage.

"We could keep her in my room with the door shut," I say. "It's only for a month—"

"Are you not hearing my words, child? I said no."

"You owe me!" I snap. She did *not* just call me *child* in front of Daniel. "You wanted to move and you used what happened at Bailey as an excuse to without even asking me! So you owe me!" Ugh, why am I saying this in front of Daniel?

Mom's face turns stormy. "Don't give me that bull. You said you were glad to move!"

"That doesn't mean—" Crap, she's right. "You didn't *ask* me about it, you *told* me. Like it didn't even cross your mind that I might have an opinion!"

"I had to get you out of there. That stubborn jerk of a superintendent wasn't willing to do what it would take to keep you safe—"

"I know how to take care of myself!" I can't even look in Daniel's direction, I'm so angry at her for saying no and mad at myself for losing my temper. "I don't need you to swoop in and rescue me!"

"If any of those boys had been carrying a weapon instead of—"

"Oh my god, stop! Just stop talking!" I steal a glance at Daniel, but there's no Daniel. I see a flash of Chewbarka's fur as he pulls our door shut behind him. I glare at Mom. "Great, he just bailed 'cause he thinks I'm a nutcase!"

Her eye roll makes me even madder. "I'm sure he doesn't think—"

"You don't get it!" I dump her drink down the sink and go after Daniel, slamming the door behind me.

6

Impress the Girl

Daniel

I don't know if Chewbarka is shaking harder or I am, but we're both in bad shape as I carry her down the steps. All I want is to get back to the tent and let out the flood of tears trying to come up my throat.

A hand touches my shoulder as I reach the building's door. Ash is holding her mom's empty glass and looking as miserable as I feel. "I'm really sorry," she says. "I didn't mean to fight with my mom in front of you."

"It's fine." Talking makes the tears think it's go time. I turn and push through the door so Ash won't see my watering eyes. Chewbarka shivers and I hug her. The adrenaline is wearing off and I feel so drained my knees barely work.

"I still want to help with Chewbarka." Ash sticks close.

"You don't have to. She's not your problem." The kids at the playground ahead of us go all swimmy in my vision. I blink fast.

"She wasn't yours either, but you're helping her, even though it's put you in a mess. Plus Booper's a good judge of character." She does a little hop-skip to keep up. "You're a good person. I want to help."

"I'm not. I'm an overemotional mess. Ask anybody." Anybody would tell her I'm the kid who ran out of the cafeteria crying the second week of school. The dope who cries at every dog food commercial and has bathroom breakdowns on the regular. The dork whose mom has started to rub her forehead every time the tears come up because *honestly, Daniel, you're almost fourteen.*

"Did you even see me up there?" Ashley says. "I'm the definition of overly emotional. I'm hotheaded and I cry when I'm mad and there are songs I love so much I think all my atoms are gonna explode in every direction when I listen to them." She laughs like she's embarrassed and holds up the glass. "Like why do I have this? I don't even remember taking it." She sets it by the trash can. "But it's not all bad, right? If you weren't an emotional, sympathetic person, Tina wouldn't have been able to leave right away to be with her daughter. So sometimes it's good to be a moody little cuss. Boom." She claps her hands, snaps her fingers, and points at me like that settles it.

The choked-up feeling recedes. "Maybe the only thing helping Tina proves is that I make bad snap judgments."

"Boy, you really know how to sell yourself." She pokes my arm. "Look, how about you show me where the tent is? I'll tell Mom I'm spending the night at Griffey's. He lives four buildings over." She points toward the back of the complex. "Mom's going out with her BFF, Renu, later anyway. I'll chill with Chewbarka tonight so you can go home and sleep. Which, whoa, you clearly need to do." She waves both palms at me like tiredness is written all over me.

Relief tries to rush back in, but I'm wary now. "You really don't need to—"

"I *want* to. I want you to sleep so you don't up and die of tired."

I trip on a sidewalk crack. Chewbarka thrashes in my arms at my sudden unsteadiness. I put her down and slip the leash over her neck. She sniffs the air and looks up at me like she didn't just try to kick Booper's little beagle butt. "What was that, Chewy?" I ask. "He was a good boy. He wasn't going to hurt you."

She sneezes and turns in a circle, then barks so hard her front feet come off the ground.

"Aw, look, Chewbarka has strong emotions like us." Ash fakes a sneeze, turns in a circle, and barks as she does a little hop.

I laugh. "You're even funnier than Co—ohhurgh." The smile falls off my face.

"Who's Co—ohhurgh?"

"No one. Just this kid I used to be friends with."

Ash nods. She leans down to pet Chewbarka like she knows I need a second to get over that stabbing reminder of a dead friendship.

When she stands back up, I look at her. Like really *look* at her, full-on, for the first time. I look at her pale skin and hazel eyes and weird edgy haircut with the purple streaks and the faint spray of freckles over her nose. I look at her straight, even eyebrows and her lips starting to curve into a crooked, self-conscious smile. I look at the dimple that pops out in one cheek but not the other. At the blackberry seed stuck in her teeth.

If it weren't for my Italian complexion, I'd be blushing right along with her. I thought she was cute before, when I'd only stolen glances at her. But now . . . I almost kind of want to take her picture. She's more than cute. She's maybe even . . .

"What?" she says. "Why are you looking at me like that?"

"You're a good person too," I blurt.

"Sweet. I knew you'd let me stay with Chewbarka." She gives my arm a squeeze. "Wait here for like three minutes. I'm gonna run upstairs and throw a bag together. Ninety-nine percent chance my mom's in the shower, 'cause she always showers after her mocktail. Even though I sort of dumped it down the sink just now." She pauses like she's thinking. "I'll tell her you left and I'm going over to Griffey's to cool my jets 'cause I'm mad, then I'll text her later and say I'm staying at Griff's overnight. Sound good?"

"Good," I say like a reflex, only realizing after she's scooped up the cocktail glass and bounded away that I just agreed to show her the tent. That she'll be out in the woods all alone getting peed on tonight, and maybe that's not the greatest way to impress a girl.

I walk to the bike rack by the playground and unlock my bike. I shouldn't be pulling Ash into this messed-up situation any more than I already have. Plus it's going to

74

take forever for us to get to the tent with me pushing my bike and her walking.

I'm not even halfway done stressing about it when she comes running across the playground with a backpack and a rolled-up sleeping bag. "Wow, that was fast," I say.

"Mom was in the shower, as predicted." She's out of breath. "Which is good, 'cause I just yelled the plan through the bathroom door and she was like, 'Fine, but eat something healthy before you go!'" Ash holds up an Atkins bar. "Want some? Kinda chalky, TBH, but these suckers fill you up for like three or four hours. They make you thirsty as heck, though, and sometimes they give you the hot farts." She blushes and bites her bottom lip like she's trying to make herself stop talking.

"I ate a protein bar at home. Part of one." I clear my throat. "So . . . any chance you have a bike?" If we can bike instead of walk, I might have time to get home before Mom does. Barely.

She points at a rusty mountain bike chained to the end of the rack. "He's a real Cadillac, lemme tell ya. Cost hundreds of cents at Goodwill. Name's Sir Reginald Bevis the Steadfast."

A laugh bursts out. "Seriously?"

"Doesn't your bike have a name?" She studies my blue road bike. "Looks fast. How 'bout Vlad the Rapid?"

"I love it." I grin as I put my backpack on my front and tuck Chewbarka into it. "Your mom lets you stay at a boy's overnight? My mom would flip if I texted her and said I was spending the night with a girl."

"Mom's a free-range parent about me and Griff." She unlocks Sir Reginald Bevis.

"Your mom seems selectively free-range." I didn't catch everything they were shouting, but it sounded like something bad happened at Ashley's old school and that's why they moved.

"Yeah." Her cute face turns stormy. "Sometimes she's way too up in my business." She kicks at a chunk of mulch that's migrated out of the playground. "But she's also like my best friend. My dad says we got a real love-hate thing going and we oughta stick our heads in a freezer twice a day to help us keep our cool."

I smile. "Sounds like he's where you got your goofiness from."

"Please, sir." She pretends to brush dust off her sleeves. "I am not *goofy*. I am . . . shoot, what's the word. Dignified. I am the paragon of dignified." She giggles. "Whatever a paragon is. My mom said it earlier. Do you know? It sounds like geometry."

"I think like . . . the most. The top."

"I am the top of dignified." She tilts her head and sticks her nose in the air. Then she makes a raspberry sound and laughs.

Hope feels so dangerous. But oh my gosh.

7

One Step at a Time

Ash

Chewbarka is so small that I'm picturing a one-person tent. But the green-and-white behemoth Daniel leads me to could just about fit a car in it. "It's like this tiny dog has her own mansion," I say as he plucks a blanket out of a bush. "Was it hard to set this up by yourself?"

He shakes leaves off the blanket. "I can't even tell you what a pain it was. I might've said some words that would get me grounded for a year. Mostly while I was breaking off honeysuckle branches to make room." He unzips the door and a strong pee smell comes out. He gives me a guilty glance. "You really don't have to do this."

I try not to cough on the stinky-stank as I step inside. Most of the smell seems to be coming from a corner at the back. Another corner has a few rolls of paper towels, a plastic tub of dog food with a snap-on lid, and a food-water combo bowl that says *Frankie*. I unzip a window and a breeze drifts in. "It's not that bad," I lie. "I'll open the windows."

"I'll help." Daniel sets Chewbarka down and zips the door shut so she can't run off. We open all six windows while she does that adorable flopping-on-her-back thing dogs do when they're itchy. I unroll my sleeping bag and Daniel folds the stanky-blanky that must be her bed. "Are you sure you'll be okay by yourself all night?" he asks. "I feel bad leaving you here."

"Dude, it's fine." I hide a grimace. I only say *dude* when I *am* a dude, and I'm pretty sure I said it after the dogs fought too.

"I could check on you," he offers. "I could set an alarm and come to the tent at three a.m. to make sure you're okay."

"That would defeat the whole purpose of me staying here so you can sleep. Plus it would interrupt *me* sleeping, which could be hazardous to your health." Chewbarka puts her front paws on my leg and looks hopefully up at me. I scratch her ears.

"But . . ." He looks uncomfortable. "You're . . . well, it just seems weird to leave a girl alone in a tent all night."

"I have Chewbarka the ferocious guard dog." I thought I'd be relieved to know Daniel thinks I'm a girl. But part of me is bothered. "And I have this." I flick open the Smith & Wesson Special Ops pocketknife Dad gave me when I turned ten. "I'm not a delicate flower or whatever, okay? So calm your tush."

Daniel laughs, looking both relieved and tired. "You're one tough chick, Ash."

I fold the knife shut and tuck it back into my jeans, making a face that's supposed to say *Darn right* but probably looks more like *Don't call me a chick.* "I gotta use the little dog-sitter's room." I unzip the tent door. An end-of-summer cicada is trilling in a nearby tree. The loopy shape of its song makes me think of kids playing leapfrog.

Daniel follows me out of the tent. "There's a gas station over there." He points through the honeysuckle. "If you go thirty feet that way, you'll see the back of it." He yawns. "Probably easier than peeing in the woods. Mom says that's a major pain for girls."

"Yep. Back in a few." I set off.

As soon as I'm out of sight of the tent, I lean on a tree, take a deep breath, and unclench my fists. I think my fake-confidence thing is working, but it's definitely fake. I gotta keep telling myself that Daniel's nothing like Tyler. He's *not*. Tyler set off warning bells in my brain from the day he moved to our old apartment complex back in June. Bells I heard even through my raging crush all summer. Bells I should've listened to, like I should've listened to Mom saying he was bad news. Like I should've listened when Booper growled at him. When my friend Camille told me he had *warning* written all over him.

But I didn't. Because he was ridiculously cute, and because I was stupid enough to hope he'd still like me once he learned I'm not always a girl. The night before school started in August, I sent him a link to my Insta, where I try out different looks. I wanted it to come from me. I didn't want him to find out from the other kids that I'm the flip-flop freak, the kid who can't pick a gender.

That I only had one friend at school, Camille, because once Griffey wasn't there to defend me anymore, everyone except her acted like I had chronic cooties.

He wrote back **Cool thx** right away. Like before he could've had a chance to look at the link. And then there was nothing. I spent a while drawing a few measures of his favorite song. I didn't really like his music taste, but I'd told him about my weird thing where I see sounds and sometimes draw cartoon versions of them, and he said it would be cool to see what that song looked like. I decorated the sketch with music symbols instead of the silly stick figures I started adding to my drawings in sixth grade round one when Mom and Dad were fighting a ton and I needed a distraction. I didn't want Tyler to think I was making fun of the song. I planned to give him the drawing at the bus stop in the morning.

Turns out the more you like a guy, the worse it sucks when he turns on you.

My phone pings with a text. I blink back to the woods and the green and the trilling cicada. Mom wants to know if I ate something healthy.

A protein bar, I tell her. *I will not shrivel away to nothing.*

Sorry it didn't work out with the dog, she writes. **I love you even when you're a stubborn cuss. Tell Griff I said hi.**

Love you too, even when you stink like truck grease. I pocket my phone and head for the gas station. It's not like I'm crushing on Daniel as hard as I crushed on Tyler. At least not yet. And Booper liked Daniel.

Loved him, really. Like so recklessly it kinda embarrassed me.

I gotta take this one step at a time, like Mom's always saying. *Don't eat your lunch for breakfast* is one of her favorite sayings. *Be where you are. Life isn't a problem to solve; it's a reality to experience.* She's got a million of them from a meditation app she's addicted to. Mostly it annoys me when she whips them out, but sometimes . . . they're legit useful. Like now, when I'm not sure what I'm feeling. What I want. What I *am*.

The gas station has one unisex bathroom, which

solves that problem before it gets off the ground. I do my business, then text Griffey and ask him to cover for me if my mom texts him tonight. I tell him I'll explain later. I refill my water bottle and head back to the tent.

When I get there, I hear a soft little snore. I unzip the door as quietly as I can. Daniel is zonked out with Chewbarka on his chest, his hands resting on her back. She's looking at me like she's found her place in the world and if I wanna come in that's cool, but I better not move her off this excellent boy who is definitely *hers*, thank you very much.

I smile and pull my sleeping bag over the half of Daniel that isn't being used as a dog bed. I lie down next to them. I'm not glad that stuff with Tyler turned into a way-too-public nightmare that chased me out of the school district. But at least it led me to this smelly tent in a patch of honeysuckle woods, watching a fascinating boy sleep with his mouth hanging open.

His lips look so . . . I don't know. So soft.

I wonder what it would be like to kiss them.

8

The Shape of a Snore

Daniel

I wake up with a start, confused about where I am and what this warm pile of orange fluff on my chest is and why my cheek is wet—

Oh god, I'm drooling.

I sit up fast, wiping it off with my arm. Chewbarka tumbles onto Ashley's Darth Vader sleeping bag with a grunt of surprise.

Ash is holding a small sketchbook and grinning at me. "Did you know you snore?"

"Umf. I guess I know now." I pat my face to make sure I got all the spit. "You must think I'm the coolest kid at Oakmont. Darkroom hysterics, dog drama, drooling."

"So far, yes, I do." She says it like she means it. "You snore like waves. It's . . . delicate."

"What?" I pull Chewbarka into my arms. I can't even snore in a manly way? Jeez.

Ash hesitates, then turns her sketchbook and shows me a pattern of waves. "This is your exhale." She traces the bottom of the first wave as it swoops up. "Then your inhale gets stuck on some flappy whatever valve in your throat, and it makes this choppier noise." She points at the tops of the waves. "It happens a couple times, like a stone skipping on a pond. Then you exhale and it's smooth again." Her finger follows the downslope of the last wave, which has a little stick figure surfing on it. "Super-arty snores. Nice work."

A grin spreads across my face. "That is the weirdest thing anyone's ever said to me right when I woke up."

She flips the sketchbook closed and jams it back in her bag.

"No, don't be embarrassed. It's cool. Actually . . . could I have it? The drawing?"

She looks at me sideways like she's trying to hide a smile. Then she tears the page out and hands it to me.

I examine the stick figure surfing my snore. "Do you draw sounds a lot?"

She nods. "I, um . . . I see sounds in my mind when I hear them. The drawings are like cartoon versions, 'cause the shapes are more involved than my art skills can handle." She looks like she's bracing to be called a freak. "It's called synesthesia. There are different kinds."

"Like what?" And why is she so adorable when she's blushing? And is it wrong that I want to keep saying stuff that makes her blush?

"Well . . . so, for some people, every letter is a different color. Or like some people taste shapes. Or hear colors or smell sounds. Basically two senses get linked." Her shoulders are up. "It's not that weird. My mom said five percent of people have some form of it."

Now I feel guilty that I lied to her about why I have Chewbarka. She's being honest with me, even though it's making her uncomfortable. And she's *here*. Helping me.

I clear my throat and check my phone. It's almost six already. There's a text from Mom to me and Mitchell: **I'm stopping at the grocery then picking up Thai food for us. So don't go stuffing your hungry faces with whatever's left in the fridge. Love you, see you soon.**

I breathe a sigh of relief. **Love you**, I write back. She usually gets home around six, so if she's making two stops, that'll add at least half an hour. I check the weather. "Looks like you'll be warm enough tonight with ol' Darth here," I tell Ash. The weekend forecast looks fine, but next week, it's going to get cold at night, down into the thirties. "I have to go. My mom will blow up my phone with texts if I'm not there. Plus Mitch will start talking crap about me to her."

"Okay." Ash looks disappointed I'm leaving. "Mitch is your brother?"

"My twin." I wait for her to ask the same dumb questions everyone asks: *Can you read each other's minds? If I poke you does he feel it? Which one of you is older? Are you the good twin or the evil twin?*

"Did you really beat him at *Super Smash*? Fiona didn't seem convinced."

"Nope. Mitch kicks my butt at that game. But I clean up the track with him in *Mario Kart*."

Ash smiles. "Text me tomorrow before you come back. I'll turn my volume up so it wakes me."

"Sure." I kind of want to see her asleep. It's only fair after she caught me drooling and snoring. "Um . . . do you need anything else?"

"I'm good. I put a bagel and a flashlight and a book

in my bag. I'm kinda looking forward to snuggling a dog and reading."

"Okay, good. Then, um, I guess . . . have a good night?"

"You too." She picks up Chewbarka and hugs her, then uses her hand to wave one of Chewbarka's paws at me. "Thanks for taking care of me," she says in a squeaky voice.

I scratch Chewbarka under the chin. She licks my hand.

"Yeah, I'm not licking your hand," Ash laughs. "Go on. We'll be fine."

"Okay. Thanks. Like times a million kabillion. You're awesome."

The last thing I see is her lopsided grin before she pushes me out the door and zips it shut.

I make it home at 6:28. Mom isn't there yet, thank the lord. Mitchell asks where I was. "Kennel," I lie.

"Why'd you wait so long to go there? You usually bike over right after school."

I shrug. "I needed to digest my protein bar."

"You ate like one bite of it."

"You were all pushy and annoying and ruined my appetite."

"Why are you wearing an empty backpack on your front? I know you went somewhere."

"Oh my god, Mitch. Do you have nothing better to do on a Friday than track me?"

He looks like he's going to say something snide, but then his shoulders slump. "Zach ditched me to hang with Lily," he mumbles.

"Oh." I think that's been happening a lot lately. Which . . . I know that feel. Erin edged into my friendship with Cole in a similar way last year. "Sucks." Especially since we both feel abandoned by Dad too. A double-suck whammy.

Mitch makes a noncommittal sound. "Bet you five bucks Mom'll subject us to *Moana* tonight."

"She watched *Wreck-It Ralph* last night. My money's on *Ralph Breaks the Internet*." Mom's always been a Disney fiend, but since Dad left, she's gotten obsessive. It's a good thing Disney+ is unlimited. Otherwise she'd break the bank streaming movies nonstop.

"I'll take that bet," Mitch says. "She watches chick flicks on Fridays. She watched *Tangled* and both *Frozen*s the last three Fridays. Tonight will be *Moana*." He pulls a few crumpled bills out of his pocket. "Wait, make it a three-dollar bet."

"I'm not betting money." I only have two bucks

anyway. Dad's the one who gives us our allowance, and that hasn't happened the last three weeks.

"Then bet me something else. A chore."

I kick my shoes off. "I'm. Not. Betting."

"'Cause you know you'll lose."

"Why do you have to turn everything into a contest?" It annoys me to no end.

He grins. "Because you're so easy to beat."

"Oh, right. I keep forgetting you got all the good genes. Despite us being identical."

"Nope, I just stole all the resources in the womb. It was easy. You were a sappy pushover before we were even born."

"Are you seriously arguing about Mom's womb? You're not right in the head, Mitch."

"We're arguing about me being the dominant winner twin and you being the—"

"Can it, boys," Mom says as she opens the back door. "I could hear you arguing from outside." She drops two takeout bags on the counter. "There's groceries in the trunk. Hop to it."

Mitch and I go outside, jabbing each other in the ribs. He grabs a package of TP and some paper towels, leaving me the two heavy bags full of milk and frozen stuff. I sigh and haul them into the house. The extra weight makes it hurt like the dickens when I step on a rock with my bare heel.

Mom plates our Thai food while Mitch and I put the groceries away. She sets up the TV trays in the living room and carries the food out there. "Get it while it's hot," she says. "The pantry stuff can wait." She turns on Disney+.

Mitch shoots me a look. *Moana*, he mouths.

I shake my head and sit on the couch. "Thanks for the food, Mom. This looks great." A twinge of guilt goes through me thinking of Ash in the tent with a bagel and a sweet but smelly dog.

"Didn't feel like cooking." Mom navigates to the *Because You Watched* recommendations. *Moana* and *Ralph Breaks the Internet* are both listed. She chooses *Moana*.

I don't look at Mitch. I can feel his stupid smug grin trying to smack the side of my head. While I eat, I keep checking my phone, hoping next week's forecast will change.

"Daniel, why the sudden interest in the weather?" Mom asks the third time I refresh the page.

"Birds," I say without thinking. I miss when she used to call me *Danny*. "And squirrels and stuff. We should put out food for them. It's gonna get really cold. They're tiny and they lose body heat fast."

Mitch laughs like scissors snapping on empty air. "You're worried about squirrels now? You seriously need to grow a thicker shell."

Mom smiles too, like she's privately laughing in her head. I fake a laugh like I know they're right, I'm being sensitive again, I should forget it. I should worry about normal stuff like grades and girls and school shootings and our family falling apart. Pretend *Daniel* doesn't bother me even though it feels like she's telling me to grow up every time she says it.

I push the rest of my food around until the part where Moana's grandma is on her deathbed. I've seen this dumb movie twice and cried both times when she died. I take my food to the kitchen and cover it with foil, pretending I don't hear Moana's grandma giving her the shell thingy. I put my food in the fridge and go back to my room.

I spend twenty more minutes looking for Tina on social. It occurs to me that maybe she's checked in at the vet, or posted a photo taken there, so I go to Dr. Snyder's business page. But so many people have checked in there it's useless.

If I knew what part of town she lives in, it would be easier. But this whole city-suburb metropolitan area has like three million people. She could live anywhere.

I keep searching until I've narrowed the list of Tina Martins to three. One has a flower profile photo, one has a cat, and one has a sunset. Then I create a Facebook account and message each of them: *Hi, it's Daniel. I hope everything is OK with your daughter. What should I do about the dog? I can't keep her. Please answer quickly. Thanks.*

I don't know how it's possible to have insomnia when I'm this tired. I can't stop looking at my cartoon snore and thinking about Ash in the tent by herself. I was there alone last night, but it was my choices that led to that. Now she's roped into my drama.

On the other side of my bedroom wall, I hear Mitchell watching debate videos on his laptop. Fiona, captain of the junior debate club they're in, is arguing about climate change. I close my eyes and focus on the sound. She's taking her usual tactic of mixing passion for her argument with facts and evidence.

She's so good at it. Mitch is good too, but he's cold and calculating. Like a giant blorp of data comes out of his mouth. But Fiona can make you believe. Make you *care*.

I need to be more like that. To use my emotions like

a tool, a source of information, instead of having them spill out everywhere and take up all the air in a room, then leave me drowning in guilt for overreacting. I mean good lord, crying in the cafeteria? I can't blame Mitch for giving me crap about that. Or Cole for sighing and turning away like he was sick to death of it. *You always make everything about you,* he'd said. *It's* my *birthday you forgot. I'm the one who's mad. And now the subject is right back to* you *and how bad* you *feel.*

Maybe losing him would be easier if he was wrong.

But he's not.

It's still dark when I wake up, too early to text Ash. I check Facebook—no responses—then quietly slip into the kitchen and put some food in a plastic bag for her: an apple, a block of cheddar, a piece of the Italian bread Mom brought home last night.

Mom comes in while I'm tying the bag shut. She's wearing her pajamas that have Joy from *Inside Out* on the shirt. "Morning, honey," she says. "You're up early." She sets her laptop on the table, then wraps an arm around my shoulder and kisses the side of my head. She used to kiss the top where my cowlick is, but now I'm taller than her. Which I'm totally not used to yet. "You feeling better? You've seemed so tired this week."

"I'm okay. Thought I'd help out at the kennel. It's always extra busy on Saturday mornings." I'm not lying; I do want to go, after I check on Ash. A high school kid comes in to feed and walk the dogs, but he's always glad when I show up to help because he can get through everything faster and leave early. Then I get the animals all to myself for a while.

"You know you can talk to me, Daniel. About whatever. Dad. School. Girls." She glances at her laptop.

"I'm fine. Do you have to do work stuff?"

"Unfortunately." She's a project manager at an ad agency and often has to finish the week's tasks on Saturday morning. "That's why I stopped at the grocery last night. I needed to look at something other than an Excel sheet. Now I'm fresh and ready again." She rolls her eyes.

"Sorry to hear it." I know she'd rather curl up on the couch with a book and a mug of tea.

"At least I don't have to volunteer at a swim meet this weekend." She glances guiltily at Mitchell's closed door. "Don't tell him I said that."

"I won't." Tempting, after how bad he always tries to make me feel for spending time with Dad without him. But I don't need to play his game.

Mom runs her hand over her black ponytail with its

gray streaks, fills a glass with water, and glances wist-
fully at the coffeemaker. Dad's the coffee drinker, not
her, but she loves the smell of it. Now the kitchen smells
only of the lemony bleach wipes she cleans with every
day.

Sadness leaks out of the silence. I wonder what shape
it is. How Ash would draw it.

I take the bag of food and leave.

9

Punk and Pricey Diapers

Ash

I wake up like a shot with a dog tongue so deep in my ear it's practically licking my eardrum. "What the cuss!"

Chewbarka seems to translate this to *Yay, it's playtime!* because she does that bark-and-turn-in-a-circle thing again. A little spray of pee shoots out around her.

"All right, outside with you." I shimmy out of my sleeping bag and discover the whole edge of it is damp. Looks like I'm doing laundry later.

The cool morning air smells sweet and fresh when I open the tent. It makes me realize how bad it smells inside, even with all the windows open. I set Chewbarka on the ground. She waddles over to a tree, dripping pee all the way. I yawn and tie my hair back. I look like a dude this way, but there's no one around and I want it out of my face.

Chewbarka returns and sniffs at a plastic bag next to the tent door. I pick it up and find it's full of food. I check my phone and find a text from Griffey asking what the heck I'm doing that needs a cover story, and one from Daniel from 8:41. It's almost ten now. **Brought you some breakfast**, Daniel's text says. **I'm at the kennel. If you need to go home, go ahead. I'll let Chewbarka out when I'm done. THANK YOU AGAIN, you're the all-time greatest ♥**

I stare at the purple heart for way too long. Then I pocket my phone and dig into the food, trying to push away my dread about lunch with Dad today.

Mom's been on me about going to a PFLAG meeting with her tomorrow and I know she'll bring it up the minute I get home. I leave my sleeping bag in a patch of sun to dry, then slip Chewbarka's leash around her neck and head out to the road. It seems weird that she doesn't have a collar or tags. I'm sure there's a good reason, though. Maybe Tina took them off while Chewbarka was in the cage at the vet so they didn't get stuck on the bars.

There's a PetSmart in the strip mall out on the main drag where we got Booper's food the week we moved to Oakmont. I check my pocket and find six bucks, all that's left of the twenty Mom gave me for lunch a week ago. I don't know how much dog diapers cost. Probably more than six bucks.

As soon as we're out of the woods, a text from Mom comes in. **Noticed when I went out for groceries that Sir Reginald Bevis isn't in the bike rack. You and Griff out terrorizing the town?**

More like terrorizing the Frisbee golf course at the park. I bite my lip. I don't like lying to her. I've done it way too much since yesterday.

Your helmet's still in your room. Make sure you wear it next time, please.

Oops. Sorry.

I keep an eye on my screen as I walk, but she doesn't say anything else. I sigh in relief and pocket my phone. After a few minutes of walking, I notice Chewbarka has a limp. I pick her up and carry her. By the time we're at the store, my arms feel like lead, so I put her back down.

It takes two seconds of shopping to confirm that dog diapers are out of my budget. I find a bin of discount treats wrapped in plastic, take one, and head for the checkout.

A German shepherd on a retractable leash comes around a shelf and Chewbarka freezes. I quickly scoop her up to avoid another dogfight. The shepherd is followed by a girl from my English class who's wearing a Snarky Carcasses shirt. I'm pretty sure her name is Zoey.

"Rex, quit pulling!" she says as she attempts to reel her dog in. She looks up and sees me holding Chewbarka away from Rex's sniffing nose. "Sorry, just a sec!" She tugs Rex back in and finally gets the leash locked. "Sit, Rex!"

Rex obediently sits next to her foot. He raises his paw like he wants to shake my hand, but I can't really take his paw. Chewbarka is shaking like a leaf.

"Good boy," Zoey tells Rex as she pushes her blonde hair out of her eyes. She's one of the few girls at Oakmont who has short hair, and she's a total dude magnet because of her, uh, build. "What's your dog's name?" She tries to pet Chewbarka's head but Chewbarka ducks away.

"Booper." I mentally facepalm. "I mean Chewbarka. Booper's my beagle. This dog isn't actually mine. I'm—uh, dog-sitting."

Zoey laughs, but not in a mean way. "So is this one Barka or Chewbooper?"

"Chewbarka." She's trying to climb up to my shoulder. "She's not great with other dogs."

"Aw, poor thing. Rex is big, but he's really chill with other dogs."

Chewbarka scratches my neck with her frantic paws. "Can you translate that into dog and tell her?"

"Arwoo-arf bark bark awooo!" Zoey says. "Good dog, Chewbooperbarka. Ar-wooo!"

I grin at her. "Love the shirt. I heard they're gonna tour for their new album."

Zoey's eyes widen. "You like the Snarky Carcasses?"

"What's not to like about an all-girl punk-cover band?" I love them when I'm a dude, but rarely listen to them when I'm a girl. "Their version of 'I Wanna Be Sedated' is one of my favorites." Chewbarka finds a spot near my left shoulder that seems to make her feel secure.

"That song rules," Zoey says. "My band's been working on it but we suck."

A warm trickle goes down my shirt. I shift Chewbarka to hide it. "What kind of music do you guys play?"

"Punk. We're not good, but boy, we're loud. We're called Tyrannosaurus Rocks. We're practicing tonight, if you wanna come watch."

"Seriously? I'd *love* that." The band name's a little on the nose for punk, but it would be awesome to check them out. I try to get my phone out without dropping Chewbarka, but I drop the phone.

A tall blonde woman in a short skirt comes around the shelf carrying a giant bag of dog food. She's followed by a towheaded kid in a soccer uniform. The kid looks like he's about eight and the woman looks like Zoey if Zoey did CrossFit twelve days a week. "For god's sake, I've been looking everywhere," she says to Zoey. "We don't have time for you to flirt with boys. Alan's game starts in ten minutes. Let's go."

My face burns. I shift Chewbarka again.

"Mom, god! Ashley's a girl."

I cringe and then try to hide it with a fake smile.

"Sorry," Zoey's mom says like she's not. "Now, kiddo."

Zoey picks up my phone and hands it to me. "Mom, can she come to band practice tonight?"

"As long as she can get a ride. I'm done being a taxi."

"I'll ask my mom." I open my contacts with a shaking hand. "Zoey, put your number in?"

"Yep." Zoey types it in and hands my phone back. "Text me and I'll give you the address and time and stuff. See ya!" She follows her mom and brother to the checkout line.

I yank the hair band loose the second they're out of

sight. Chewbarka licks my neck like she's saying thanks for keeping her safe from big, scary Rex. We lurk in the clearance aisle till I hear Zoey and her family leave. Then I pay for my treat and head back to the tent, wondering how Sam from Rainbow Alliance reacts when someone's mom assumes their gender. Probably a lot better than I just did.

Maybe I should see if they give lessons. In dealing with other people. In being confident.

I call Griffey while I'm walking and ask if he knows Zoey. He doesn't, which isn't surprising since Oakmont's so huge. "Hey, so why'd you ask me to cover for you?" he asks.

I explain about Daniel getting stuck with Chewbarka and needing help, and about me fighting with Mom and staying in the tent. "Oh, and you and I are out Frisbee-golfing if my mom texts you," I tell him. I doubt she will, but better play it safe.

"Wow, so you've got a thing with Daniel now." He pauses long enough for me to realize he's about to ask the question I don't want to answer. "Are you gonna tell him?"

"No!" I practically shout. But then I hesitate. "I mean . . . not yet. I don't know. I think, like, things aren't that far yet. Like, I like him, like I *like*-like him, but I'm just, like—"

His laugh cuts me off. "Can you cram more 'likes' into one sentence?"

"Shut your trap, turd huffer. You sound stupid too when you talk about Jacob."

"Ugh, I know. It's like my IQ drops twenty points when I'm around him."

"I just wish I knew more about Daniel. At least with Tyler I knew his family was a bratty pack of hell-raisers, so I should've seen it coming how stuff turned out." Not that your family sucking means you suck too, but in his case, it was definitely a clue. I totally should've listened to Camille. And Booper. And Mom.

"Do you follow Daniel on Insta?"

"No, what's his account?"

"It's called The_Ugly_Twinn, with underscores and two n's. It's not a meme account like everyone else has. It's like legit good photography. I don't think he's posted in a while, though."

"I'll look it up. I'm at the tent, I gotta deal with the dog. I'll call you tonight and tell you about lunch with my dad and how the band thing goes."

"Cool." He sounds disappointed, like he was hoping to hang out. "Good luck with your dad. Later, tater hater."

In the tent, I attempt to tie my wrinkled Imagine Dragons T-shirt around Chewbarka like a diaper. It doesn't really work, and I don't want her to pee all over my shirt even though I'm no longer the raging Imagine Dragons fan I used to be. I take her outside and we curl up on my dry but still-stanky sleeping bag in the sun. I put on some wistful, sad music that looks like silk blowing in the wind, then open Insta to search for Daniel's account. I haven't opened the app since the day of The Tyler Disaster, when I made my account private to everyone except Griffey. There's one new notification on the last selfie I posted, a comment from Griff that says Miss your face on here xoxoxo.

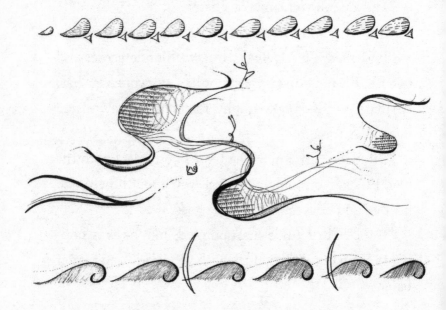

I search for The_Ugly_Twinn. It shows up right away, and my breath catches. Daniel's pictures are lovely and lonely: a sunset with a single cloud catching the light. An empty field of golden grass under a heavy gray sky. A flower being sucked into a flooding creek. A dead tree with one leaf still stuck to a branch. A tarnished silver teapot sitting beside a road with a bunch of fast-food trash. A cracked snail shell nestled into a bed of moss.

I could take a hundred pictures of a snail shell on moss and it would look like I just snapped it with my phone. But Daniel obviously used that rule-of-thirds thing Ms. Bernstein was talking about. He's so good I don't know why he's taking photography. He's already won at it.

Halfway through looking at all his stuff, I find a selfie. It's a simple mirror shot taken in what might be his bedroom. He has one eyebrow up and he's half smiling.

I zoom in. His lips look so . . . ugh. So ridiculously *kissable.*

I'm *not* going to kiss him. I'm Ashley to him, not Asher. Dad said once that girls aren't supposed to make the first move. Besides, I've never kissed anyone. I don't know how it works.

But good lord. I'm blushing just thinking about it and no one's even around.

I curl up and hug Chewbarka, turning over Griffey's question about telling Daniel. I saw a TikTok a few weeks ago of a girl sitting on a floor looking at her phone. A guy in the background notices her and starts dancing toward her like he wants to ask her out. Some dude runs into the frame and whispers, "Don't do it, she's trans!" in the dancing guy's ear. But he just shrugs the dude off and keeps dancing toward the girl.

I cried when I saw it. I don't even know if I'm trans. Like whatever I decide I am for good, Ashley or Asher, one of those will make me trans and one won't. Plus, if I'm Asher I'll be gay, and I'll be straight if I'm Ashley.

But that meme is exactly what I hope will happen: A guy will see me for *me*. He'll shrug at my whatever-whatever gender mess and keep dancing toward me like *woop woop cutie-boo!*

Daniel really is nothing like Tyler. But liking him is an intense mix of exciting and scary, and I'm feeling even less girly than I did yesterday. If I wake up tomorrow in full-on dude mode, it'll suck to fake being a girl. I've tried faking before. It's like someone's rubbing my eyebrows the wrong way.

I don't want to be fake with Daniel. But if he only

likes girls, I'll lose whatever this thing is that might be starting. This feeling that I want to make his life easier, that I want to be the one he comes to when he's sad or lonely. This feeling that he might look past my outsides and see me for *me*. A task so challenging my own freaking dad can barely do it.

I hug Chewbarka. "Dogs are so lucky," I tell her. "You don't gotta worry 'bout this crap."

She licks my arm and pees on me.

10

Hazel Surprise

Daniel

While the morning kennel worker is cleaning the cages in room B, I sneak a look in the supply closet. There's so much stuff in there, old blankets and bags of food from past boarders, extra leashes, flea dip solution, toenail clippers, cat litter. On a top shelf near the back, I find what I'm looking for: a plastic bin of disposable dog diapers. I fish through it as fast as I can, searching for one small enough to fit Chewbarka. I finally find a couple at the bottom. I roll them up and shove them into my pocket along with a dog brush. Then I duck into the employee bathroom and check Facebook. There's a reply to one of my messages. My heart leaps, but when I tap the message, it says *I have no idea what you're talking about.*

I wish I could ask someone upstairs to look up Tina's number. But Saturdays are chaos up there and I doubt anyone would have time for me. The only front-office worker whose name I know is that Gavin guy, and he doesn't come in on Saturdays. Besides, maybe they *can't* give me her number. At my last checkup at the doctor, we had to wait forever and I read the HIPAA paperwork because I was so bored and it made it sound like you can never, ever give someone's personal information away without their consent. What if I ask and they say, *Sorry that's illegal*, and then get too curious about why I want Tina's number?

I'm playing with a basenji in the kennel yard an hour later when I have a brain wave: Maybe I *could* ask Dad to help. He backed Mom on the no-getting-another-dog thing, but his heart wasn't in it. He loved Frankie as much as I did.

I hate that there's so much everyone in my family keeps hidden lately. I know what's going on with Mitch, getting ditched by his friend who has a girlfriend now, plus losing Dad and hitting puberty and crushing on a girl who's not into him. And Mom's . . . well, whatever she is about Dad. Sad? Disappointed? Relieved? Mad?

It seems like all of it at the same time. I keep looking back at the last few years and how Dad's slowly been withdrawing from us and I worry it's my fault somehow, because I'm so emotionally over the top. The inside of my head keeps getting bigger and more complicated and it seems harder and harder to share the full truth of it with anyone, especially when everyone already thinks I'm way too in my feelings.

I just miss Dad. A lot. I missed him before he left and I miss him more now. All of us have huge private struggles, and none of us talk about them. We keep big parts of ourselves locked away.

But maybe Chewbarka could fit into Dad's separate, hidden part. Just for a few weeks.

My mind churns as I put the basenji back in her cage. I can't bike all the way to Dad's with Chewy in the backpack. It's awkward to ride that way. But we still have our old bike trailer from when me and Mitch were little. I could bike Chewbarka to Dad's apartment tomorrow while Mom's doing her church stuff. I've never pulled the trailer, and there are busy roads between our house and Dad's apartment, but maybe I can find a back way.

Maybe I can make this work.

It's an imperfect solution. But if I have to go through another week like the one I just had, I'm going to crack and cry and spill my guts to Mom, and it will doom the dear little doggo I've fallen in love with.

After I've walked all the dogs, I bike back to the patch of woods. I jam Vlad the Rapid into the underbrush next to Sir Reginald Bevis and pick my way toward the tent. Ash is curled up on her sleeping bag outside it with Chewbarka in her arms. She must not hear me, because she's staring up at the trees with a sad, worried look on her face. "Hi," I say softly so I don't startle her.

"Oh!" She sits up fast and smiles. "Hi! Welcome home. Or welcome back. Whichever. Thanks for the food. Especially the cheese. Cheese is my favorite food."

I smile at her blush. "Look what I got." I hold up the diapers and brush.

She giggles. "Are those for your rule-of-thirds photo assignment?"

"Totally. I'll stage them on a peed-on blanket."

"I tried to make a diaper out of my T-shirt. It didn't work out so great."

We give Chewy a good brushing and get some of the mats out of her fur. As we're trying to figure out how the diaper goes on, I tell Ash my Dad Plan for tomorrow. Our hands keep brushing together as we put Chewbarka's legs through the leg holes. When I pull her fuzzy tail through, Ash's wrist bumps mine and a wave of heat goes through me.

Once the diaper's on, we both crack up. It's flattened Chewbarka's back-end fuzziness and her butt looks super tiny compared to the rest of her. "That's so adorable," Ash says. "And sad. Sad-dorable. Oh! Check out what I discovered." She gently touches Chewbarka's nose and Chewy's tongue falls out the side of her mouth. "You boops the snoot, you gets the blep!"

Both of us laugh. I reach out and squeeze Ash's hand, then quickly let go. I don't know if she's more surprised by it or I am. "I wish I could bike you to your apartment. But my mom's probably wondering why I'm not home yet."

"It's fine," she says. "I have junk I gotta get done today. Lunch with my dad and I'm gonna go see this girl Zoey's band tonight." While she rolls up Darth Vader, she tells me about running into Zoey at PetSmart and getting invited to her band practice. She stands up and brushes Chewbarka's hair off her shirt. "Do you think your dad will understand? Or do you think he'll tell your mom?"

I kick at a stick. "I don't know. I can't tell him what's really up, you know?"

"Why not? You haven't done anything wrong."

"Well—" I press my arms to my chest. "It's sort

114

of . . . it's maybe more complicated than I told you."

Ashley's brow furrows.

I press my lips together and look down. My eyes are starting to sting. "I, um." I take a deep breath. "So some guy brought Chewbarka to the vet to be killed." I spill the story, explaining how I not only have to protect Chewbarka but Tina too, and how telling any grown-ups could result in Chewbarka getting killed and Tina getting fired. I can't look at Ash while I'm talking. My throat closes up and my eyes water when I explain I wasn't sure who I could trust, that I just wanted to keep Chewbarka safe.

The tears spill over when I think about that guy walking away from his sweet little leaky, lovey-dovey dog he paid to have killed. I turn away and wipe my face. "I'm sorry," I say with my back to Ash. "I'm sorry I didn't tell you before."

She's silent for a moment. And then I feel her hand on my shoulder. "I get it," she says softly. "And I'm even more glad I could help." I hear her kneel and pick up Chewbarka. She moves in front of me, holding the dog. "I want to help. When you take her to your dad tomorrow."

"You don't have to." I smear my face, light-years beyond embarrassed.

"I know I don't have to. But I *want* to. I care about Chewbarka too, you know."

It would be so good to have her along. "Really?"

She nods. "Where should we meet? What time?"

I half gulp. She's actually going to help me. "My mom leaves for church at eight fifteen. How about by the dollar store on the corner of Kenmere and Montgomery at eight thirty?"

"I'm there like a mama bear." She laughs. "I don't even know what that means."

I smile. "Seriously, Ash, thank you. It's good to have a friend again."

"Again?"

"Yeah." I take a breath. "As long as I'm spilling my guts . . . I had a best friend for like forever. Cole." Where do I even start with this? "So, last spring, he started hanging around with this girl Erin Rogers." I explain how I thought he liked her, but he said he was crushing on Fiona, and that he decided to throw an end-of-year party with a spin-the-bottle game so he'd maybe get to kiss her. And how awkward it was that Mitch liked Fiona too, and that Cole had invited him not knowing that. I tell Ash I didn't want to play the game, but everyone else was and it looked weird that I wasn't. I tell her how when Fiona spun it stopped on me, and how no one else had backed out and I didn't want Fiona to feel rejected, and that the kiss was quick but still sort of had some tongue because that's what everyone else was jokingly doing, and that it was just enough to enrage both Cole *and* Mitchell. I tell her Cole didn't talk to me for the rest of the party, that he texted me while Mom was driving me and Mitchell home and said, **You French-kissed the girl you knew I liked RIGHT IN FRONT OF ME.**

"Well . . . what were you supposed to do?"

"Right?" I'm glad she understands. "Then Cole was always 'busy' over the summer. I wound up hanging out with my dog, Frankie, all of June and hiding from Mitchell and listening to my parents argue, until Frankie got so sick in July that he couldn't eat or walk anymore and we had to have him put to sleep—" My throat closes and I cough. "And Dad moved out in August right when school started"—oh lord, I gotta talk about something else—"so I felt awful and I really wanted to patch stuff up with Cole, right, so when school started I sat with him and Erin at lunch, which was awkward because I have nothing in common with her, or whatever, and Cole was a lot more interested in talking to her than talking to me, so they excluded me a lot. Which sucked. One day neither of them were responding to anything

117

I said, and I just kept babbling about Frankie and my dad. By the end of the lunch bell, Cole was staring daggers at me and I was like, 'Just tell me what you're mad about.' Erin looked at me like I was dirt and said, 'You invited yourself to our table and talked about your dad and your dead dog for half an hour and didn't even tell him happy birthday.'" I grimace at how stupid and selfish I felt. *Still* feel. "It was such a facepalm moment. I said I was sorry, but he laid into me. I got the idea he'd had it pent up for a long time. He said all I ever focused on was myself and I never paid attention when other people felt stuff and he was tired of it and no offense, but how about I sit somewhere else at lunch from now on. I ran to the bathroom crying like a freaking idiot. I haven't talked to him since, even though we have a class together and I see him in the hallways and—well." I clear my throat again, but the choked-up feeling just gets worse.

"And your dog died and your dad left and now you're taking care of Chewbarka on top of everything else," Ash says. "That's way too much all at once."

I cross my arms and look at my feet. If I lean into her sympathy, I'll turn into a blubbering puddle.

"Daniel . . ." She sets Chewbarka down, steps close, and puts her hands on my shoulders. "Feeling stuff really hard doesn't mean you're selfish."

For a frozen, stretched-out moment, I look into her eyes. They're warm brown at the edges and fade to a pale green by her pupils.

I never realized how interesting *hazel* is. Like it's a word for a collection, a spectrum, instead of a word for a color.

Ashley pulls me closer and kisses me.

I blink in surprise at the warmth of her lips on mine. Then I lean in and kiss her back, and it's everything I ever hoped a kiss would be: so sweet and sudden and wonderful that everything else disappears. It only lasts a moment before she ends it and I make an accidental *mwah* sound and Ash starts laughing.

"What?" I cover my mouth, afraid I did it badly again, that I suck at kissing—

"It's better from this side!" she says through her laughter. "*So* much better!"

I must look confused, because she explains how she's always disliked hearing people kiss because the shape of the sound was so doofy, but that the shape is different when it's happening to her, with her mouth, in her head. She grins and blushes the whole time she's explaining it, and I can't help smiling too, sucked into her light and laughter.

"Should we do it again?" I ask.

"Heck yes." We kiss again, and it's just as magical till Ash ends with an intentional *mwah*, and she dissolves in giggles and so do I and all my problems with my friends and my family and my fear disappear.

Just for a minute. Just enough that I can breathe again.

11

Boy Skirt Girl Punk

Ash

Mom pulls into the parking lot of the Mexican restaurant at 1:33. Dad steps out of his car wearing a button-down shirt with khakis instead of his usual white tee and jeans. He pointedly looks at his watch.

I suppress a sigh. If he's already mad that we're three minutes late, this could be rough.

"Don't let him give you a bunch of crap," Mom says. "He can't talk to you like you're eight years old anymore."

"He'll try." Mom and Dad never got along beautifully—according to her, they first connected because they were both leftists who enjoyed arguing politics, and they each understood where the other was coming from even if they didn't agree on specifics—but Dad's changed a lot since the divorce. "I just hope he lets me finish my food this time." Dad has a habit of assuming that when he's done eating, the meal is over.

"Good luck, baby. I'll see you when he drops you off, okay?"

"Yep." I take a deep breath, then get out and cross the lot to Dad.

"Hey, kid." Dad pulls me into a hug. For a moment, it's nice—he's tall and strong and he hugs fierce, and it's easy to feel safe. But that quickly changes to feeling suffocated. "What's the flavor of the day?" He lets me go.

I hate how that question reduces me to only my gender. "Um, girl still." I guess.

He gives my neutral outfit a once-over and we go inside. As I trail after him, I notice he smells different than usual. More . . . I don't know, soapy. Once we're seated in a booth, I see he's neatly trimmed his salt-and-pepper goatee as well.

Does he look all polished because he has a date tonight? Eew.

A stooped, gray-haired man with warm brown eyes hands us menus and asks what we'd like to drink. I request lemonade and Dad gets a Diet Coke, which is odd. He usually goes for the full-sugar stuff.

"So how's school?" he asks in his clipped way as soon as the waiter leaves.

"Good. I'm making new friends."

"Glad to hear it, kiddo. Oakmont seems like a big change from Bailey. More accepting."

"It is. And it's more diverse, which I like." I wish he'd use my name instead of *kiddo*.

"Have you joined any clubs yet? Your mom said they're big on extracurriculars."

I open my mouth to say *Rainbow Alliance*, but quickly change my mind. "Not yet. But I got invited to this girl Zoey's band practice tonight. I'm sort of hoping they'll invite me to join." Even if they suck, I've always wanted to be in a band.

Dad gives me a genuine smile. "I'm sure once they realize how talented you are, you'll be a shoo-in."

"Thanks. I hope so." His words make me feel good. But if Mom were here, she'd say calling me *talented* robs me of the credit I deserve for putting in the work to get skilled. "How are things at the doctor's office?" He's a medical technician at a cardiologist's office and does EKGs all day.

"Same old." A smile quirks at the corner of his mouth, like he's having a private thought he doesn't want to share.

"Have you seen any interesting cases lately?"

"People aren't *cases*," he says, straightening his collar. "Every heart is different. Like every person is different."

Uh-oh, here we go. "But . . . hearts behave in predictable ways, right? Like unhealthy choices make your heart unhealthy?"

"Sometimes. If you want to reduce it that way." He twists in the booth to make his back crack. It used to drive Mom nuts.

The waiter brings our drinks and takes our orders. Dad says he'll have the tilapia tacos and I ask for the deluxe vegetarian burrito. While we wait, Dad tells me about a book he's reading on the Boston Tea Party, a topic that's always fascinated him and bored me to tears.

The food arrives. My burrito is cheesy-gooey-excellent, but it's hard to enjoy it when Dad keeps glancing at his watch and then looking at me like there's something he wants to bring up. He finishes his tacos and asks the waiter for a box for my leftovers, even though I'm not done. When the guy brings it, Dad boxes up my food like I'm a child incapable of doing it myself.

I break a tortilla chip into tiny bits. He's about to drop a "fatherly wisdom" bomb on me in the vein of *If you don't take my criticism with gratitude, you're an immature child.*

He puts the box on his side of the table and looks out the window. "Have you been presenting as a consistent gender at school so far?"

My lungs try to suck in a steadying breath. I keep my shoulders still to hide it. "Girl."

"Your mom mentioned there's a school dance coming up."

I'm not sure what he wants me to say. "I saw a poster for it."

"Are you thinking of asking anyone?"

I go on high alert. "Um . . . sort of?" I *was* just kissing a cute guy two hours ago . . .

Dad studies my blush like he knows what I'm thinking about. "Well. Keep in mind that usually it's the guy who asks the girl. Not the other way around."

My blush deepens. What would he say if he knew I started the kiss with Daniel? "I'm pretty sure girls can ask guys—"

"They *can*. But they normally *don't*. If you want to be consistently perceived as a girl, you need to act feminine. Not just dress that way. Remember when I told you boys don't usually giggle at *My Little Pony*? And girls don't get obsessed with *Fortnite*? Same concept."

"But I mean . . . they *can* do those things."

He flicks his straw in irritation. "I'm telling you how

kids *usually* behave, since that seems to elude you. You can't put on khakis and a baseball hat and say you're a boy, or a dress and say you're a girl, if you're not consistently coding your behavior accordingly."

He's going all big-words on me to show he's smarter than me. "Why does it matter?"

He closes his eyes like I'm totally dense. "I'll simplify it. Would you put on a boy outfit and ask a new guy friend to watch *Frozen* with you?"

"I guess not." It would depend on the guy. Griffey loves *Frozen*.

"Would you put on a dress and ask a new female friend to, I don't know, play baseball? Or football?"

I stay silent. He knows I've never played either of those in my life.

"That's all I'm saying. If you insist on switching, at least do people the courtesy of acting like the gender you say you are. It'll make it easier for them to know how to interact with you."

"But—"

"It's all about consistency. This is something you should've figured out by now. You'd be in eighth grade already if you hadn't failed sixth."

Ouch. "I know, thanks."

"Consistency is especially important given your . . .

unusual thinking. Have you really not thought about changing your behavior along with your outfits? Come on."

"My thinking's not unusual," I mumble. I mean, Sam and Mara exist. "Mom thinks it's fine."

"I'm not saying gender roles aren't baloney. I don't go around preaching that women belong in the kitchen, for pity's sake. But your mom disregards the negative consequences your switching has with your peers. She doesn't necessarily have your best interests at heart."

I slump in my seat. "I didn't choose to be like this."

"You *choose* every day what you feel like doing. I've told you over and over how inconvenient that is for people. If you expect your new friends to change how they interact with you based on whatever your whim of the day is, you need to make it easier for them. That's why I'm explaining to you about being consistent with *behaving* like a girl and not just dressing like one." His voice is infuriatingly calm, but he's crimping an angry pattern in my Styrofoam leftover box with his thumbnail. "And honestly, you could avoid this whole mess if you'd finally get around to picking one gender and sticking to it. I'd be happy to defend you if you did that. Even if it's not the sex you were born as. You know I consider myself a trans ally."

A familiar mix of anger and shame floods me. Mom reamed the Bailey principal a new one after Camille posted the video she'd secretly taken of Tyler and those jerks jumping me. When Dad heard about it, he was mad those kids had bullied me, but he also told me it wouldn't have happened in the first place if I'd stayed one consistent gender. If I hadn't behaved in a way that made Tyler feel lied to. Which, ugh, he's right about. "It just seems like you're sort of saying I should be the one to change, instead of saying other people should stop being jerks," I say.

His expression softens. "I wish it weren't that way, kiddo. I really do. Other people should *not* be jerks. But in the real world—not the 'ideal' one your mom lives in—there will always be jerks. No matter what. I want you to be safe in the real world."

"And safe means hiding who I am."

He grimaces like he doesn't like my logic. "No. It means finally figuring out which gender you identify most with. And being *consistent*. Your life will be infinitely easier." He starts crimping the Styrofoam again.

I'm pretty sure he means *Other people will find you easier to be around*, not *You'll be happy and fulfilled*. I steel myself and ask the question I've wanted to ask for a long time: "When did you decide you were a guy?"

He cracks through the Styrofoam. "Don't be ridiculous."

"I just don't understand how you can say you're a trans ally if you only support, like, full-time trans people. And not . . . part-time ones." Is that what I am, maybe? Part-time trans?

"Don't invent new identities. And don't put words in my mouth. I'm *fine* with trans people. They make a full commitment to one gender, unlike you."

"I don't know if that's true for all trans—"

"You're a naive child who doesn't understand the concept of *trans*," Dad snaps. He sighs and rubs his forehead. "I've looked into it. Believe me. I had to arm myself for the fights your mom always wanted to have about it. *I've* done the research on the terminology. *You*"—he points like he wishes his index finger were a stick he could jab me with—"are young and impulsive. And she, for whatever reason, just goes along with it. All I can do is try not to care so much that your friendships at Bailey got so screwed up over your switching that your mom had to move you to a new district. Which means *my* child support checks are now going toward rent on *your* unnecessarily expensive new apartment." He wads up his napkin and drops it on my empty plate. "If you'll excuse me." He edges out of the booth and stalks off toward the bathrooms.

I wipe away angry tears. A retort circles my brain, too late to use: *Wow, Dad, I bet all the trans people in the world are so relieved that you're "totally fine" with them.*

I can't even imagine saying that to him. He'd have some comeback about switching and airports and inconsistency.

The waiter stops by to refill my lemonade. "Everything okay?"

I keep my face down and nod.

"Do you need help?"

I shake my head.

He hovers for a moment, then goes to another table, looking over his shoulder at me. A few moments later, he sets the bill at the end of the table. I scrape my pulverized tortilla chip into my palm and dump the crumbs into the basket. Maybe I could use a pile of disassembled tortilla chips for my rule-of-thirds assignment. It's an accurate reflection of my mental state.

By the time Dad comes back, I've calmed down and I'm folding my napkin into a rose. Dad puts his credit card on the folder with the bill. The waiter comes to get it right away. He gives Dad a once-over while he collects our empty plates, then glances at me. I fake a smile.

While we wait for the receipt, Dad spends a few minutes mansplaining the plot twist in that old Bruce Willis movie about dead people like it's even remotely relevant to my life. I nod in the right places. The waiter comes back, Dad signs the receipt and leaves a stingy 10 percent tip, and we slide out of the booth. I grab the pen and write *Thank You* on the napkin rose's petals while Dad pockets his wallet and digs out his keys.

It takes a hundred years to decide what to wear to Zoey's punk-band practice. Punk is guy music to me, but Zoey reads me as a girl. I don't want to rock the boat before it even leaves the dock. I'm feeling gun-shy of boat rocking after that lousy lunch.

I turn my thoughts to Daniel. I still can't believe I kissed him. Like *boom*, jump in like a dude, Ash! Don't wait till you're sure he likes you, or till he knows you're not always a girl! Don't be *smart* about it!

I doodled the shape of that *mwah* a thousand times when I got home. I drew stick figures of us too, what we looked like—two people standing together—and what it felt like. Two people rising up from the ground. Falling through the sky. Dancing the tango. I drew the one I'm afraid of, where Daniel stays on the ground and I grow wings and float up without him.

I pull on my vintage Ramones shirt and look in the mirror. Guy-me wants to wear it. But I need to hold on to the fast-fading girl feeling. Because Zoey thinks I'm a girl. Because I'm gonna need to feel like a girl tomorrow when I spend hours with Daniel.

Maybe wearing a skirt will help. I put on a layered fall-colors one I got at Goodwill with Mom a few weeks ago.

It feels so freaking wrong. So not-me.

Mom raps on my bedroom door. "You gonna be ready sometime this century?"

I scowl at my reflection. My shirt and skirt do *not* go together. I pull off the shirt, put on a plain black tee and grab the purple purse Mom cross-stitched with *I am Groot* under a picture of Baby Groot doing the Rosie the Riveter pose. Fiona would like it. "Ready."

In the car, I pick at my chipped nail polish. I feel like a dude in a skirt. I keep thinking about Sam at Rainbow

Alliance, who said pronouns aren't important to them, and Mara, who looks like a girl but uses he/him pronouns.

I want to be as laid-back about gender as they are. But I'm not laid-back at all, thanks to Dad. I'm Ashley or I'm Asher and that's that. While I'm switching, for that week or so, everything feels gross and inside out and bass-ackward until I can settle into what I'm switching to. That "identify as airport" thing Dad said was icky, but it also hit the nail on the head. I *hate* being in between. It's like when a lousy radio DJ doesn't know how to fade one song into another. That few seconds when both songs are playing but the beats aren't blending and you're like, *Oh my god, go back to DJ school.*

It makes no sense to me how anyone can hang out in between. Or be so comfortable with looking the opposite of how they feel that they're like, *This is who I am.*

Mom gives me a sideways glance at a stoplight. "Everything okay?"

"Fine." The car does the *screeeee—ping!* sound that always makes me worry a wheel's gonna fall off. Mom likes to joke that her car is old enough to legally vote.

"You've seemed a little . . . conflicted. Since lunch." She lets the silence stretch till the light turns green. "You really don't have to pick—"

"Yes, I *do*." We've had this argument so many times. "My life would be so much easier."

"Your dad wants you to see things as black-and-white, like he does. But life's not like that. *You're* not like that. No one is."

"Can we not talk about Dad?"

She makes a face. "I know. Puts me right off my tea and crumpets too. It just makes me sad that he tries to cram all his faulty thinking down your throat."

I keep my face aimed out the window. It's hard to consider Dad's thinking entirely faulty when there are so many things he's right about: that I wouldn't have gotten bullied if I'd been consistent. That Tyler felt lied to. That it's a pain for other people to keep up with my changing gender. That my problems are my own fault. You can't insist to everyone at school that you're a girl one week and a boy the next, and switch it over and over, without picking up a nasty nickname and more than a few bruises.

I just don't know any other way to be. I've wished on every birthday candle since I was eight that I could stop switching. Kids at school would quit calling me names and shouldering me out of group projects and ignoring me at recess. Dad would quit yelling at Mom that all the switching was driving him nuts and I'd stop bringing this mess down on my head if I'd just pick one and stick to it. He said it was impossible to parent a wishy-washy kid like me.

Mom says the divorce wasn't my fault. That they had a ton of other problems that had built up over time. That the "current political climate" that "discourages rational discourse" didn't help matters.

But it *is* my fault. Because when I was in sixth grade round one, I begged and begged Mom to legally change my name to Ash, which is totally different from my very gendered birth name. Dad was against changing it because he said I was too young to decide something so important—which, hello, does not jive *at all* with him saying I'm too old to not know what I am.

Mom changed my name without telling him. Dad was arguing with a doctor after my appendicitis surgery about the wrong name being on my chart when Mom told him. By the time I got home from the hospital, he'd moved out.

I'm still not sure if he went on his own or if Mom kicked him out.

When we get to Zoey's huge house, she's in the open three-car garage. One corner of it is full of musical equipment and has posters of dinosaurs all over the walls. Zoey's plugging a cherry-red Fender into an amp. She introduces the two other girls there as Olivia and Jordan. Olivia's a skinny redhead with glasses and freckles and Jordan is a tall girl with amber-brown skin, nearly shorn hair, and black fingernails with white skulls on them. "Together we're Tyrannosaurus Rocks, the baddest band to rock Oakmont Middle," Zoey finishes theatrically.

"Emphasis on the 'bad,'" Jordan snickers. "Especially you."

"Bite me," Zoey says. "You only know like five notes."

Rex comes over wagging his tail and noses my hand so I'll pet him. Mom asks if I'm good, and leaves when I give her a nod.

Jordan grins at Zoey. "At least Olivia has a boyfriend."

"Guys are garbage." Zoey pops her gum. "Every single one makes eye contact with my boobs before they look at my face."

"If you hate your boobs so much, donate some to me," Olivia says. "I need major help in that department."

"Me too," I say quickly. Rex sits at my feet and looks adoringly up at Zoey.

"Trust me, this is a problem you do *not* want. Every

guy looks at me like I'm a piece of meat." Zoey pushes a wheeled stool over to me and tells me about meeting Olivia and Jordan in sixth grade, about how the three of them became best friends immediately since they all like punk and hate country music and they all have a younger sister and an older brother and they're all good at math. She's dizzying to follow, but her energy is electric. By the time she's done talking, I'm pumped up and ready to rock.

"That skirt is literal fire," Jordan tells me as she tunes her bass. "I love the colors."

"Thanks. I got it at Goodwill for three bucks." I blush. I realized last year when Jackson said something about my "thrift-store trash outfit" that not everyone thinks thrifting is cool.

Jordan doesn't bat an eye, though. We talk about punk bands while Olivia bangs out a messy rhythm on the drum set. Rex startles at the sound and goes back into the house via a doggy door. As Jordan and I talk, I study her, trying to figure out if her works-with-any-gender name and her short hair mean she's like me. But then she says she's the only Black girl at school who's hard-core into punk, so I guess she's all female. She and Olivia and Zoey start talking about why girl punk bands are infinitely cooler than boy punk bands. I sit on my hands and pretend the guy bashing isn't bothering me.

"What are we starting with?" Olivia finally asks.

"Let's do 'Typical Girls,'" Zoey says. "Ready?"

"So ready."

The girls crash into a sloppy rendition of the song. Zoey's A string is tuned too low, Olivia's barely on the beat, and Jordan has more energy than skill, but they're having such a blast as they shout into their mics that it barely matters. I spin on my stool and play air guitar and sing along to the gritty, jangled steel-wool shapes of Zoey's guitar chords. The song's about girl stereotypes and the blasting punk shapes are shaking the boy feeling through my blood and bones, but I don't even care. When they finish the song, I go wild with applause. They all bow and laugh. I point to a dusty keyboard in the corner. "Does that work? I could join you."

"Sure, let's plug you in. Do you know 'Rebel Girl' by Bikini Kill?"

I've listened to the song a few times because Mom likes it. "Is that . . . A, G, G sharp, A?"

Zoey laughs. "Are you a legit musician? Like you know how to read music, not just tab?"

"I took piano lessons for a kajillion years." Zoey plugs me in and I play a scale. The jack is janky and static crackles every time I come down hard on a note.

"Wow!" Zoey watches my fingers fly. "You play any other instruments?"

"Guitar." I'm proficient, but not as good as I am at piano.

My nerves flutter as Zoey strums the chords for "Rebel Girl." I find a voice on the keyboard called "Overdrive" that looks like wiry hair with a curving metallic ribbon in it. Jordan and Olivia fool around for a moment, and then Zoey says, "Okay, go!" and plows in.

It takes a few measures for us to line up. I don't have a mic, but I shout the lyrics I know. I can almost hear my voice over the noise. Goose bumps prickle my skin as we head for the chorus. This sound is a living, breathing creature coming out of us, like we're calling it into being. I throw myself into the music, banging the keyboard and shouting the lyrics and breaking the best sweat I've ever sweated, losing myself in the wild joy of shoving all these jaggy excellent shapes into the world's empty spaces.

"Holy heck, I am *hooked*!" I say when the song's over. My ears are ringing and my heart is hammering. "That made writing laptop music feel like playing with Legos!" I wipe sweat off my forehead. "Does Tyranno-saurus Rocks have room for a fourth?"

"Hmm," Zoey says, tapping her chin and looking at Olivia and Jordan.

Their faces go flat and blank.

My stomach dips. It was way too forward to ask to join their band. And what's going to happen when girl fades all the way out and dude barges in? What if I can't fake female and they turn on me? What if they tell everyone I'm a liar? What if—

"You're so in," Zoey says. Olivia and Jordan melt into laughter. "But you gotta teach us how to read music."

I grin. "Totally can do that. I can show you how to use GarageBand too if you want."

"Oh heck yes!" Zoey looks at Jordan and Olivia. They both nod and she turns back to me. "So there's this thing next month called Girls Who Rock the Future. It's a fundraiser for a women's shelter my aunt volunteers at. Basically a battle of the bands for local under-eighteen girl groups. My aunt got us a spot and we're supposed to play two songs. You think you could maybe help us? Like teach us to play better?"

My heart leaps. "I would *love* to help you!"

"Awesome. My mom was gonna get me lessons, but I'll tell her you'll help us instead."

Yikes. I don't know if I'm good enough to fill that role. "Do you, um, do you have your songs picked out?"

"We're supposed to do one cover and one original. We're thinking about 'Rebel Girl' for the cover, but, well . . . we're not doing too hot on writing an original song." Her shoulders slump and she makes a face. "None of us are there yet."

I suck in my breath and hold it for half a moment. Boy-me wants to jump in and run this show. Girl-me is feeling intimidated. I need to shift my mindset if I want this to work. "I can write a song to fit everyone's skill level," I blurt.

Zoey brightens. "Holy cheese and crackers. You're our new best friend."

Olivia and Jordan laugh. To say I'm suddenly on cloud nine is a vast understatement. This is the *perfect* antidote to lunch with Dad. And wow, it feels good to give into the boy feeling I've been fighting. Even if it's just for a little while. And sort of undercover.

"The judges at Girls Who Rock will pick the three best bands," Zoey says. "Those bands get to go to a camp over winter break that teaches you branding and how to get gigs and stuff. We're all dying to get in."

"Mom said she'll get me a decent bass if we make the cut," Jordan says. "Instead of this crappy used one we got off Craigslist."

"Well, then, let's see about getting you a new bass," boy-me says.

We practice "Rebel Girl" twice, then stop for cheese puffs and Mountain Dew. While we eat, I explain the basics of reading notes on a treble clef. By the time Mom arrives to pick me up, confident Asher is running the show, explaining the difference between major and minor chords and how volume makes a sound louder but gain makes it bigger. Correcting Olivia's beats. Even showing off a little on the keyboard. I thank Zoey for an awesome time and tell the girls they rocked my face right off.

It takes only the short car ride home for the war between *girl* and *punk* and *boy* and *skirt* to start raging inside me. By the time we're home, Dad's words are ringing in my head and I'm more torn than ever about what I am. About who gets to make the first move. About which gender *confident punk-rock songwriter* is, and why I have it in my head that only boy-me can handle that role when Mom would say my gender doesn't matter a whit for something like that.

It's so freaking complicated. A math equation with too many variables.

Griffey sighs as he watches me pull my sleeping bag out of the washer and shove it in a dryer. He went on what he called "the world's most awkward bumper-bowling date" tonight with a dude from his English class and needed to vent about the disaster, so I told him to meet me at the laundry room on the first floor of building F. For the past ten minutes, he's been explaining exactly how stupid boys are.

It's making me feel gross after the boy bashing at Zoey's band practice. But I'm not gonna ask him to stop. This was his first actual date and it's a big deal to him. The least I can do is ignore my problems and listen to his.

"Sooooo," he finally says. "Did you tell Daniel yet?"

"Ugh, no." I put my empty laundry basket upside down on my head and squat on the floor. "I'm just gonna hide in here till I figure out if I'm a boy or a girl."

He pulls his arms inside his hoodie and twists so the sleeves flop. "You're neither. Your gender is turtle."

I snort a laugh. "Guess that's better than airport. But maybe I should be yours. Wacky waving inflatable tube dude."

"Ignoring your problems just gives them a chance to level up."

"Did you get that off a motivational poster at school?" I take the basket off my head and feed the dryer a few quarters. "I want to go with Daniel tomorrow to bring Chewbarka to his dad's. But Mom wants me to go to a PFLAG meeting with her. Which, like, I don't even know if I'm gay." I guess I'm headed that way, though. Being a guy, liking a guy . . . it adds up.

And I don't think Daniel's gay.

Griffey whacks my arm with his empty sleeve. "I'd shave off an eyebrow to have a mom who wanted me to go to any kind of LGBT support meeting with her."

I twist the knob on the dryer. I feel guilty that my mom's so supportive, even if maybe she's *too* support-ive, when Griffey's mom is super religious and regularly tells him he's going to hell for liking boys. "You could go in my place. I'm pretty sure my mom thinks of you as her auxiliary kid."

"I wish I could just *have* your mom." He shoves his hands through his sleeves, then gives me a let's-strike-a-deal look. "Tell you what. If you promise to tell Daniel the truth tomorrow, I'll tell your mom I got rejected by a boy and need your support in the form of another over-night."

I start the dyer. "It's like you're helping, but you're not helping."

"I just don't want you to get hurt. That video Camille took of those buttwads made me realize I might actually be capable of strangling another human being." He grimaces. "I *hate* what they did to you."

"They didn't hurt me." Not really. "And I don't think Daniel would do . . . that. But it still freaks me out wondering what he'd do if he found out."

"Since you kissed him already, you sort of have to tell him. Don't you think?"

I hop up and sit on the dryer. "What part of 'You're not helping' did you miss?"

"The part where I don't want some jerk to turn on you when he finds out you're not always a girl. Or did you miss that?"

"We're talking in circles."

Griff wrinkles his nose and his glasses slide down. "There's an easy way to solve that. You know what's great about being out? Literally everything. You should try it."

"I did. It did not go well." I never really *came out* at me and Griff's elementary school. I just obliviously assumed it was fine to go to school dressed like a boy some days and a girl other days, because in first and second grade, no one seemed to care. But the older we got, the more my gender became a Big Freakin' Deal. "What if you felt like you had to choose a side?" I ask. "What if people gave you a bunch of crap when you switched?"

"Ash. Your dad's a flaming jerk. Okay? You don't have to decide. For him or anyone else. You can be in between, or one sometimes and the other sometimes. Or a mix. Look at Sam and Mara. They don't give a crap what people say about them." He flicks a lint ball at me. "Just think about coming out, okay? To Daniel, to everyone. You could be so much happier."

Funny how Dad said I would be happier if I'd pick-and-stick. How Mom tells me I'll be happier if I do cross-country. It's like everyone has an idea of what will make my life better. "I constantly think about it. But I'll think harder."

"I know. It's complicated and I'm being a stubborn butt." He yanks my shoelace untied. "'I'll think about it' is good enough for me. I'll cover for you tomorrow so you can do the dog thing with Daniel."

I sigh in relief. "Thanks, Griff. I owe you like ten million." I retie my shoe.

"Yep. You're one lucky son-of-a-cuss to have a friend like me." He starts singing the genie's song from

Aladdin. I join in while drumming the dryer lid with my knuckles until someone in the apartment above the laundry room stomps their foot and yells, "Skip track!" and we laugh so hard I nearly pee myself like an ancient Pomeranian.

12

Closed for Business

Daniel

Early Sunday morning, Mitchell scares the bejesus out of me while I'm pumping the bike trailer's tires in the garage. "What are you doing?"

"Inventing sliced bread."

"You've been weird lately. Something's up."

"I'm—" Ugh, I'm no good at thinking fast. "I'm taking Frankie's old bed to the kennel. Since Mom says we can't get another dog. They can use it."

"Why don't you just ask Mom to drive it? Duh."

"You know what would be great? If you'd stop acting like you're looking for a chance to throw me under a bus."

His eyes narrow as he watches me hook the trailer to Vlad the Rapid. "So." He crosses his arms. "I know for a fact that Fiona's not busy this morning. You set me up on a blind date with her, and I won't tell Mom you're sneaking—"

"Mitch. Fiona has a boyfriend."

"The guy's a jerk who takes her for granted. She deserves better."

"You're better?"

"*Yes.*" He kicks the garage doorframe. "You're friends with her. If you tell her you want to meet her, she'll do what you say. And then it'll be me instead of you that shows up. With this." He takes something out of his pocket and shows me. It's a tiny silver Avengers music box.

"I'm not lying to her. She's my friend."

"Fine, I'll tell Mom you've been sneaking out at night. And that I found your hoodie behind the shed and it smelled like pee."

I look up at him. He looks back at me evenly, his arms still crossed. His jaw set.

He knows this is messed up. And he's doing it anyway because he's that tied in knots over this girl.

I grit my teeth. Mitch has a competitive streak a mile wide. He once told me I'd spent thirteen and a half hours doing stuff with Dad during Christmas break, and that Dad had only spent six hours with him. He lives to get even. I can't tell him no or he'll bust me and Chewbarka will be killed.

But man, I do *not* want to do this to Fiona. It's so unfair to her. I focus on the trailer tires, trying to think up some other solution that won't involve lying to her.

Mitchell takes out his phone. "I could text Mom right now."

"Fine," I snap at him. "Just . . . ugh. Really? *Really?*"

He at least has the decency to look a little sick that his gross plan worked. "Tell her you want to meet at Frosty Stop. Eleven o'clock."

I curse Mitchell out mentally, then text Fiona: **Can you meet me at Frosty Stop at 11? Need to ask you something**. I am a complete freaking jerk.

I guess, Fiona writes back. **Everything cool?**

Yup, will tell you what's up when I see you. She's going to destroy me for this. And I'm going to deserve it. "She's in," I tell Mitch. "If I'm not back before Mom gets home from church and volunteering, tell her I went to the kennel."

"You didn't put Frankie's bed in the trailer. Are you actually going there?"

"Do you actually care?"

Mitch steps into the shadows of the garage. He picks at a chunk of dried dirt on an empty pot and looks at me sideways. "I've thought of like fifty reasons for you to sneak out every night and come home reeking of outhouse. None of them are good. Are you like . . . okay?"

I wheel Vlad and the trailer out of the garage and yank the door down behind me. I am never, ever playing spin the bottle again.

Sometimes when I'm biking, my brain spits out an insight I belatedly realize has been stewing in the back of my head. Like a computer program solving an equation while the user does something else, and then boom: an answer. On the way to meet Ash, while I'm thinking over everything I told her about Cole, it occurs to me that saying *I'm sorry* and crying was just me doing the same thing that drove him to drop me in the first place: focusing on myself. On how I felt. I felt sorry, I felt regret, I felt guilty. And I expressed that.

What I should have done was what he always did for me. I should have said I understood where he was coming from. Cole is brilliant at repeating what someone says so they know he's understood them. I should have done that in June, when he was mad I kissed Fiona. I should have said *I didn't think about how much it would hurt you to watch that happen.*

There's more I need to think about with this, but I'm nearly to the corner where I agreed to meet Ash. The second I see her, a surge of nerves hits. She's on Sir Reginald Bevis the Steadfast, one foot on the ground and the other on a pedal, rolling back and forth. A purple helmet that matches her frilly purple shirt dangles from the bike's handlebars. She sees me and her face lights up.

My heart does the same thing. It's . . . surprising. And reassuring. I was starting to think something was wrong with me since I've never caught feels for someone the way it seems like everyone around me has already.

Then again, I also never thought I'd be hauling an incontinent Pomeranian in a bike trailer halfway across town to an apartment my dad lives in because he doesn't live with us anymore. But here we are.

"Morning!" Ash says brightly as I approach. "How's Chewy digging the trailer?"

"She cried at first and I felt terrible. But she calmed down." I glance inside the netting. She's panting and has a doggy smile. "You ready for a long ride?" I ask Ash.

"Abso-posi-toot-ley." She puts the helmet on. "Lead the way, noble rescuer of cute leaky doggo!"

* * *

It doesn't take long for my legs to burn and my butt to hurt from the bike seat. I Google Mapped a back way that keeps us off the busy roads, but hauling the trailer, even though there's only an eight-pound Pom in it, is tiring. I keep slowing to pull down the hoodie around my waist so it's over the bike seat to provide extra butt padding.

Six miles in, we stop for drinks at a gas station. We pull our bikes behind the dumpster and lock them together. It's shady and cool back here, even though it stinks. We take our helmets off and head inside. "What'd you tell your mom you were doing this morning?" Ash asks.

"Nothing yet. She does church and then volunteers at a food bank, so she won't be back till like two or three. How about you?"

"*Minecraft Bed Wars* tournament with Griff. She wasn't thrilled, but she didn't demand I come home, so." Ash shrugs.

In the store, I'm debating between blue Gatorade and red and Ash is looking at the snacks when she glances at two people at the end of the aisle and goes tense. Her eyes dart to the plain black hoodie around my waist. "Can I borrow that a sec?"

I hand it to her, curious. It's not cold in here.

She pulls it on and ties her hair back as a kid comes

over. He looks about our age and says "Sup" to Ashley like he knows her.

"Hey," she answers stiffly.

The kid seems like he wants to say something. He shifts his bag of chips from one hand to the other and looks at me like he's trying to figure out what the deal is with me and Ash.

I'm tempted to step closer and take her hand. But something makes me stop. She seems taller all of a sudden, almost as tall as me, and she's holding her shoulders rigid. She looks different with her hair tied back. Like . . . really different. Older, or something.

"Tyler's a total scumbag," the kid says. "Him and Jackson have been—"

"It's fine," Ash says quickly. Her voice is deeper, sharper. "I don't need to know."

The kid glances at the woman he came in with. "Well. We're getting hammered at the meets this year. Our team scores suck without you."

Ash opens the fridge case and takes an orange juice off the shelf with a shaking hand. I notice she's not wearing nail polish anymore. She doesn't look at the kid. She's blushing so hard her neck is red.

"Okay, um," the kid says. "I guess good luck at the new school or whatever."

Ash nods, still without looking at him. She beelines for the cash register like a girl on a mission.

As soon as we're out of the store, she yanks out the hair tie. She takes off the hoodie and gives it back to me without eye contact.

"So . . ." I don't know what to say. It seems weird to not acknowledge whatever just happened. "Why'd you ask for my hoodie?"

She looks like she doesn't know if she wants to kick the dumpster or burst into tears. "It was cold in there." She kneels by the trailer. "Hey, pupper. Doing okay?"

I busy myself with unlocking our bikes, a million questions in my mind. I start to ask who the kid was, how she knows him, why she made herself look different. Sort of like a guy. What kind of team he was talking about. Why she didn't want to talk to him.

But when I look at Ash again, she's getting on Sir Reginald Bevis and avoiding my eyes. She might as well have hung a Closed sign around her neck.

I don't want to upset her. So I don't ask.

13

Dude Mode: Activate

Ash

Daniel's unasked questions drift behind him on the warm fall breeze as we get back on the road. The longer he goes without saying anything, the more I want to tell him everything.

Well. Not everything. Just enough to explain, sort of, why seeing Nate freaked me out. I can't tell Daniel how right it felt to be a boy out loud, just for those few seconds, even inside the awkwardness. How right it felt to be *myself*, and how that feeling banged up hard against how much I like Daniel and want him to think I'm a girl. And how that locked me all up and turned me into a socially awkward robot in front of Nate, who thinks of me as a weird dude who dresses like a chick sometimes and not a chick who's a tomboy sometimes.

Maybe I could tell Daniel how I wound up at Oakmont. Without the details. I promised Griffey I'd at least think about telling Daniel the truth.

So as we ride, I start talking. I tell him about my appendix going kablooey, and that my parents' fighting got way worse when that happened, and how they split up while I was in the hospital. I tell him about Griffey moving to Oakmont when his dad got a better job here. I tell Daniel I failed sixth grade, and that everyone made fun of me for it—which they did, even if their focus was my flip-flopping gender, a detail I definitely *don't* tell Daniel—and I tell him how I only had one friend, Camille, and we weren't super close but she was kind to me. I tell him the bullying got bad at the start of this school year. Which isn't a lie. And that it got so bad that my mom decided we'd move, which also isn't a lie. And that Oakmont seemed better to her than Bailey in a hundred ways. Plus Griffey was here and she loves Griffey almost as much as I do. Which *also* isn't a lie.

I fall into silence and drop my gaze to my pedaling feet. I just gave Daniel like 30 percent of the real story. I left out everything about why Dad bailed. I left out that the only reason Camille was my friend was because she was the only person I knew at Bailey who was comfortable being herself out loud—like she was open about being bi and about being a total Wings of Fire fangirl—and who didn't also make a hobby of policing other people's identities. I left out Tyler and the song I drew and what he did to me. I left out Camille filming it and posting it in an effort to get adults to finally see how bad I was getting bullied. I didn't tell Daniel how the video spread like wildfire on social and wound up with Mom cussing out the superintendent and yanking me out of school.

Nothing I said just now was a lie. But it was such a small part of the truth.

It occurs to me as we pedal that I could just . . . say it. All that's keeping me trapped in this dumb girl act is me. I don't want to be wearing this frilly shirt, I don't want my hair down, I don't want to have on these fitted jeans with fake front pockets and stupid sequins on the butt. I'm wearing a girl costume over boy-me so Daniel will like me.

It's so fake. So wrong. Like I'm in drag against my will.

I look up, on the verge of telling him. But I have no idea where we are. He could turn on me as fast as Tyler did. Maybe faster, because I never kissed Tyler and I have kissed Daniel, and maybe that'll make him furious. He doesn't seem like the type to get furious, but I didn't think Tyler was either, and boy, should I have taken a cue from how he acted when his little sister cracked his phone case to know how he'd respond when he felt lied to. Even though I never lied to him. Not exactly. I just didn't tell him everything.

Like I'm not telling Daniel everything.

Daniel won't do what Tyler did. He won't pretend everything's fine and then turn on me when no grown-ups are around. He *won't*.

Anyway, Tyler would never have gone to so much trouble to save a dog.

Ahead of me, Daniel's foot slips off the pedal and he bashes his shin into it. He sucks his breath in and I realize that the jagged shapes dancing through my head, the ones I haven't been paying attention to because I was focused on myself, are the sounds of his breathing getting choppier. "Are you okay?" I ask.

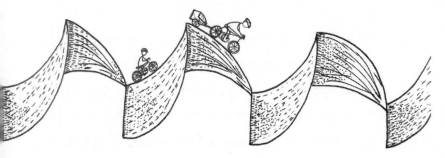

"No. Yes. Fine." He gets his foot on the pedal. His back is to me, so I can't see his face, but he sounds like he's doing that gasp thing people do when they're trying not to cry.

"You want to stop for a minute? Or trade? I can haul the trailer." I'm not sure I could, really. Sir Reginald Bevis isn't that steadfast. He's rusty and his shifters don't work. It takes about all I have to keep up.

Daniel doesn't answer. He slows to a stop. I put my kickstand down and walk to him. He smears his face with his sleeve and turns like he doesn't want me to see.

"Hey," I say quietly. "What's up?"

"That sucks that all that stuff happened to you. I'm really sorry."

"That's why you're upset?" Jeez. I should've kept my mouth shut.

"No, I just—I mean yes, I'm upset that people were mean to you. That's awful."

"But . . ." I'm getting the idea that's not why he's crying.

"I don't want to screw this up," he blurts. "I've seen Dad twice since he moved and both times I cried like a stupid little kid and I'm gonna do it again and I just—" He turns away, wiping at his face with both wrists. He barks out a triangular laugh. "I'm basically

160

a five-year-old. Or, like, a toddler throwing a fit at the grocery store. That's my maturity level. Fit-pitching toddler." He laughs again, but it's more cry than laugh.

I want to pull him into my arms and fold up around him and protect him from all the ways the world makes you feel bad for having feelings. But he's standing with his back and shoulders all stiff like if I do he's not going to be able to keep the epic meltdown in, and it'll make this even harder.

"We need a story," I say to distract him. "Since the truth could end in . . . well . . ." I glance at Chewbarka watching us with her cloudy eyes, her pink tongue poking out of her mouth.

Daniel takes a deep breath. "Yeah. I've been thinking about that." He wipes his face. "So I thought—" His voice cracks. He clears his throat. "I thought I could say Tina found her in the woods behind the kennel. And that she stuck her in a cage till she could figure out what to do with her. And then the car wreck thing, and I can say I sort of blurted out that I would take care of Chewbarka. But that I've been hiding her from Mom because Mom's so against getting a dog. But I'd say it's only been since Friday. Not all week."

"Right, good. That's good." It incorporates pieces of truth. Like I just did. "Except don't use Chewbarka's name? Because if she didn't have tags, you wouldn't know it."

"I didn't think of that." Daniel cracks a small smile. "I'm glad you came along."

A burst of joy spreads through me. "Would he ask why the dog couldn't stay at the kennel till Tina came back?"

Daniel's smile fades. "Oh. Yeah, I guess he will." His face goes glum. But then he brightens. "Or, wait. I was in the kennel once when Gavin the office guy was giving a customer a tour. He said that to be boarded, a dog has to be up to date on shots. So like, you wouldn't know that about a stray, right? So a stray couldn't stay there." He nods like he's agreeing with himself. "Yes. Yeah." He blinks and focuses on my face. "I'm glad you thought of that too. You're a genius, Ash."

My skin's going pink, but for once, I don't care. "Will he ask if you tried to call Tina?"

Daniel nods. "I actually thought of that. I've been trying to find her on Facebook but there's so many Tina Martins. I messaged three I thought might be her. Only got one answer, from someone who didn't know what I was talking about." He checks his phone. "Make that two someones who don't know. Still no answer from the third."

162

"Who's the genius now?"

"You. Still you. Definitely."

I laugh. I feel so light and free and happy that I lean forward to kiss him again. But our helmets knock together and our chins bump and we both crack up.

"Awkward!" I practically shout.

Daniel looks embarrassed but happy. "So, um. When we get there . . . can you help me explain? I don't think I'll cry like a two-year-old, but"— he waves his hand— "let's be realistic, it's probably gonna happen." He looks pained.

"Of course," I say.

"Thank you." Daniel smiles sadly. "My mom said once that her and Dad always wanted a daughter. I guess my life would be easier if I were a Danielle instead. It's fine if girls cry at the drop of a hat. But for guys, once you're past preschool . . ." He shrugs and forces a laugh.

I do too. It sounds like I tripped over a goat. Daniel says something about Mitch and Fiona that I'm too confuzzled to catch, and then we get back on our bikes and ride, and I can't get the image of him as a girl out of my head.

If I found out he really *was* a girl, and I thought I'd kissed a girl instead of a guy, would I be mad? Or upset?

I think I would.

I think I'd feel like I'd been lied to.

I don't know what to do with that. So I just keep pedaling.

14

Bodily Function

Daniel

I thought I was ready, I thought after joking about being a Danielle, I thought after we came up with a story, that I'd be cool. That I wouldn't immediately melt down and beg Dad to please come home so my life feels like a complete picture again instead of a puzzle with pieces missing. So I can sleep at night and do photography and return to my regular level of freaked out instead of this DEFCON 1 nonsense.

But standing at his door at 10:42 a.m., holding a smelly, diapered Pomeranian whose tongue won't stay in her mouth, I'm suddenly . . . not ready for this.

I can't even knock.

Ashley lifts her hand toward the door. She raises her eyebrows to ask if I want her to knock for me.

I nod. She nods too. Then she waits a minute like she's aware I need it.

She always knows exactly what to do. How to be around me without making me feel bad for feeling.

Cole used to be like that.

Ash knocks.

My heart pounds hard. I don't even know if Dad's here. Which, wow, how did it not occur to me until this minute that he might not be here? He's a creative director at an ad agency and sometimes has to go out to LA to direct commercials. For all I know, he's not even in town.

Footsteps inside, and the door opens, and he's so extremely here that I freeze up and can't even say hi. I just stare at his blue-gray eyes, level with mine, which is *so weird*, like he's been bigger than me my whole life and then I barely see him for two months and I'm as tall as him now? Have his shoulders always seemed so small?

The familiar lines of his face morph from surprise to confusion and then alarm.

"Hi! I'm Ash." Ashley sticks out her hand.

Dad shakes it, looking at me with one eyebrow up. "I'm Luke," he tells her. "Actually, make that Mr. Sanders. Daniel, what are you doing here? Whose dog is that?"

"This is Ch—" Oh crap. "Uh, it's sort of a long story. Can we come in?"

Dad glances into his apartment, then turns to me with an expression I can't read. "Yeah," he says like he wants to say no. He steps aside and we go in.

I stop dead. A woman with pale skin and long dark hair and dark eyes is on the couch, holding a tissue and a mostly empty glass of water. Like she's been there awhile. Her eyes are puffy like she has allergies. The TV is paused on *Mad Men*. Dad's favorite show.

"Daniel, this is Grace. Grace, this is my son Daniel. And—sorry, what was it? Ashley?"

"Just Ash. It's nice to meet you both."

Oops. I assumed *Ash* was short for *Ashley*.

"How'd you get here?" Dad asks me. "Did your mom bring you?"

"We biked," I croak. My throat is a desert. Not just from running out of water on the ride.

Dad looks alarmed. "On busy roads? With a dog? How'd you—"

"We took back roads through neighborhoods," Ash says. "Totally safe, don't worry."

"But that's—what is that, fifteen miles?" Dad tilts his head at me. "I think I need an explanation. Please."

My heart starts unraveling. When Mitch or I mess

up, Mom's like a school principal, all disciplinarian, ready to get us back in line. Dad's not like that. He wants to know where we're coming from, what we were thinking that made us do whatever we did. If we can't see how what we did could've turned out badly, he explains it, patiently. It works so much better than Mom's methods of taking away our phones or giving us extra chores or whatever.

I want to melt into that. To connect. To know he cares, even though he's gone.

Nothing comes out my mouth. I stare at Grace. She's pretty. Like prettier than Mom. Young-looking. Asking Dad with her eyes why his kid is staring at her like she has three heads.

Dad glances at her and then back to me. "It's not what it looks like," he says in a low voice, too quiet for her to hear. "She's my coworker. She's having a rough time with her kid and needed somebody to talk to. That's all."

My eyes move to the box of tissues on the coffee table. To the crumpled tissue in Grace's hand. I look at her eyes again. Not puffy like allergies. Puffy like tears. Her nose is faintly red.

But they're watching *Mad Men*. On Dad's couch.

Grace stands and brushes off her black jeans. "I need

to be getting back," she says to Dad. "I'm sure Mason has the sitter tearing her hair out by now. Thanks again, Luke." She picks up a set of keys on the table by the door. She nods at me and Ash, then steps out and closes the door behind her.

I watch Dad's face as the door closes. Is that disappointment? Frustration?

He looks at the dog in my arms. "So. You biked fifteen miles here and you brought a dog. I suspect I'm about to be asked a big question."

"Tina found her," I say. "Um—the lady at the kennel. A vet tech. Who works there." My brain is scrambled eggs. "Um, the dog was in the woods at the—behind the kennel. There's like a patch of woods back there past the field." My throat's doing the thing it does right before I start crying. Maybe if I talk faster I can stay ahead of it. "She's a stray. The dog I mean. And Tina's daughter got in a car wreck, so Tina had to leave and I said I'd—I would—" I push Chewbarka into Ash's arms. "I gotta pee," I blurt, and stumble down the hall. I close the bathroom door as Ash launches into the story we came up with.

The flood of tears that comes out my face is like the blorp of Mitchell debating. Like barfing. Like an earthquake. It's fast and intense and it's hard to keep it quiet.

I sit on the edge of the tub, pull a towel off the hook, and shove my face in it to muffle the sounds.

The towel smells like Dad's aftershave.

I throw it into the tub and finish my stupid meltdown with my fist jammed against my teeth. It doesn't take long to finish crying. But as soon as the last sob shakes its way out, guilt hits like a truck.

I lost it again. At a really freaking bad time to lose it.

I press my forehead to my knees and close my eyes and fantasize about living without being ashamed of this. Without constantly needing to apologize for feeling too hard. Without beating myself up every single day for having Big Huge Hairy Heinous Feelings. I wish so hard that people could cry whenever we need to and then get on with the day. Like sneezing or burping or getting the hiccups. A bodily function.

Maybe that's how it is in some other universe. Where dogs are in charge instead of humans. Dogs just feel what they feel. They're straightforward. They don't bother with guilt for being scared during thunderstorms or peeing when they can't help it or stealing every last bit of your heart.

I splash cold water on my face. It occurs to me that when I see Mom later today, it's going to feel like lying to not tell her about Grace.

But there's no way to tell her about Grace without telling her I came here. No way to tell her I came here without bringing up the dog. No way to explain the dog without disastrous consequences. For Chewbarka. For Tina. For me.

There's no way to make this easier.

Except . . . well. Ash is here.

Ash who cares about this messed-up dog as much as I do. Ash who doesn't mind my meltdowns. Ash who's patient and funny and smart and kind and fiery and the best sort of surprise.

I'm not alone. She's here with me.

It sucks that she's gone through so much. All the bullying, being sick, her parents splitting up, having to move—it's *so* much.

But she's okay. She went through all that and she's okay. Maybe not as happy as she could be, maybe with a little less faith in humanity. But she can still laugh and draw snores and joke about mutant zebra-platypus dogs and help me with Chewbarka.

She's brave enough and strong enough to keep going, even after all that.

I dry my face on Dad's aftershave towel, hang it up, and leave the bathroom.

15

Bargain

Ash

I want so bad to follow Daniel down the hall, since he's obvs two seconds from meltdown, but here I am holding this dog with Mr. Sanders looking at me all kinds of confused and upset and somebody's got to start explaining, so here we go.

I tell him the story we came up with. While I talk, I try to yank myself out of dude mode and back into girl, because I don't know, maybe that will help since Daniel said his dad wanted a daughter? But it feels so wrong after the gas station. Like those few minutes wearing Daniel's hoodie flipped the switch for good, and now I'm wearing someone else's ill-fitting clothes, someone else's broken-in shoes. I feel wrong in my skin.

When I finish explaining and ask if he'd maybe be willing to take the dog just till Tina gets back, Mr. Sanders looks at the closed bathroom door like he's more worried about Daniel. "Did he try to call Tina?"

"He's been trying to reach her on social. No answer. I guess she's pretty preoccupied with her daughter and all." I glance at the wall in the living room, covered in framed prints of Daniel's photos from his The_Ugly_ Twinn account.

Mr. Sanders starts to say something. But then he changes his mind. "Did he take the dog to a shelter to see if she has a microchip?"

"Oh. Um. I don't think so?" Shoot shoot shoot. Should've said yes.

He looks at me sort of the way Daniel did the other day. Like he's really seeing me. He has the same eye shape as Daniel, deep-set and intense, but his mouth is grim where Daniel's seems ready to quirk into a sad smile at any second. Maybe it's just grim because his kid busted him with another woman. He has the hang-dog face of that dude who plays the Hulk when he's not Hulked out. Guilty and sorta sick. Like he's done something he's not proud of.

The bathroom door opens. Daniel comes down the

hall looking like he ate something from the back of the fridge that should've been chucked a few weeks ago.

"Are you okay?" Mr. Sanders asks him.

"Fine," Daniel says, not meeting his eyes. He was definitely crying in there.

"There's a shelter ten minutes away," Mr. Sanders says. "With any luck, the dog's chipped and we can solve this right now."

Daniel takes Chewbarka from me, looking miserable.

In the back of Mr. Sanders's car, which has the same funky mold-in-the-AC smell Mom's car has, Daniel holds Chewbarka and looks out the window. He buries his nose in the fur at the back of her neck. She shifts in his arms like he's holding her too tight.

I reach out and take his hand. He folds his fingers through mine but doesn't look at me.

The shelter smells like bleach and pee and stressed-out dog. Chewbarka clearly hates it. She tries to claw her way up Daniel's neck and leaves a big red scratch on his skin. I try to take her from him, but she's not having it.

The gray-haired Black lady at the front desk looks wiped out, like she's cared about homeless animals too hard for too long. Mr. Sanders explains the situation to her, or at least the fake situation. He takes a struggling Chewbarka from Daniel as he talks.

"All right, let's see him." The lady beckons for Mr. Sanders to hand her over.

"Her," Daniel corrects. "She's a girl."

"Oh—I'm so sorry, sweetie. You're a girl! Yes, you are!" The lady cuddles Chewy and ruffles her ears. I feel a little sick. I wish people would apologize like that for misgendering me. Instead, if Mom corrects them, they usually get all flustered and defensive.

Daniel hugs his ribs and looks through the glass doors at the rows of cages full of abandoned dogs. I don't need to be a mind reader to know his heart is breaking as much as mine at the thought of all those animals who are gonna wind up dead because humans suck.

The shelter lady puts a thing that looks like a grocery-store scanner on the back of Chewbarka's neck. The scanner beeps. "Name's Chewbarka," the shelter lady says. "Belongs to a guy named Mark McBrenner." She sits back in her creaky desk chair and scribbles the phone number and address from the scanner on a Post-it.

"There you go," Mr. Sanders tells Daniel. "Problem solved."

The woman holds out the Post-it. Mr. Sanders reaches for it, but Daniel plucks it from her hand. "I'll call them," he says quickly.

Mr. Sanders looks at him suspiciously, but doesn't press it. He thanks the lady and we leave. "Are you two hungry? We can stop there." He points at the McDonald's across the street.

Daniel gets into the back of the car without answering. His silence says everything.

"I'm not really hungry either," I lie. I'm upset about how that went down too, but . . . that was a heckin' long bike ride and I've worked up an appetite.

Once we're all in the car, Mr. Sanders turns to face us, looking pained. "Daniel . . . if you need to talk about anything, I'm here. Okay? I hope you know that."

"*Here* isn't at home with us. Where you belong." Daniel sounds like he's about to cry again. Guy-me wants to jump in and stab his sadness with a lightsaber. Girl-me wants to cuddle the heck out of him and tell him it's okay to be sad when your parent is disappointing you.

Guy-me is definitely winning right now. My shoulders are up. Everything is tense.

"Let me see the Post-it, please," Mr. Sanders says. "We'll drop off the dog."

"What? I said I'd take care of it!"

"We can do it now."

"But *I* want to do it!" Daniel sputters. His eyes are wide, his hands gripping Chewbarka so tightly I hope he's not hurting her. "I'm the one who's been taking care of her. I want to bring her back myself!"

He's not the only one reeling. I have no idea what we'd tell that Mark McBrenner dude. He thinks his dog is dead.

Daniel's dad frowns. "How exactly do you plan to do that? On your bike?"

"Yes!"

"I'm saving you a trip. I don't understand why you're getting so worked up."

"It's not about the dog!" Tears leak from Daniel's eyes. He wipes his nose like he's angry with himself. "You ignore us for two months, and suddenly you want to be a dad and help me?"

Mr. Sanders lets a moment go by. Then he takes out his wallet and gives me a twenty. "Ash, would you mind going to McDonald's and getting us a couple burgers for lunch? Or whatever you want. I'm sure you'll both feel better after some food."

"Uh, sure." I'm totally being invited out. "Daniel . . . are you okay?"

He nods curtly without looking at me. I want to take Chewbarka, but I can't go in the restaurant with her, so I get out of the car. "Good luck," I murmur before closing the door.

I don't think Daniel can talk his way out of this one.

16

Chewbarka's Person

Daniel

My heart sinks as the door closes behind Ash. She's on my side. I want her here. But I don't want her to see this meltdown.

Dad faces the front, exhales, and grips the steering wheel. He's still wearing his wedding ring. He turns to face me. "What you've done today is not safe. You're not biking home alone."

"I'm not alone. Ash is with me."

"I'm calling your mother." He reaches for his phone.

"Do you want me to tell her about Grace?" I blurt.

Dad pauses. He presses his lips together.

"I actually did want to see you." I smear at my face

with my sleeve. "I didn't come here just to ask about the dog. But please don't tell Mom about her. She'll get mad at me for being 'irrational' or whatever." My drippy state isn't helping my case. "I can get Chewbarka back to her owner. I don't need your help."

Dad takes another deep breath. I feel like a burden. "How's school going?"

I blink at the sudden subject change. "What?"

"You got some bad quiz scores this week. You look exhausted. Have you really only had that dog since Friday?"

"You look at GradeFolder?"

"Every day."

"Instead of, I don't know, actually talking to us?"

"I called you every day the first week I was in the apartment. You answered your phone exactly once and gave me one-word answers."

I hug Chewbarka.

"You've always hated talking on the phone. But that's not what was going on. Was it?"

"I didn't . . ." I didn't know what to say. It seemed mundane to discuss my day-to-day life. To tell him about getting a typical B-plus on a science quiz. About doing my math homework. Missing Frankie. And if I couldn't talk about the boring stuff, how could I talk about the important stuff?

"I'm concerned about you," Dad says. "I want you to be happy. I can see that you're not."

"Then come home." I sound petulant. "Mitchell's a mess without you. He needs you around." It's easier than saying I need him too.

"We told you, this move knocks forty minutes off my commute each way. It's practical."

"Do you think we can't put two and two together? Are you that hard up for free time that you literally abandoned your family?"

He closes his eyes. "Let's not be dramatic. Nobody's abandoning anyone."

"Why don't you just tell me and Mitch the truth? That you guys are getting a divorce?"

"Who said anything about a divorce?"

"Maybe Mom will when she finds out about Grace."

Dad rubs his forehead the same way Mom does when she's stressed. I wonder which of them picked up the habit from the other, or if they've both always done it. "Okay," Dad says. "Fine. Sort out the dog situation on your own, since you clearly don't want my help. But I'm not letting you two bike back home. It's too far. I'll drive you."

"Our bikes and the trailer won't fit in your car."

"The trailer's collapsible. We'll put the back seats down. You can sit up front holding the dog. Ash is a little smaller, so she can squeeze in the back with the bikes. We'll manage."

I pull my knees up and curl around Chewbarka.

"I'm sorry you feel like I'm letting you down," Dad says. "Believe it or not, I'm human. Sometimes I unintentionally hurt or upset the people I love."

I'm sorry you feel bad that I hurt you is not an actual apology. "Then stop."

"The circumstances are complicated. It's not that easy."

"It looks easy from here." All he has to do is come home. Give up his new apartment, give up whatever's happening with Grace. Then we could be a family again. I want to say that, but I don't want to tip him into not letting me handle Chewbarka on my own. "I know it's complicated," I concede. "I feel like everything is way too complicated."

"Well." Dad's shoulders slump. "It's not a fun lesson to learn. But yeah. Everything is generally way too complicated. It only gets more so as you grow up."

"That's encouraging."

"Complicated isn't always bad." He nods at Ash hurrying across the road with a McDonald's bag. "Are things simple and straightforward with her?"

"They're—" I don't know. They are and they aren't.

Ash reaches us and stands looking at me and Dad in the car like she's not sure if she's interrupting. Dad rolls down the window. "Come on, get in."

She opens the back door and sits next to me. Chewbarka sniffs the scent of burgers and fries floating from the bag. "I got Quarter Pounders," Ash says. "And two large fries. I didn't get drinks because you didn't say to. Is that okay?"

"It's perfect." Dad holds his hand out. She hands over the bag with his change. He puts the change in the console, then takes a wrapped burger from the bag and tries to hand it to me.

"No thanks."

He pauses like he's annoyed. But then he gives me a sympathetic look that surprises me. He hands the burger to Ash. "Want fries?" he asks her.

"Yes, please."

He gives them to her and starts the car. "Buckle up, kids."

We buckle our belts. "What's the plan?" Ash murmurs to me.

"He's gonna drive us back to my house."

Her expression turns relieved and she nods. "Thank

183

you for driving us home, Mr. Sanders. My butt was killing me."

Dad laughs, but it sounds fake. "That's a long ride even if you're used to long rides."

"Which I'm not. I'm usually a runner."

"Usually?"

Regret crosses her face. "I ran cross-country at my old school."

"When did you move here?"

"Just a few weeks ago." They talk about the differences between Ash's old school and Oakmont for a minute, and then an awkward silence settles in.

"I'm sorry I've been calling you Ashley," I tell her. "I just assumed."

"It's fine."

We're quiet the rest of the way back to Dad's. I keep looking at the back of Ash's head while she looks out the window. When I was a kid, Mom said to Dad at the dinner table once that watching me and Mitchell felt like seeing her heart walking around outside her body. I didn't understand what she meant, but her words stayed with me because the visual was so gory and intense and funny. That was before things with her and Dad got cold and quiet. Before me and Mitch grew out of Legos and getting along. Before Frankie died and Cole ditched me and I figured out that life can seriously short out your fuses sometimes.

Now I get what Mom meant: Love is wildly dangerous. But you can't help it. Your heart says *yes, this* and that's that.

My heart has said *yes, this* to Chewbarka.

I'm afraid it's starting to say it to Ash too. I feel so much better when she's around.

Back at Dad's apartment, we unlock our bikes and spend ten minutes collapsing the trailer and folding down car seats and finagling Vlad and Sir Reginald Bevis into the back of the car. I tell Ash to take the front seat so she'll be comfortable, but she squeezes in the back so she's sitting on top of a folded-down seat with her feet resting on the frame of my bike.

Nobody talks on the car ride. About five minutes in, my phone pings with a text from Ash: **I was thinking, it seems weird a grown dude would name his dog Chewbarka. I looked up the name the shelter lady gave you. Chewbarka has a family and one of the kids goes to Oakmont Middle. Her name's Bella McBrenner. Do you know her?**

Doesn't sound familiar, I write.

I found her Insta. Ash sends the link.

185

I uninstalled the app, sorry.

A few minutes go by, then Ash sends a bunch of screen grabs. I don't know the blonde girl in the selfies, but it's clear she loves her dog. Chewbarka is in every one of them.

Do you think we should talk to her? Ash asks. **Tell her we have her dog?**

No way. What if she tells her dad? Chewy would be killed and Tina would get fired. I've blown so much stuff lately. I don't need to blow this.

"Are you two texting each other?" Dad asks. "You're sitting two feet apart."

Ash giggles. Another text comes in: **Maybe Bella wouldn't tell her dad.** She sends a screen grab of a post from eight days ago. It's a Chewbarka collage, from her puppyhood all the way through her face starting to go gray and her eyes cloudy. **Can't believe she's gone,** the caption says. **RIP baby girl xoxoxo your so loved.**

Guilt goes through me. I didn't post about Frankie before I deleted Insta. I was too sad.

Looks like Bella got Chewy when she was two, Ash writes. **Most of C's teeth were pulled a few years ago. That's why her tongue doesn't stay in her mouth. Her eyes are cloudy b/c she has cataracts. She limps and she's scared of other dogs b/c a stray attacked her**

186

and Bella's dad didn't want to pay for surgery to fix her torn ACL. And he got mad when Chewy had an accident in a hotel a year ago and C. wasn't allowed on family vacations after that. There's a pause, then Ash writes, I think it's safe to say Bella's obsessed with her dog.

I wrap my body around Chewbarka. It sounds like Bella felt she had to protect Chewy from her dad. Maybe telling Bella would be a bad idea, because if her dad found out . . .

Ugh. Chewbarka must miss Bella so much. It's obvious from the photos that she's Chewbarka's person, the way I was Frankie's person. He belonged to our whole family, but I was his. He slept with me every night. I fed him and gave him his medicine. I carried him outside and pulled him around in our old wagon when he got so old and feeble he could barely walk.

I can't even imagine how I'd feel if I found out he was still alive.

I know he's not. Putting Frankie to sleep was the last thing our family did together before Dad moved out. I felt Frankie's heart stop under my palm. I've worried for two months that my complete sobbing hysterics afterward are the reason Dad hasn't come home, the reason Mom's been extra hard on me about being so emotional.

But what if Mom or Dad had taken Frankie to that vet appointment without me or Mitchell? What if it turned out Frankie just needed a new kind of medicine or something, and someone else had him, and I found out he was still alive?

I asked Griffey if he knows Bella, Ash texts. **They're in jazz band together. He says she's in seventh grade and she plays clarinet like a boss but can't read sheet music to save her life.**

I nestle my nose into the back of Chewbarka's neck. I don't know what to do.

17

Fold It Up, Shove It Down

Ash

Daniel asks Mr. Sanders to drop us off at my apartment building. He doesn't look thrilled, but he glances at his Apple Watch and says okay. Maybe he wants to invite Grace back over for dinner later.

After we extract everything from the car in my parking lot, Mr. Sanders looks at Daniel on the curb holding Chewbarka. "You okay, Danny?"

Daniel nods. "Thanks for the ride. It was . . ." He bites his lip. "It was good to see you."

Mr. Sanders grabs him in a sudden hug. "I miss you, kid."

I can't see Daniel's face. His shoulders go stiff like he

wants to lean in, but he's not letting himself.

I get it. Part of me still craves Dad's approval.

After Daniel's dad leaves, Daniel gets Chewbarka settled into the trailer. "Thank you for coming with me today," he says. "It meant a lot."

"It seems like more is bothering you than the dog situation." I stick my hand in and ruffle Chewbarka's fuzzy ears before snapping the last part of the trailer's screen in place.

"I just . . . I can't believe my dad's seeing . . ." His voice is tight and he sits down hard on the curb. "I can't tell Mom. She'll know I biked to Dad's, which she'll freak out about, and she'll want to know why I went and then she'll find out about Chewbarka. But I don't even *want* to tell her about Dad because what if it means my parents are really, actually gonna get divorced?" He gives Chewbarka a longing glance like he wants to pick her up and hug her. "If I tell her about Grace and they split up, it'll be my fault. What if I get so freaked out that as soon as I see Mom I cry and tell her everything? It's totally something I'd do."

I sit next to him and scrape my shoe over the concrete. The shape it makes has a satisfying texture, like granite. I want Daniel to trust me. But that means being honest with him, which means, maybe, losing this. Whatever this is. "I'm sorry," I tell him. "I know what it feels like to be the reason your parents split."

Daniel looks at me sideways. Like he wants to know but he's too shy to ask.

I stand up. "It's survivable. And it was nice that your dad had your photos on his wall."

"What?"

"In the living room. You didn't see?"

"No." Daniel looks like his heart's breaking. "He did?"

"Yeah, like six or seven at least. Framed."

"Oh." His eyes are still aimed at my face, but I don't think he's seeing me.

"Um . . . do you want any water before you bike home?"

He blinks, then takes a second to fold up what he feels so it'll stop leaking out his face. "Yeah, actually.

Chewy's probably thirsty too."

I hop up. "Sit. Stay. Good boy! I'll get some water." I head for our building's door. I tuck my helmet under the steps so Mom won't know I was out biking.

"How goes the *Minecraft* tournament?" she asks when I go into our apartment. She's at the kitchen table flipping through her old Moosewood cookbook.

"Done. Just grabbing a book Griff wants to borrow."

"Hungarian bean soup for dinner? With sausage?"

"Sound good and gassy." I fill a water bottle at the tap, then grab a book from my room. "Be right back." Hopefully she won't look out the window.

Outside, I hand Daniel the water bottle. He thanks me for everything I've done. I ask if he's going to talk to Bella. He puts on his helmet without answering.

"I mean . . . maybe she knows someone who could help. A friend, or someone else in her family. Like an aunt or cousin or something."

He rubs his forehead like his dad did. "I need to think."

I take his other hand. "Daniel . . ." My stomach dips when he looks into my eyes. "I love how much you care about Chewbarka. It's really sweet."

He laughs like he's embarrassed. "It's not convenient."

"That doesn't matter. I mean it matters, but . . . the

192

fact that you're doing so much for her . . . well." I lean in to kiss him, angling so I don't bump his helmet.

He turns his face at the last second and I get his cheek.

I let go of his hand and step back. "Sorry," I mumble. My face is *flaming*. I must look like an overboiled hot dog.

"Don't be. I'm just like . . . this thing with Dad and Grace . . . it's a lot. You know?" He takes my hands again. "But I can't imagine how much harder it would be without you."

A rush of warmth hits me. "Well. It's important to have somebody to talk to. I talked Griffey's ear off while my folks were splitting. Not that yours will!" I say quickly when his face sinks. "It always seems like there's a ton of crap we can't control, 'cause we're kids. But having someone who knows what's going on in your life can help." Aaaand there goes my mouth.

"Yeah, you're right." Daniel looks at his feet, then at me. "It's hard to screw up a hug, though, right? I probably wouldn't, the way I'd screw it up if—"

"You ain't screwed nothin' up." I fling myself at him and wrap my arms around him tight, like I can squeeze all the sadness out. I hook my chin over his shoulder. "It's gonna be okay," I say, even though I have no idea if it will be okay, even though there's a big honking chance

193

it's *not* gonna be okay. Whatever "okay" even looks like. A non-dead dog, for starters, and a Daniel who isn't stressed out and exhausted.

"I hope you're right," he says like he's scared I'm wrong.

After Daniel leaves, I go back upstairs. Before I enter our apartment, I tuck the book I grabbed under my shirt. This whole dog situation is turning me into a liar. I feel gross about it.

But not gross enough to come clean.

While Mom does a cross-stitch and watches Netflix, I work out more of the punk song I started writing after the Tyrannosaurus Rocks practice last night. It's so good to think I can help them with Girls Who Rock the Future. To know they trust me after one jam session. I'm *going* to get this song right. It has to be simple enough that they can play it, and it definitely has to be about girl power in some way.

But not so girl power that I'll feel wrong singing it.

It's a weird balance. Punk is dude music to me. Even though there are tons of good girl punk bands. I just never listen to punk when I'm a girl.

I want to be part of Tyrannosaurus Rocks so bad my teeth hurt. That feeling I got when we were all playing and the sounds were lining up was just so . . . *big*. So good and real and *right*.

I want Daniel and me to feel that way with each other too.

18

Happy Fun Sunshine Time

Daniel

Back at the tent, while I'm getting Chewbarka settled and filling her dishes, my phone pings. I reach for it, hoping it's Ash. Wanting that sense of calm I felt when she hugged me.

But it's Fiona: **I thought you were cool. WOW, WRONG.**

I'm sorry, I answer. **Mitch made me do it or he was gonna bust me for something.**

I am NOT a bargaining chip in some STUPID FIGHT you have with your JERK brother who KNOWS I HAVE A BOYFRIEND. She sends three of the angry-face emoji with the profanity over the mouth.

I know, I write. **I really am sorry. I didn't know what else to do.**

How about take the heat for whatever you did! How about NOT pulling me into it!

You're right. You are. I'm so sorry.

She doesn't answer.

At home, Mom's car isn't in the driveway yet, which is a relief. I guess it's good Dad drove us home. I put Vlad the Rapid and the trailer in the shed and go inside. Mitch's door is closed and everything feels cold and hollow and wrong.

I miss my family. Even my stupid self-absorbed brother, who under all his dumb ideas and bad plans just wants the girl he likes to like him back. Wants his dad to come home.

I open the fridge. I'm not hungry, but maybe I'll feel better if I eat. Or at least less . . . empty. The only thing that doesn't require cooking is my leftover Thai from the other night.

Mitch comes in while I'm microwaving it. He sits at the table and crosses his arms, his face stormy. "She hates me now."

"She's mad at me too." The microwave beeps and I take my food out.

He kicks the table leg. "Why'd you let me do that?"

"*Let* you? Do you even remember how that conversation went?"

"I looked so stupid! She right away was like, 'Is this some dumb white-boy twin-swap crap?' and I was like, 'No, it's me giving you this,' and I handed her the music box and she—"

"I don't need the details." It's too pathetic to even think about.

He drops his head to the table. "I am such. An. Idiot." He thumps his head on the oak surface with each word.

I'm not gonna argue with that. I poke my rice with a fork. I should eat, but . . . ugh. To the infinite power.

I check the weather on my phone. Tonight's forecast has changed. It's supposed to get colder sooner, and now it's going to rain too.

Mitch sits up and eyes my screen. "What the flip is up with your weather obsession?"

"None of your business." I shove the phone in my pocket and leave the kitchen.

Mom comes home from volunteering at the food bank in a quiet mood, like she usually does after so much socializing, so Mitch and I are spared her all-up-in-your-business game. She just reminds us to get our weekend homework done and make our lunches, and then she spends the rest of the afternoon curled up on the couch with a book. The cover has a woman in yoga pants sitting cross-legged in a photoshopped flower.

I bring my homework to the living room and settle into the chair by the window. Mitchell's angst is leaking through my bedroom wall. I can't deal with his vibe.

My English assignment is straightforward, a worksheet that'll be the basis for an essay, but I keep yawning and sneaking glances at Mom. She looks so . . . unbothered, reading with her legs tucked under her. Not like someone whose husband moved out so he could see another woman. Not like the parent of one kid who doesn't get girls' boundaries and another kid who's been sneaking out every night and lying and is always two seconds from breakdown.

Her chill would be so crashed if she knew about Dad. They'd get divorced, probably sell the house. We might live in an apartment, which I've never done. Maybe there would be a custody battle. Or maybe not, because Dad doesn't seem like he wants us. It's not like he tried that hard to connect today. He just dodged the dog problem and drove us home.

I wonder how I didn't notice my photos on his wall.
Well. Grace.
I read the last question on the worksheet for the

hundredth time and fail to answer it. Again. I can't stop thinking about Chewbarka all alone in that stinky tent. It's killing me.

Mitchell tells Mom his homework is done and asks if he can go to Zach's house. She says to be back by six thirty for dinner. I'm exhausted after the ride, so I bluff my way through the last question and go collapse in a sorry heap on my bed. The next thing I know, I'm waking up groggy and confused to the sound of Mom calling me for dinner.

I check the forecast again: still cold and rainy. Still no reply from the last Tina Martin.

Apparently while I was asleep, Mom looked at Grade-Folder, because she's back to grilling me and Mitch about homework. Trying to manage us like we're projects at her job. I tell her what she wants to hear while I stare at Dad's empty chair and think about him having dinner with Grace. Drinking wine. Smiling. Playing footsie under the table.

It's hard to eat.

I blunder through my math homework after, then pretend to get ready for bed. Mom comes in while I'm climbing under the covers and says she's glad I took a nap, that I look more rested than I have and that she hopes I had a good weekend.

"I hope you did too," I say. "How was volunteering?"

She talks for a while about a family who just lost their apartment because of a rent raise and another where the single mom lost her job. It's depressing. I listen to the rain on the roof, to the wind picking up. It's hard to focus on her words while I'm thinking of Chewbarka. What if she's scared of rain and thunderstorms like Frankie was? What if she's trying to claw her way out of the tent? What if she *does* claw out?

"—distracted."

I blink back to the bedroom. "What?"

She studies me for an uncomfortable moment. Finally she gives me a fake smile. "Is it a girl?" She ruffles my hair.

I slump in relief. If she thinks it's that, she'll tease me instead of hassling me for being emotional. "Sort of."

"Tell me about her."

"Well. She's . . ." I lean against the headboard. "She's smart, and funny, and . . . you know, all those good things people say." Heat rises in my chest when I think of Ash hugging me. "She listens to me. Like she *sees* me. She doesn't just wait for me to stop talking so it's her turn."

Mom's smile shifts from fake to warm. "Anyone who does that is a keeper. Friends, girls, parents . . ." She looks out my window and her smile fades. "I know it's been rough since—Cole."

She was going to say *Dad*. I shift, not knowing where to look. Where to put my hands. I wish I had Chewbarka to hold.

"Has he talked to you at school at all? Or texted or called?"

"No."

"Have you tried to talk to him?"

"No."

"Nothing will change if you don't make an effort." She's back to project-manager Mom, solving my problems for me.

"I know."

She gives me The Mom Look, then sighs. "Mitch is kicking himself about something. But of course he won't tell me."

I fake a smile. "It's definitely a girl."

"Ah." Her face clears like at least one mystery is solved. "Fiona again?"

"I'm . . . uh, not at liberty to answer." I crack my knuckles. "As you like to say, 'Puberty is upon us.'"

"So it is." She sighs. "Well. It's good to talk with you. Or to talk around things again." She gives me a last look like she's thinking of bringing up something neither of us wants to discuss, but then she squeezes my shoulder. "Sleep tight."

"You too." I get under the blankets as she leaves. She starts to pull the door shut. "Leave it open?" I need to hear when she goes to sleep.

"Sure." She leaves.

When she's done putting her lunch together and setting out her clothes for tomorrow, I listen to her watching *Brave* on her tablet for the hundredth time. She calls it her "comfort movie." She's been watching it a lot since Dad left.

She watches the whole freaking movie.

I pace so I won't fall asleep. I watch YouTube on mute. I google *Tina Martin* for the tenth useless time. I nod off looking through the results I've looked at ten times already.

I snap awake at 11:52. It's pouring outside. Mom's light is finally out.

The hall closet door squeaks like the devil, so I don't risk getting my raincoat. I'm soaked by the time I make it to the tent on Vlad. Chewy is huddled in a ball, shivering. "Oh no. I'm so sorry. I'm so, so sorry." I pull her into my arms and wrap the smelly, awful blanket around us, curl up on the cold tent floor, and hold her close. My soggy clothes make her pee stink even worse. It must be so awful for her. Dogs have a way stronger sense of smell than humans do.

When she finally stops shaking, I text Ash: **Thank you for coming today. I'm sorry it didn't work. I'm going to try to find a way to reach Tina.** Maybe I can . . . I don't know, tell one of the receptionists I want to call her and see how her daughter is doing. Would that be weird?

Yeah. But I'm gonna have to suck it up and be weird. I'm running out of options.

Ash surprises me by answering, even though it's nearly one a.m.: **I think you should tell Bella. I bet she can help.**

I tighten my arms around Chewbarka. **I can't take that chance. Is this a girl-solidarity thing?** As soon as I send it, I realize it was a crappy thing to say.

No. I'm trying to help you.

I'm sorry, I answer. **This mess has me all messed up.**

If you were in her shoes, you'd want to know your dog was still alive. Wouldn't you?

I don't answer. I curl up with Chewy and gently try to tug apart some of the mats forming in her long, thick fur.

Did you put extra blankets in the tent? Ash writes. **It got so cold out. I have a bunch of quarters. I can help with washing stuff tomorrow if you want.**

Sort of, I say. **If you consider me a blanket.**

You're there now??? Dude it's wicked cold.

I noticed. I pull the blanket tighter around us. I like when Ash says *dude.* I don't know why. It's . . . familiar. Like we're really good friends.

She's quiet for a while, then: **Do you want me to bring Darth Vader to you?**

Of course I want her to bring her sleeping bag. I want her to bring *her.* But she's already done so much, and it's so late. **We're fine. Thanks though.**

Okay. There's a long pause, and I think that's it. Then she writes, **Isn't it funny that to dogs, we're basically magical giants who live for hundreds of dog years?**

I send back a smiley. **Never thought of it that way.**

I had a good time this weekend, she writes. **Not like a happy fun sunshine time, but I enjoyed it. Parts of it. The parts with you. I mean it was nice to spend time with you.** Another pause, followed by **I'm gonna shut up now.**

I liked those parts too, I write. I can't help smiling. It takes the ache out of the cold.

19

Sneet Snart

Ash

Monday morning, I wake up snuggling the wrong end of Booper. I'm so wiped out from texting Daniel at one a.m. and working on the T-Rocks song that I move like molasses and barely make it to the bus. Once I'm on, I open my bag to check if I have all my stuff. My pencil case and homework folder are missing. We have a quiz in algebra first period. Of course Mr. Simmons makes us trade one of our shoes to borrow a pencil. And of course I'm wearing the socks Mom cross-stitched corgi butts and cuss words on, because as she says, *Sometimes you gotta stick it to the Man even if the Man can't see it.* Which is how I felt when I put them on last night thinking of Daniel's dad doing that jerk thing and my dad being a jerk and how I don't want to be a dude like that, I want to be a dude like *me*, a new breed of dude who doesn't suck.

I take off my right shoe and turn my sock inside out as the bus is pulling up to school. I finish tying my shoe just in time to be the last one off the bus.

As I push through the crowded lobby, trying to get up to the 700 hallway so I can dig through my locker for a pencil, I see the back of a familiar head. "Daniel!" I call. But it's so loud and crowded he doesn't hear me. He works his way toward the eighth-grade wing and I follow. I finally grab his shoulder as he breaks free of the herd. "Hey!" I say.

He turns around, and whoa, it's not Daniel. It's someone who looks exactly like him. Or not *exactly* like him. Just . . . almost. "You're not Daniel," I say intelligently.

He looks at my Chainsmokers shirt and wrinkles his nose like he finds me gross. He turns and goes down the hallway while I stand there like an idiot. He moves nothing like Daniel. How on earth could I have mistaken him?

"Hi," a familiar voice says next to me.

I whirl to face Daniel. "You didn't say you guys were

identical!" It sounds like an accusation. "I mean—uh. That's Mitch?"

He nods. He looks again like he did on Friday, like he's barely staying upright. A faint pee smell comes off him.

"You stayed with her all night again. Didn't you."

"Shh." He looks around like someone's going to bust him. "She was cold. It's fine."

"It's not fine, dude. You look like death on toast. I'm legit worried."

"I need to go to my locker." He turns away.

"Daniel . . ."

He looks back at me, his face made of hope and wariness. I want to hug him like I did on the sidewalk, when I imagined squeezing the sad out of him. "I love how much you love her. You're a big softie."

He flinches like I just hit him.

"I'm sorry," I say quickly. "I didn't mean it like . . . I don't know. It's just something I really like about you. That you care so hard."

"You're the only person who likes that about me." He looks away like he wants to leave.

"You should tell Bella. So you can sleep again."

He doesn't meet my eyes. "I have to go. See you in photo class." He walks away before I can ask if he has a pencil I can borrow.

My locker turns out to be pencil-less. When I ask Mr. Simmons for a pencil, I can't remember which foot has the inside-out sock, and I take off the wrong shoe. He gets one look at the corgi butts and cuss words and gives me a lunch detention. Which is a case I could *totally* argue, because it's not like anyone could see my socks before I had to take off my shoe and who the flaming poop wants a shoe for a pencil anyway?

He tells me to turn my sock inside out. Right there in front of everyone.

I try to ignore the snickers. At least I'll match now. Even if all the cuss words are aimed at me instead of at the Man. Who is definitely Mr. Simmons.

Maybe for my rule-of-thirds assignment, I could use two inside-out socks covered in cuss words. That sure feels "personally significant" right now.

In English class when Mrs. Ellis breaks us into groups to discuss *The House of Dies Drear*, Zoey beelines for me with Jordan in tow. "Here." She thrusts a paper at me. It's full of songs by girl punk bands. "Now that we have a good musician—that's you, duh—we can up our game. You think you can teach us how to play these songs before Girls Who Rock?"

I look over her list. I know about half the songs, but

I only like two or three of them. "Probably. Which do you wanna start with?"

"I'll number them." She starts scribbling numbers next to the songs.

Mrs. Ellis taps her desk. "Zoey, it's time to work, not arrange a playlist."

"Sure thing." Zoey keeps numbering while Mrs. Ellis glares. I tense, thinking I'm gonna get in extra trouble since I already have a lunch detention. Zoey finally gives me the paper. "We'll talk after class."

"That's right," Mrs. Ellis says. "Because now you're *in* class. Where you do *work*." She gives me, Zoey, and Jordan a stern look and goes off to harass another group.

Zoey rolls her eyes. "She's totally uptight. She def needs to rock out."

Jordan grins. "Can you imagine her screaming into a mic?"

"She wouldn't be able to stop." I doodle a stick figure of her screaming out the jagged shape of punk chords. "All her pent-up rage would come flying out. Her hair would frizz and sweat would fly and she'd be so spent after that she'd fall over."

"That's a punk show I'd pay to see," Zoey says.

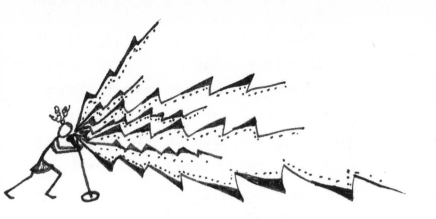

I stop at the cafeteria to get my lunch to take to detention. Griffey's not at our usual seat when I come out of the line. I scan the crowded cafeteria and spot him sitting near the condiment station. I take my tray to him. "What are you doing over here?"

He shrugs and bites his sandwich. I follow his eyes to our usual spot, where a cute guy is eating a wrap and looking around like he's trying to find someone. "Don't look at him," Griffey says. He shifts so his back is to the kid. "If he comes over, I'm gonna have a massive attack of awkward."

"Is that bumper-bowling dude?"

"Ugh, yes."

"You left out the part about him being cute."

"Cute doesn't mean squat when it's attached to a guy with the personality of a toenail clipping!" He shudders.

"Are you coming to Rainbow Alliance today? Because I do actually need moral support."

I don't want to go because, ugh, *gender*. And I'd rather help Daniel. But I really do owe Griffey for covering for me this weekend. Twice. Plus he was there for me when my parents were splitting, even though he had his own chaos going on with moving to Oakmont. "Yeah," I say, trying not to sound reluctant. "I'll go with you."

"You're the best." He flashes a grin. But then his face falls. "He's coming over here. Save me!"

"Sorry, dude. I gotta go to detention."

"What I wouldn't give for a DT. Ugh, I don't know how to handle this!" His face goes from dread to fake smile. "Heeeeyyyy," he says as the guy sits next to him.

I duck out. I feel bad abandoning him, but I don't want to get in even more trouble.

Detention turns out to be a nice change of pace. It's quiet, just six or seven of us delinquents sitting at desks, no talking, no phones. We're allowed to do homework or read.

I never realized how tense I am in the cafeteria. I guess it's 'cause of the massive number of people in there. This is a million times better.

I wonder if I could get lunch DT every day. And if Griffey could too. That'd be sweet.

I spend most of the time drawing a silly picture of Chewbarka. When the bell rings and I get my phone back, I text it to Daniel as I'm hurrying to history. In the flow of kids, right before I reach my classroom, I get a response. It's an adorable photo of Chewbarka in the tent. She's looking at the camera with her head tilted as if she's hearing a high-pitched noise. I zoom in and look at her cute tongue-blep.

"Hey," a girl says right behind me. "You. With the purple hair."

I turn and see a face I know only from Instagram. "Bella?"

"Why is my dog on your phone? And how do you know my name?"

Oh crap. "Um, what? This is my friend's dog."

"Bull. It was Chewy. I know that white splotch on

213

her head. And her tongue was sticking out." She reaches for my phone.

I pocket it. "I don't know what you're talking about."

"Then why are you hiding your phone? If that's really your friend's dog, prove it. Let me see the photo."

Panic mode. Zero words come out of my mouth.

Bella's eyes go wide. "No way." She half shakes her head like she can't believe it. Then her face darkens like she's about to haul off and deck me. "Explain. Now."

"Um—"

"Is she alive?"

I bite my lip and hug my ribs.

"Do you have her? Is she hurt? My dad said she got hit by a car. Did you find her?" Her blue eyes fill with angry tears. "Answer me! Is she okay?"

"She's fine." I press my back into the wall next to the history room door. I suddenly feel how I felt at Bailey Middle. Small, vulnerable. Afraid.

"Then how do you have her photo on your phone?"

The only action between my ears is fear. "Um—your dad, um, brought her to the vet to be put to sleep. But it sort of didn't go as planned?"

Bella's face goes through a million emotions before landing on a mix of rage and hope. "What the *actual*—" Her eyes dig into me like she's going after all my secrets.

"Where *is* she?"

"Um—someone I know is taking care of her."

She steps close. Like really close. "Who? Where?"

"A friend." No way am I telling her.

"What friend?" She leans even closer, her face almost touching mine. "What friend?!"

The bell rings. I edge away and duck into my history classroom.

She follows me in. "What friend!" she yells.

Ms. Jenkins looks at us. "Ash, you're cutting it a little close to the bell," she says. "And Miss McBrenner, this is seventh period, not third. Or did you not get enough of the Civil War this morning?"

"Ash what?" Bella demands. "What's your last name?"

Someone in the front row says "Haley" just as someone else makes a fart sound. Bella blinks like she's coming out of a trance. She gives me a narrow-eyed look like *I'm gonna get what I want.* She turns and leaves.

I sink into my desk, glad to be off my shaking legs.

Daniel's a mess in photography. We're supposed to write a plan for what we're going to photograph with our pinhole cameras and why and how long the exposure will be, but he keeps glancing at Fiona, who seems mad at him, and then staring off into space. He barely

215

meets my eyes. Which is good, because I'm having a hard time looking at him, thinking of how betrayed he's going to feel when he finds out I accidentally told Bella her dog's alive.

When our writing time is up, Ms. Bernstein tells us to share our plans with our table while she walks around and listens in.

Fiona reads hers out with her voice and shoulders all stiff. Daniel tries to compliment her, but she gives him a frosty stare. I have no idea what's going on. Braden tells us about the shop-room band saw he's gonna photograph, making it sound like it's stupid to photograph anything that's not a power tool. Ms. Bernstein comes over as it's Daniel's turn to share. He tries to read what he wrote, but struggles to read his own messy handwriting.

Ms. Bernstein tells him his plan needs work. He slumps.

When class is over, he's out the door before I can ask if he wants help today.

The Rainbow Alliance room is just as rowdy as the first meeting I went to with Griff. As soon as we go in, Sam, who's eating an apple, waves us over to a desk. "Hey, Griff. Ash, right?"

I blush like a doofus. "Um, yeah. Hi."

Sam takes a bite of apple, makes eye contact with Griffey, and nods. "I caught you staring at me here last week."

Oh god, Griffey's staged an intervention. "Sorry," I mumble with my face down. "I'm new here, I just, I'm trying to, like . . . get my footing, I guess."

"It's okay."

I glance up. Sam and Griffey are both smiling. "People stare at me all the time," Sam says. "I always ask why. They usually say they're trying to figure out what I am."

"Um." I glance at Griffey. "People do that to me too. Sometimes. I'm . . . like you. I think." I chip at a scratch on the desk. "I don't always dress like my birth gender."

"Yes!" Griffey practically shouts. "Jeebus, I thought it would never happen."

"Shut up!" I hiss at him.

Sam is laughing. "People don't have a birth gender. We're assigned a birth *sex*."

"I know," I say quickly. I glance around. The nearest kids are laughing at someone's phone. "My mom told me they're different."

"Gender's just, like, socially overemphasized decoration. Fun to play with." They point at their face. "Like today I'm feeling a little girly. Hence the mascara. But guy's there too, so I thickened my eyebrows with a brow pencil."

"But—" My brain is shorting out. Sam is a walking, talking example of all the stuff Mom tries to tell me. "You wear makeup to look like a guy?"

Sam takes another bite of apple. It still has a sticker on it. "I wear makeup so my outsides match my insides. I'm into coordination. You are too, yeah? You've got the red blush to go with your red Chucks."

Curse my fair skin. "What do you call yourself?"

"Sam. Nice to meet you." They hold out their hand and Griffey laughs.

I shake it awkwardly. "I mean . . . what label do you use?"

"I don't label myself. But other people like to label me. Enby, genderqueer, nonbinary, freak, agender, whatever. I get it all."

"But—are those accurate? I mean, except for freak. You aren't a freak."

"If you like being defined by something you're not, they're technically accurate." Sam takes another bite that just barely misses the sticker. "You like playing chess?"

Griffey laughs. "Ash sucks at chess. No offense, but you do."

"So are you non-chess?" Sam asks. "Chess-queer? Are you a-chess?"

I'm not sure if I'm being made fun of. "I guess?"

Sam shrugs. "Zero people will die if you don't label yourself. Or if you don't want to define something that shifts."

It's the kind of thing Mom would say. "I know," I say again, even though I don't, entirely. "It's just that the world's set up like it's one thing or the other. Are eight billion people wrong?" That's a big sticking point for Dad.

Sam leans in, their dark eyes looking right into me. "Yeah, they hella freaking *are*."

I shrink a little under Sam's intensity. "Do you— do you use the neutral bathroom?" My face is on fire. "Wait, that's too personal. Forget I asked. Sorry."

"I use whatever's closest when I need to pee. So yeah, sometimes."

"But—do people freak out at you?"

Sam shrugs. "Who cares? I just suggest they download the Genderbread Person so they can explore their identity, since their interest in my junk might mean they're more fluid than they think. Works like a charm." Sam notices the sticker. They pluck it off and stick it to Griffey's sleeve. "People get weird when your identity conflicts with how they think the world works."

"I've noticed," I say. "Which is why I'm, like . . . not out here. I'm not embarrassed, I'm just . . . I don't really know what I am. I'm not ready to—"

"I won't tell." Sam looks me in the eyes. "Promise. I'd never out anyone unless they specifically asked me to."

I slump in relief. "He knows, obviously." I nod at Griffey. "And my parents. That's all." And the kids at my last school. I'm "out" to them as the "flip-flop freak." As "it."

Mara joins our group. "Hey, guys."

"Hey, babe." Sam gives Mara a peck on the cheek that makes me blush, then turns to me. "All I'm saying is, nobody has to pick between two opposites. It's a spectrum, not a binary. You can be on both ends at the same time, or neither end. Hang out anywhere you want on the whole glorious continuum. You don't have to look like a guy to be a guy, or a girl to be a girl."

Mara nods. "Preach."

"I second that. I mean third it," Griffey says.

"Then it's settled." Sam chucks the apple core at the trash can by Mr. Lockhart's desk. It misses and bounces across the floor, leaving smears. "Oops." They get up to retrieve it.

Mr. Lockhart calls the room to order and asks us to

shove the desks into a circle. I wind up between Griffey and Esme, the girl who's pre-HRT MTF. Mr. Lockhart hands everyone an index card. He drags an empty desk to the middle of the room and puts a big bin of markers on it. We're supposed to look up the pride flag that best represents us at this moment, then draw it on our index card. He says if we don't know what flag is right for us or don't feel like making one, we can write an inspirational quote.

I steal a glance at Sam, who rolls their eyes and mouths *labels*, then grins.

Everyone gets to work, talking and laughing. Griff starts on a rainbow. Esme uses pink and blue to make the trans flag. I look over at Sam. I can't tell what other colors they're using than the purple they're holding.

I stare at my blank card. There's no flag for *just plain dude*. Which is what I am "at this moment," which is what Mr. Lockhart said we should do. And I don't think any of Mom's cross-stitches count as "inspirational" quotes.

Griffey shows me his phone. "How about this one?" His screen has a flag labeled *Gender Fluid* with five colors on it. He nods at Sam. "That's probably what they're doing."

"I'm not that right now," I say. "I'm just a guy."

"And you like a guy, right? So go with a rainbow. It

covers everything anyway."

I guess he's right. I borrow his red marker and start the first stripe.

I'm so stressed about the Daniel-Chewbarka-Bella situation that I barely pay attention to the conversations around me. I don't snap out of it until I look up and realize everyone's putting their flags in a pile. Mr. Lockhart says he's going to make a collage to put in the school lobby.

Esme tells Griffey and Sam how she pronounced *peninsula* as "pe-*nin*-sweh-*lah*" when she was reading from the textbook in social studies today. "It's spelled the same as it is in Tagalog, and that's how my mom would say it in Tagalog. It was so freaking embarrassing. Everyone laughed and that's how I realized I said it wrong."

"It sounds way cooler than peninsula," Griffey says. "Like you'd go to the pe-*nin*-sweh-*lah* to party."

Sam laughs. "I'd party on the pe-*nin*-sweh-*lah* with you folks any day."

The conversation drifts for a while. Esme starts talking about how she goes to thrift stores with her friend on the weekends and buys girl clothes, then hides them at home because her parents insist she's sick for saying she's a girl. She leaves her house wearing guy clothes every morning and changes in the neutral bathroom here. She starts crying as she says her dad found her expensive makeup and chucked it. She'd saved the money to buy it by mowing lawns all summer, even though it made her dysphoria wicked bad. Her dad told her if he ever found out she was dressing like a girl again, he would send her to live with her aunt in Texas.

Sam tells her that's a horrible thing for a parent to do. "Like grade-A actual worst."

"Totally," I agree. "You win the crappy-dad contest." At least mine never threatened to throw me out.

Esme sniffles. "Sometimes I think there's a universal law. Dads are required to suck."

"You want me to punch his lights out?" I push up the sleeve of my Chainsmokers shirt to show my nonexistent bicep.

She laughs through her tears. "He spends every night drinking Bud Light and watching ESPN. You could totally take him."

"Well. Probably I need to do more push-ups first." I pull my sleeve back down.

Sam snaps their gum. "It's such a load of smelly bull for a parent to make their kid feel bad about who they are. I'm sorry you have to deal with that."

Esme gives us a grateful smile. "*So* hot and smelly."

She wipes her face. "Thanks. For real. You're cool, Ash. Even without the push-ups."

I feel my cheeks turn pink, which is so not a dude color. I gotta get the focus off me fast. "Did you know 'trans teens' spelled backward is 'sneet snart'?"

Sam, Esme, and Griffey burst out laughing. I take out my phone and pretend to be fascinated by my wallpaper. My face is so red I'm sure people can see the glow from Kansas.

While Mom's driving me to Zoey's, she mentions she got a voice mail from school that I had a lunch DT. "What was it for?"

"Wearing socks with cuss words on them."

She makes a raspberry sound. "Guess it's a relief you weren't setting off smoke bombs in the teachers' lounge. Maybe I shouldn't have encouraged you to wear those particular socks to school."

"Yeah, probably not." I keep trying to pop my already popped knuckles. I texted Daniel after school to ask how Chewbarka was, and he said *Cute as ever* and sent a few pictures. I can't stop thinking about what's gonna happen when he finds out I told Bella. And what will happen if Bella goes looking for me on social and finds the Gatorade video.

"You're awfully quiet," Mom says after a while.

"Just tired." I look at the weather. It's gonna get stupid cold tonight.

"How's Griff?"

"Fine." Whoops. "For getting rejected. I met the kid at lunch. Cute but dumb."

She gives me the side-eye. "Well. It's important to support the people you love."

"I know." Was that a dig? Because I didn't go to the meeting for PFLAG so she could "support" me by shoving me into a social situation I don't want to be in?

Keeping my mouth shut is the best strategy. Luckily, the rest of the ride is short.

Rex the shepherd is happy to see me when we get to Zoey's. He noses my hand again and sniffs all the Booper smells on my jeans. "You must be a dog person," Zoey says. "He's usually standoffish when people come over."

"I love dogs." More than people, usually. I hug Rex. When Olivia starts banging the drums, he startles like last time and goes back into the house.

Practice doesn't go great. My head's not in the girlpunk groove. My mind's too busy holding up everything Sam said against what Dad said at lunch. Trying to figure out who's right. If they both are. If I should stop thinking because it's all baffling and I feel gross about not having anything figured out. It's killing my confidence.

Zoey keeps giving me weird looks, like she's confused I'm not as excited as I was last week. I realize I must seem like a different person than I was then, when I was jumping around all pumped up on the music.

I pull it together enough to be sort of convincingly enthused. When we're done playing "Rebel Girl" for the third time (they're improving, but slowly), I take my phone out and start walking the girls through how to use GarageBand to layer tracks. Zoey and Jordan follow along on their iPhones, but Olivia has an Android. She keeps losing interest and wandering off to play drums. Zoey gets annoyed with her for making noise while I'm talking and tells her to get her head in the game, that we won't be ready for Girls Who Rock if everyone's not on the same page. Olivia sighs and comes over to watch me explain how to add in a beat. "Let me hear that one again," she says while I'm showing Zoey the presets.

I turn my phone volume up and loop it for her. She sits at the drum set and starts trying to play along with it. She's got the general idea, but the specifics are eluding her.

Zoey asks how the song I'm writing for the fundraiser is coming along.

"It's getting there. I'm mostly focused on the bridge now. It's a little tricky."

"What's a bridge?"

It's hard to believe someone who has a punk band doesn't know what a bridge is. "It's that part after the chorus repeats for the second or third time that changes the mood. Like it can be in a different key, or faster or slower or whatever. So you come to the final chorus with a different take on it." I try to think of a punk example, but of course my brain spits out a Disney one. "You know in 'Let It Go' from *Frozen*, that part where Elsa's singing about her soul spiraling in frozen fractals? That's a bridge."

Zoey laughs. "I haven't watched that movie since I was like six. So the bridge part is harder to write?"

"It can be. There are so many different ways you can go with it." Like my whole life right now. My gender. Whatever the heck is gonna happen with Daniel. This Girls Who Rock the Future thing that I'm probably gonna be a boy for. "I'll figure it out."

"Can you play what you have so far?"

I pick out the chord progression on the keyboard.

But I didn't practice it enough to play it perfectly. I miss a note with my left hand, then lose the beat trying to recover. "Sorry, I'm super tired. I promise it's better than this."

Zoey looks disappointed. I'm saved from feeling like a total idiot by the arrival of Olivia's and Jordan's moms, and mine right after.

"Chug a Rockstar before practice next time," Zoey tells me. "Punk's all about energy. You were kinda lacking in that department tonight."

I look down at my hands in my lap. "I know. I'm sorry."

Zoey shrugs. "I'm not mad or whatever. I just really wanna kick butt at this Girls Who Rock thing and get into that camp. I've been dreaming about it for months."

"For real," Jordan says. "It would kick so much butt. Not to mention it would prove to my annoying brother that Black girls can *totally* rock some punk."

"Totally," I echo hollowly.

"Sweet." Zoey gives all of us a fist bump and we leave.

I keep my headphones in all the way home so I don't have to talk to Mom.

20

What If?

Daniel

I'm a sleepwalking mess Tuesday morning when I leave for the tent. I brought two more blankets there on last night's late-night run, and I wrapped Chewbarka in them before I went home. But when I unzip the door this morning, I find she's peed through her last stolen diaper and both blankets are damp. She's sluggish, like the cold has seeped into her bones and she's too chilled to even shiver.

I hold her for as long as I can before I have to go home, working on her mats with the borrowed brush. My warmth slowly sinks into her. She finally looks up at me and licks my arm.

It's so hard to leave to get ready for school. It's only going to be in the mid-forties today. She's old and cold and must be sick to death of this stinky tent and maybe Ash is right that I should tell Bella, even though that's the last thing I want to do because what if? What if?

But I might have to take the chance. Because freezing alone in a tent overnight with pee-soaked blankets when it's thirty-eight degrees is a worse way to die than euthanasia.

At school, I steel myself and head for Ash's locker. As I approach, I see someone yelling at her, a girl whose back is to me. I step up my pace.

"—found that video of you," the girl says.

"What's going on?" I ask.

The girl turns and faces me. I recognize her from the Insta screenshots Ash sent me. "Do you know where my dog is?" she demands. "Because this loser won't tell me a thing." She jerks her thumb in Ash's direction.

I slump against the lockers. Ash told her behind my back? "No." I can't meet Bella's eyes. "I don't know what you're talking about."

Bella scowls and turns back to Ash. "If you don't tell me where she is by tomorrow, I'm sharing that Gatorade video with everyone. And then maybe the same thing will happen to you here." She takes off down the hall.

I look at Ash. Her face has gone pale. "What is she—"

"It's nothing." She spins her combination lock, not looking at me.

"Why'd you tell her?" I hug my stomach.

"I didn't mean to." She sounds like she's going to cry. "I didn't tell her where the dog is, I promise. Or anything else."

"What Gatorade video? What's that mean?"

"Nothing." Her voice is faint. Her hands shake as she slides a book into her bag. She closes her locker and ducks across the hall into her homeroom.

All through first-period chemistry, I avoid looking at Cole and Erin, as usual. I imagine the conversation between Ash and Bella. How could she have done that when this isn't even her problem? She's not the one barely sleeping, getting up at five a.m., constantly hiding a lie from her mom. She hasn't been in contact with so much dog pee it's probably stuck to her for life.

She's said so many times that she wants to help.

She *has* helped. On Friday night, and then going to Dad's with me.

But she just straight-up told Bella. Without asking me first.

I feel stabbed in the back. Everything is even more

out of my control now. All I want is for Chewbarka to be safe. And warm. And not dead.

When the bell rings, I'm too caught up in my head to notice I'm right behind Cole. Just as we're about to go out the door, he looks back at me. I suddenly recall my bike-ride revelation about apologizing to him the right way.

I open my mouth, but then stop. I haven't thought it out enough. I need to do it *right*.

He goes out the door and the moment is gone.

In English, Erin sits on the other side of the room and, like always, ignores my presence. I'm used to it now. But it still hurts. Especially when I'm already feeling stung. Betrayed. Scared that my attempt to help a dog is going to get the dog killed.

She looks so happy, talking to Tatianna. I keep hearing snippets of their conversation about dress shopping for the fall dance. The one Erin's going to with Cole.

The whole "dance" thing is so dumb. The janitors cover the gym floor with thick black plastic so our shoes don't mess it up. There'll be punch and bad junk food, like unsalted pretzels and stale marshmallows. Some kids wear jeans and hoodies and some kids get dressed up and it feels weird, like you're in two realities at once. It's never helped by the creepy mix of awful gym fluorescents combined with cheap spotlights that spin colored beams over the plastic floor. One of the bus drivers is the DJ. He'll play "Baby Shark" at least twice.

I still don't get why Cole connects with Erin. They're so different. She's all sportsball and fashion and doesn't like dogs, and he loves dogs almost as much as I do. It seems weird that they're dating now when Erin's not Cole's type. Whatever his type is. Who even knows.

Maybe Ash is *my* type. Maybe I'm down on the dance because I was sort of hoping in the back of my mind that I might ask Ash.

There's no way I'm asking her now. Even if she is cute and funny and loves dogs and I'm sure she'd say yes. I can't *believe* she told Bella. If it gets Chewbarka killed . . .

That can't happen.

But I've run out of options and time. I *need* to get in touch with Tina. She's the only adult who might be able to help now.

All through second period, I work on drumming up some guts to call the vet office by thinking about how much Chewbarka needs me. When the bell rings, I duck into the bathroom and dial, my heart pounding and my palms sweating.

A receptionist answers the phone. I stumble through

explaining that I'm the kid who volunteers in the afternoons, that I'm wondering if she can give me Tina's number because I want to see how her daughter's doing. I hear another phone line ringing, and people talking.

"Sorry, kid, it's busy here," the woman says. "No time to chase down a number. I'll have someone call you later."

"Okay," I say quickly and hang up.

Crap. I didn't give her my number.

I thump my head on the stall door. I wonder how much trouble I'd be in if I just walked out of school and went to the tent. If the trouble would be worth Chewbarka's life.

21

Confession

Ash

By lunchtime, I can't keep it in anymore. I sit with Griffey and everything pours out: how Bella found the Gatorade video and is gonna blackmail me. How Daniel hates me now and all I wanted to do was help save this dog and keep Daniel from falling apart. How I feel like *I'm* falling apart now, and I was going to tell Daniel, I really was, about not being a girl, but now he'll find out from someone else and I can't even—

"Whoa, calm down." Griffey grabs my arms and looks at my face. "Just so I have this right . . . Bella's threatening to out you if you don't tell her where the dog is?"

"Yes." I'm practically hyperventilating. "And Daniel will see it and he'll hear those kids deadnaming me and calling me the flip-flop freak and he'll know I'm not always a girl—like I'm not anymore, I'm a guy now—" I hiccup on the fear. "And what if he pulls a Tyler? What if Bella's dad finds out and Chewbarka gets killed and it's all my fault?" I cover my face and try to get a full breath in. Crying is *not* an Asher thing. It's all Ashley.

"Lord, boy." Griff pulls me in for a hug. He's the very best friend on earth because he knows exactly how long he can do it before I crack. He pushes me away at just the right second. "How'd she find the video?"

"I don't know. It's everywhere on social. It couldn't have been hard to find a purple-haired Oakmont kid named Ash Haley who can't pick a gender."

"We're gonna fix this," Griff says with certainty.

"How?" I ask, reeling my freak-out in.

His eyes narrow and he gets that hint of a smile before he does something that winds up with him in trouble. "You'll see," he says.

He won't tell me anything else.

I don't know if I feel better or not.

In photography class, we finally get to take our pinhole cameras out of the room to do our photos. I'm getting big ol' leave-me-alone vibes from Daniel, so I go left out of the room, even though the plan I wrote yesterday involves the mural by the cafeteria and now I'm walking the wrong way. I glance back to see if Daniel's gone yet. He's way at the other end of the hall, looking like he wants to talk to me. But then he steps around the corner and is gone.

I slide down the wall, hug my oatmeal box, watch the clock, and wait. If I used my pinhole camera right now to make a selfie, I could title my photo *Angsty teen boy huddled in hallway*, tag it #emo, and collect a slew of likes from other angsty kids.

I doubt there are many middle schoolers with this particular flavor of angst. I don't want to lie to Daniel about being a girl anymore. It feels like I'm wearing a mask over the truth of who I am. But I don't want to lose him either. He's one of the most caring people I've ever met. He cares even when it hurts him. When it's inconvenient. When it gets him in trouble and costs him his friends. I *love* that about him.

I hope his compassion means there's a future where I can be who I am without losing him.

Daniel doesn't show up till almost the end of the period. He sees me sitting in my angst ball on the floor and steps into the classroom.

I hurry to the mural and set up my camera. I wrote

on my plan that I'd expose it for twenty seconds, but twelve seconds in, I bump the oatmeal box with my elbow. The shot will be ruined if I don't cover the pinhole. I strap the cardboard flap over it with the rubber band and rush back to class. I'm the last one in the room. Ms. Bernstein gives me an irritated look.

The whole bus ride home, I go back and forth about what to do. By the time I get off at my stop, I know all the shouting I'm doing in my head is totally pointless, that it's time to tell Daniel. Like right now. Before Bella outs me.

I bike to the tent slow as witch's snot in January, even though I should hurry so I beat Mom home. I'm gonna lose Daniel over this. He's already mad I told Bella. I don't think he'll team up with a bunch of scumbags to pin me in the grass and yank my head back and dump Gatorade up my nose while he screams "Flip-flop freak!" at me. But I didn't think Tyler would either, and now there's a video of it all up on the interwebs where anybody can find it. Thanks to Camille, who I still haven't talked to since I yelled at her for posting it.

I should've known someone here would figure it out. That moving was only a temporary fix. That I couldn't hide it when I switched again.

I'm so doomed. My whole life is gonna be like this.

Daniel is curled up with Chewbarka by the tent, looking miserable. "Hey," I say quietly.

He nods but doesn't look up.

"Can I sit down?"

He shrugs.

"I didn't tell her you have her," I say. "She doesn't know it's you."

He looks at me sideways, then down at his feet.

I take a deep breath. "She's going to . . . tomorrow, she's going to tell people . . . about me. Um." I tuck my hands under my legs. "Like that's . . ." A flattened laugh comes out. "The price I'm paying. To keep her in the dark about you having Chewbarka. I'm gonna . . . let that happen. To keep your secret. Okay?"

Daniel just looks confused.

My heart is trying to wham its way out of me. "There was this guy. Um. At my old—where we used to live, our old apartment complex. I liked him. His name was Tyler. He—"

Daniel's phone rings the "Radiate" tone. The liquidy minor chord ripples through the air between us. He looks at the screen. "It's the vet. I have to answer."

I nod, frustrated and relieved at the same time.

"Hello?" Daniel says.

"Daniel," a guy with a deep voice says. The phone volume is turned up enough that I can hear every word. "Explain why my client Mark McBrenner says his daughter told him a kid at school has their dog. The one I euthanized last week."

Oh no.

"Um—" Daniel's voice is a squeak. He clears his throat. "Um, I'm not sure?"

"I know Tina didn't finish the euth. But she doesn't go to Oakmont Middle. You do."

"Um, what's—what's going to happen to Tina?" Daniel's gone white as a sheet. He looks like he's about to hurl.

"Tina's been fired. Where's the dog?"

"I don't—I don't know." He looks at Chewbarka sniffing a tree.

"You need to bring the dog back." The guy sounds furious, even over a tinny phone speaker. "Immediately."

"I can't," Daniel whispers. He hangs up. And right away he's sobbing. "They know," he chokes. "They're gonna kill her." He stumbles over to Chewbarka, grabs her, and hugs her tight.

Chewbarka struggles in his desperate grip. I take her from him as gently as I can. He doesn't want to let her go, but I can tell he knows he needs to so that he doesn't hug her too hard. "Look," I say as calmly as I can. "This might be the only way to save her. What if we give her to Bella and—"

"No!" He covers his face with his fists, his shoulders shaking. "How can you say that?"

"She loves her dog. She was crying when she realized Chewy was still alive. What if there's a chance she could talk her dad out of it? I don't even like Bella, but it's the only thing I can think of that might save—"

"You're just saying that so she won't tell everyone whatever you're hiding!" He presses his face to his knees. "You're just trying to save yourself!"

I lean back with the dog, feeling gut-punched. "I just told you I'm letting her out me. To protect you and Chewbarka. Did you miss that?"

"Out you? What, you're . . . are you gay? Then why'd you kiss—"

"I'm not—I mean maybe, I don't—" I groan in frustration. "I was trying to tell you. Before the vet called."

"Oh yeah. You were telling me about some guy you liked." He finally looks at me, his teary eyes all anger and confusion.

"Yeah." I swallow. It's now or never, so I guess it's now. "Tyler and some other kids pinned me down and screamed nasty stuff at me. My friend filmed it and posted it. Tyler poured purple Gatorade up my nose. Because I told him who I am."

"Wait, that's—that was the bullying? He *hurt* you?" Daniel has about a hundred expressions on his face. "What does that mean, who you are?"

"I'm—I'm Ash. That's it." My lunch wants to come back out. "Like sometimes Ashley. Sometimes Asher. But always just . . . Ash."

"You're—oh my god." He leans away from me. "You're saying you're a *guy*?"

"Not always. I mean, I am now. But I wasn't before." I sound like the flip-flop freak the Bailey bullies said I am. But . . . it's a strange relief to have it out there.

"I kissed a guy," he says. "You're telling me I kissed a guy."

"You kissed *me*," I tell him. "Or I guess I kissed you, really, but I was a girl then and . . ." I feel so sick. "But I mean—would it be so wrong? If you did kiss a guy?"

Daniel stares at me, his face unreadable. Then he goes into the tent and comes out with Chewbarka's leash. He takes her from me and puts the leash around her neck. "You should go."

Tears spring to my eyes. I feel empty and alone and so incredibly rejected and stupid and wrong I can barely breathe. "What are you going to do about Chewbarka?"

Daniel angrily smears at his face. "I don't know. There are zero good options."

"But—"

His phone rings. "Please just go."

I stand up and brush the dirt and leaves off my jeans. The woods swim in my vision. Daniel's phone rings again. "I just wanted to help you and Chewbarka," I say. "This whole time. I promise."

He won't look at me.

22

Just for Now

Daniel

The phone rings again. It's Mom. Dr. Snyder must have called her, he must have told her I have Chewbarka. She's calling to ream me out, to tell me to get my butt home this instant so she can figure out what to do with me.

I send the call to voice mail. "This isn't your problem," I tell Ash. "It never was."

"But I care about—"

"I know," I tell her. Him?

Him.

God. She lied to me. Or he did. I don't know. I just know that *I care* is true, because look at everything Ash has done to try to help me save Chewbarka.

It doesn't matter now. They're going to kill this dog, who's done nothing wrong. Who just wants someone to hold her at night when it's cold.

My throat goes tight. I turn away. "Please go."

Ash says nothing for a long time. My mind spins. I can't process. All I can do is feel. My heart has come loose and crash-landed into my spleen.

Eventually, I hear Ash walk away. Chewbarka watches him leave and whines softly.

I turn to go after Ash. To say I'm sorry, I just need a minute to compute, I'm not saying go away forever. Just for now, so I can figure out what I feel. What to do. How to be.

But I still see Ash*ley*, like Ashley the girl I assumed he was, when I look at his retreating back. And it feels like I'm losing the girl I knew.

It hurts like fiery hell. I *care* about her. Him. Whichever.

Ash the person. Not only Ash the girl. The *person*.

Who's leaving. Because I said to.

I duck back into the tent with Chewbarka. I need to get this epic tear flood out of my system so I can bring Chewbarka home to Mom and plead my case without turning into a blubbering idiot. I want so badly to talk to Cole. To Dad. Even to Mom, minus the judgment. I just need to know someone's in my corner, now that the very last person who I knew was on my side has just walked away because I told him to.

I have *got* to start fixing my relationships.

23

The Gatorade Kid

Ash

I don't know why I go looking for the Gatorade video when I get home. Maybe I want to convince myself it's not that big a deal. That losing people you care about is part of life and I should get over it.

But first I want to figure out how Bella found it. I open Insta since she probably searched *Ash Haley* on there. My profile is private but my screen name, Ash_BashCrashSmash, is still visible. The one friend we have in common is Griffey.

I check his photos. The fourth one down is a shot he took of the two of us pretending to arm wrestle. The second comment on that photo is from Camille. It says

Aaaah I miss Ash!!

"Sure you do," I mutter. I look at her profile, which is public. A few posts down is a screenshot she took of some nasty comments Tyler and Jackson left on one of her photos. She's captioned the screenshot Theydies and gentlethems, I present to you my charming classmates who bullied my friend Ash right out of school, followed by three of the eye roll emoji. The first comment is from my former cross-country teammate Nate, the one I saw at the convenience store with Daniel. It says I miss Ash! @TylerDurdenWishes and @JacksonWithTheAction are the scum of the earth. Below that, Tyler and Jackson have, predictably, defended themselves by slinging a lot of profanity at Camille and Nate.

I sigh. That didn't take much sleuthing. Bella probably followed the same trail and found Tyler's or Jackson's profiles. Griff told me Camille deleted the Gatorade video later that night, but Tyler and Jackson had already downloaded it and reposted it, bragging about what they'd done.

I never went looking. I wanted to forget the whole thing.

I don't want to risk seeing the video on Insta with a bunch of comments calling me a freak and saying I deserved what I got. I don't need to fan the flames of my wrecked self-esteem after that mess with Daniel. Instead, I open Facebook and go to the Bailey Middle PTA page, where Mom said she saw it. I scroll through the last few weeks of posts, searching. Torn between hoping I'll find it and hoping I won't.

My stomach dips when it shows up on my screen. It has 122 comments.

I look at the framed cross-stitch on my wall that says *When life shuts a door, open it. That's how doors work.*

I take a deep breath and click play, bracing for the fear and humiliation to hit again.

But it doesn't.

This time, when I watch Jackson jerk my head back and deadname me, when I see Tyler pour Gatorade up my nose, my heart fills with anger.

Not anger. *Rage.*

How could they *do* that to me? What is *wrong* with them? How screwed up do you have to be to attack someone like that? Someone who is literally *zero threat whatsoever* to you? And to do it three against one—

I sink back in my desk chair, shaking. I open Insta to tell Camille, again, exactly how furious I am at her for posting it. How she wrecked my life and it's her fault we had to move and how I thought we were friends.

But then I pause. I go back to Facebook and look at

the parents' comments.

So many are supportive. Angry on my behalf, on Mom's behalf. Blasting the principal and superintendent, saying it was a cop-out for them to claim that since it happened off school grounds there was nothing they could do. Demanding changes at Bailey. There's even a thread where parents decide they'll set up a bullying hotline. Down at the bottom, one of the oldest comments posted is from Mom asking the poster to take it down, to respect my privacy. But then a bunch of people replied and said it should stay up as evidence. That nothing would change if people didn't see what was really happening.

I take a deep breath and open my Instagram messages. I read what I said to Camille the day it happened. Throwing all my anger at her instead of at those boys, 'cause she was a target I could reach. A target I knew I could hurt.

Hey, I write. I'm sorry I said that stuff to you after you posted the video. I know you were trying to help.

Omg, she writes back immediately. I'm so sorry I posted it. I never should have. I get why you were mad.

No, it's good you did. I hope it made stuff change.

There's a long pause, and then she says, It did and it didn't. Like the teachers are all "If you see something say something" all the time. But Tyler and Jackson are still &%#*wads.

I hope they're not messing with you for trying to bust them, I write.

Not me. They're focused on a sixth grader. I keep trying to get him to own his gayness so the Scumbag Squad will stop harassing him, but he's not out yet and they're torturing him for it.

Ugh. At least if I'd stayed, Tyler and Jackson and those boys would be picking on me instead of that poor kid. I know how he feels, I say. Someone here found out I'm the Gatorade video kid and she's threatened to out me.

Oh god now I feel worse, Camille writes. I'm so sorry. I didn't think it would get so spread around. I just wanted those buttheads to get punished for what they did to you.

It's fine, I write. I needed to come out here anyway. I actually did tonight to a guy I like.

Did it go okay?

I drop my phone, cover my face, and take a few deep breaths.

I can't freaking believe how bad that went. But I also get why he wanted me to leave. If he'd been the one to kiss me first, if I found out he had girl parts under his clothes . . . I don't know. I might have been mad.

251

But maybe I wouldn't. Because he'd still be who he is. The person who saved Chewy, who's sacrificed sleep and free time and sanity to keep her safe. To try to solve this awful problem.

I guess love for a dog isn't a thing that has a gender. And that's what I like about him. His dog love is more important than what's under his clothes. And if he says he's a boy, even if he has girl parts, then to me he's a boy. I don't even know if it would matter if he had different parts than the ones I assume he has. Even though I definitely like guys and not girls.

I sigh hugely. Realizing I'd like Daniel regardless of what's under his clothes doesn't make me feel better. Because I hoped he'd like something in me that was separate from that too.

And I don't know if he does. I think maybe he doesn't.

I pick up my phone and tell Camille it didn't go great, then say I need to do my homework. She asks if I want to hang out sometime.

I hug my knees. I don't know how it would feel to see her. If I'd think of all the miserable stuff that happened at Bailey after Griffey left. If I'd be a total killjoy.

But . . . well, Camille is pretty all right, really. She might've humiliated me while trying to save me, but she meant well. And she was comfortable being herself in a way I never was. Last April in the cafeteria she asked Ellie Decker if she wanted to see the school's spring musical together, like as a date, and Ellie said, "I'm not gay," and Camille was the poster child for handling rejection. She shrugged and smiled and said it was fine, that she figured there was no harm in asking. And Ellie was cool about it because Camille was cool about it.

That's what I should've done with Daniel. Right from the start. Then at least maybe we'd be friends now. Instead of . . . whatever we are.

Nothing, probably.

Yeah, I tell Camille. I'd like that.

After the distraction of my homework is finished, I start feeling rotten about Daniel again. I sketch Chewbarka sleeping. But it doesn't do much to help me feel better.

I grab my laptop and work on the song I'm writing for Tyrannosaurus Rocks. I focus on feeling out where I want it to go, on what I want to say.

As I move pieces of it around, I realize the shapes of the chords and rhythms I'm putting in the bridge are more complicated than the girls can handle. I go back through and make it basic. I change the lyric focus of the section from victim rage to what it's like to be told as a girl that you should like princesses and unicorns instead of punk.

When I'm finished, I have a decent girl-punk anthem they should be able to play with a little practice. But it feels squashed. Not as cool as it could be. It's not my real voice.

The girls in Zoey's band are just getting started. I've been doing this stuff since I was in diapers, when my grandma gave me a two-octave keyboard. I'm lucky to have eight years of piano lessons under my belt, to have a mom who's encouraged my music even when it drives

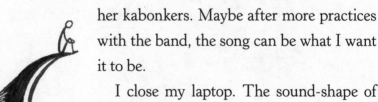

her kabonkers. Maybe after more practices with the band, the song can be what I want it to be.

I close my laptop. The sound-shape of the lid clicking shut is the exact shape of the hollow, sad satisfaction inside me.

24

We Need to Talk

Daniel

My house looks warm in the cold dusk. It's felt so empty and sad the past two months, but standing on the sidewalk with Chewbarka in my arms, knowing if she stays outside one more night in this weather, she'll die . . . well. It's enough to make my house look not so bad. Or maybe I cried so much in the tent that I'm all cried out and I don't know what to feel or think anymore. My heart and brain are fried. Frazzled. Empty.

Maybe it'll help. Mom rolls her eyes when I get teary these days. And then tortures me with her tearjerker Disney flicks playing nonstop.

While I'm trying to figure out exactly what to say, the front door opens. Mom covers her mouth. Then she rushes out like she's going to hug me, but stops short when she sees the dog. "Daniel, come inside. We need to talk."

I swallow hard and follow her into the house.

"Sit." She points at the couch.

I sit. Chewbarka seems to grasp the gravity of the situation. She's calm and still. Or maybe she thinks *she's* been told to sit.

Mom sinks into the chair across from me. "Are you okay?"

That . . . is not what I expected to come out her mouth. "Yes. I don't know. Not really. Maybe?" Good lord.

"The vet called."

I duck my head.

"Dad called."

I search her face for a sign, any sign. "He did?"

"Mitchell says you've been acting strange. Going someplace after school."

I press my lips together. Chewbarka licks my wrist with her dry little tongue.

"Daniel . . . just . . . what in the *world*?" She folds her hands and leans toward me. Her knuckles go white like each hand is gripping the other so they don't fly apart.

"You biked all the way to your dad's pulling a trailer. Without telling anyone what you were doing. Do you have any idea how dangerous that was?"

"I couldn't let her die." I sound like a pathetic mouse. Not a guy who's as tall as his dad.

Mom rubs her forehead. "Where have you been keeping her?"

There's no point in lying anymore. "Our old tent. In the woods behind the gas station."

"I know you think this dog is the most important—"

"It's not her fault!" I burst out. "She doesn't deserve to die!"

"That's not the issue—"

"I couldn't save Frankie. Or you and Dad. Or my friendship with Cole or *anything*. I had to save *something*!" My eyes water. I should enter the freaking world championships of crying. Gold medal winner right here.

Mom's face is a battleground between anger and sympathy. "I know things have been tough lately. But this—"

"You think I'm pathetic every time I cry." I grind my teeth. "You want me to be like Mitchell. Not like *me*."

Her brows go down. "I just don't want you to get hurt. You let your feelings get the best of you so much. I worry you'll—"

"You make me feel guilty about feeling stuff. Well, I don't feel bad about this. I won't let them kill her!"

Her face hardens. "You have no idea how much trouble you're in. What you've done could ruin Dr. Snyder's reputation and have a serious impact on his business. He threatened legal retaliation." She rubs the back of her neck like it hurts. "We're going to the vet's office immediately after school tomorrow. I'll have to take the afternoon off. I told him you'll return the dog and apologize."

"I can't do that—"

"You will." Her voice has an edge. "You can sleep in the basement with her tonight. She can stay in Frankie's crate tomorrow while you're at school and I'm at work." She stands up. "I'm sorry, Daniel. This is how it has to be."

I hug Chewbarka. "You're not sorry."

"There's no other choice. You *cannot* keep this dog."

The last sliver of silvery hope slips out of me. It floats up, and away, and it's gone.

I sink to the floor with Chewbarka.

Our basement has cinder-block walls and a concrete floor with a drain that smells like roadkill. I snuggle with Chewy in Dad's old sleeping bag in the corner as far as I can get from the drain. I'm exhausted and still sore from the bike ride, but my head's so full that sleep is impossible.

I can't stop thinking about how much I miss Cole. When we were friends, he'd have been the first person I went to for help with this. Even if he couldn't do anything, it would have been so good to know he cared.

I feel even worse now than when everything went sour with Cole. Than when I wrecked things with Ash.

I can't think about Ash right now. It's too big. Too confusing. I need to focus on something else. Project managing seems to keep Mom sane. I need a mental project to manage.

I can work out how to tell Cole I'm sorry. It's better than lying here hating myself.

I search *how to apologize* on my phone and find a list. *Admit you were wrong*, the first point says.

Well, I can do that. I made a mistake—or two, or actually three if you count waiting so long to try to make this right.

Describe what happened from the other person's point of view. That's encouraging at least. My bike-ride revelation about focusing on Cole and not myself when I apologize is on the right track.

Offer a plan to fix what you did wrong has me stumped. I can't un-kiss Fiona. I can't un-forget his birthday.

But . . . I could tell him I've realized I'm too self-involved, and that I'm working on paying attention to how other people feel. I want that to be true. Spending time with Ash, even though everything's messed up now, has shown me I'm capable of it. I just need to do more of it. To practice so I get better. Not only for Cole. For Ash too. For Mom and Dad. Even Mitchell.

Maybe not Mitchell. I don't know.

Ask for forgiveness.

That sounds easy. But it's hard to imagine saying *Please forgive me.* It seems so . . . vulnerable. What if he says he can't? Or he doesn't want to?

Mitchell comes down and interrupts my musings. "Mom's really ticked," he says. "Might as well have told you to man up and stop being such a basket case."

All traces of my improved mood evaporate. "Yeah, I got that."

He crosses his arms. "She's not wrong."

Ow. "It must be nice to only ever feel one emotion. Two if you count anger *and* irritation."

"That's not true about me."

"It's all you ever act like you feel." My phone buzzes with a number I don't know. I let it go to voice mail.

Mitch squats and holds his hand out to Chewbarka. "She smells like pee."

"You reek of chlorine and meanness." I should stop rising to his bait. But I'm out of tolerance for his crap.

Mitch starts to scratch the top of Chewbarka's head. She ducks away. He moves his hand under her chin.

I feel her shift her weight toward him. She leans into his palm. Just a little.

I sigh. I should take a page out of her book. Show him I understand why he acts like he does. He just makes it so freaking *difficult*.

"They're really going to kill her tomorrow?" he asks.

I don't answer. It hurts too much.

Mitch stays still with her head on his palm for a minute. Then he takes his old Spider-Man sleeping bag off the shelf, drops it over us, and heads for the stairs.

"You miss Dad too," I say. "It sucked for you when you saw us do stuff together without including you."

He goes still. I brace for whatever he's about to say. But he just stands there looking at me like he's trying to process.

"I'm sorry it made you feel bad," I tell him. "I didn't realize it then. But I do now. If he comes home, I hope we can all do things together. Or even if he doesn't come home. I want stuff to not suck."

Time stretches like a rubber band. I hope it's not a dry-rotted one that'll snap and sting me. Things with

261

Mitch have definitely felt dry-rotted lately.

"Does the dog need water or anything?" he finally asks. He puts his hands in his pockets like he doesn't know what to do with them.

I wave a hand at the water dish on the floor. "She's good."

He keeps standing there like he wants to say something else.

Then he turns and goes up the stairs.

Hours later. Still awake. Nose stuffed from a crying fit that cramped all my muscles and left me shaky and exhausted.

The voice mail was Tina. All she said was "Give me a call." I couldn't tell if she sounded mad that I got her fired, or if she was mad I took Chewbarka instead of letting someone find her and finish her off and negate this whole mess, or what. I couldn't tell if she was mad at all. She sounded as exhausted as I feel.

I didn't call her back. I'd just cry again and I can't cry any more today. I can't. My phone's down to 5 percent battery anyway, and getting all teary would bother Chewbarka. I'd rather just be here for her, holding her, on her last night alive.

Besides, Tina's fired. Even if she offered to take

Chewbarka, Mom said Dr. Snyder threatened "legal retaliation." He'd find some way to get Chewbarka back and kill her.

I listen to Chewy's faint snoring and wonder how Ash would draw it.

The guilt is so fresh and real. But I'm so deep into this sleepless night that I've thought all the other thoughts my brain can think, and now I have to think about Ash.

I don't know how to get my mind around today. He said he was a girl when he kissed me. And that he's a guy now. But how can that change? I keep thinking of when Ash-the-girl borrowed my hoodie in the gas station and tied her hair back. And seemed so different, but I couldn't put my finger on how.

The thought of a bunch of jerks pinning him down and dumping Gatorade in his face while screaming at him makes me furious. It doesn't even matter whether Ash was a girl or a boy then. Nobody deserves that. Especially not someone like Ash, who's only ever been good to me.

I think back over every moment we shared, trying to pick out the shift from girl to boy.

I can't find it. It's all just . . . Ash. The same person regardless of what gender I think he was. Is. Wants to be.

So maybe . . . I don't know. Maybe that means it doesn't matter. If I can't find it.

Or maybe it means Ash was trying to hide it from me because he was scared of how I'd react, since people literally *attacked* him for it in the past.

Or maybe I'm so shook because I liked that kiss. Like a lot. Whether it was girl-Ash or boy-Ash I kissed. And adding *Oh god, what if I'm gay or bi* to everything else now is just . . .

I laugh aloud. It's ridiculous. What does it matter? Chewbarka will be dead tomorrow. Who cares what I am? What Ash is? Who cares what other people think of us? We connected, and we worked together to help this dog. That's what's important. Not the specifics.

I hope I haven't ruined everything. Even if things aren't the same as before, I *know* I still want Ash in my life. However that looks.

I shift so Chewbarka is sleeping more comfortably. I can't fix my broken brain and heart with my broken brain and heart right now. But I can make sure this dog's last night on earth is spent warm and comfortable in the arms of someone who loves her.

25

Hump Day

Ash

Wednesday, and boy, is it a humdinger of a hump day: today's the day I gotta get over the hump of probably being outed.

It's a big honking hump. And I'm not at the top of my game after lying awake all night listening to the crickets and the traffic and the faraway night sirens, freaking out that being who I am means I'm never gonna succeed at a relationship with a boy. I hope my deodorant holds. Or I'm gonna have seriously spicy armpits when I see Daniel in photo class.

Sure enough, Bella's waiting at my locker in the crowded, noisy hallway. The second she sees me, she beelines for me. "Where's my dog? My dad knows but he won't freaking tell me."

"Somewhere safe." I try to edge around her to get to my locker.

She blocks my path. "Tell me *exactly* where she is. Like an address. Now."

I press my lips together and shake my head.

"Fine." She takes out her phone. "You made your choice."

Powerlessness invades me as she taps her screen. I might've shifted from scared to angry at Tyler and Jackson and the rest of those boys, but here I am again with my private business shoved into the light against my will. It won't be long before everyone here knows my old name and what I "really" am. Even though what I "really" am has nothing to do with my biology.

At least Daniel's secret's still safe. Even if he hates me now.

"Yo, Bella!" someone yells.

Bella's head and mine swivel. Griffey's plowing through the crowd of seventh graders like the boss eighth grader he is, Esme and Sam from Rainbow Alliance in tow. "Didn't your mom teach you it's wrong to spread bullying videos around?"

"What?" Bella sputters. "I'm not—"

"Deadnaming is *garbage*," Esme says. "It's a horrible thing to do." She's not wearing her girl clothes yet. I didn't know she was so tall, or that her voice could go so deep, and here she is using those like a shield to keep me safe when it's probably making her feel dysphoric.

Bella steps back from her. "I don't even know what deadnaming is—"

"It's cruel," Griffey says, his voice quieter than Esme's but still steely. "It takes a person's identity away from them. If you share that video, that's what you're doing."

Bella squares her shoulders. "I just want to find my dog—"

"So blackmail is cool?" Sam says. "Maybe you should think about that a little harder."

Esme stands even taller. "How would you feel if someone tried to dig up dirt on you and make it public?" Behind her, Zoey is at her locker, watching us with a puzzled expression.

I'm not wild about Esme trying to guilt Bella. But Bella's shrinking in on herself, her posture slumping. "Whatever," she says. She turns and disappears into the crowd.

Griffey grins at me. "Told you I'd fix it."

"Yeah, I guess you did." So why do I feel so sick?

Maybe because at least Bella posting that video would take care of the job of outing me, and now I have to find another way to do it. Or maybe there's just no good way to feel about any of this.

Griffey gives me a side hug. "Gotta jet, my homeroom teacher's a stickler about butts in chairs before the bell."

"Thanks," I say faintly as he and Esme and Sam leave.

Nobody in homeroom or algebra says anything about what happened. I guess that's a benefit of going to a huge school. But in English, Zoey gives me a weird look.

As class drones on, the butterflies in my stomach turn to bees. When the bell rings, Zoey's at my desk in a flash. "What was up with those gay kids defending you?"

I push my folder into my bag with shaking hands. "Well," I say. "Um." I watch Jordan leave the room.

Zoey lets the silence stretch. If she knew how to do that as a musician, she'd be a lot better.

I clear my throat as I stand up. "I'm not . . . a girl now."

Zoey's eyes narrow. "What does that even mean?"

"Gender can change. It's not based on biology."

She shakes her head like I'm an idiot. "Did you miss the part about Tyrannosaurus Rocks being a *girl* band?

Did you miss that the fundraiser's called *Girls* Who Rock the Future?"

"No. Actually. I did not miss that."

Zoey wrinkles her nose. "Thanks a lot. You came swooping in like you could make everything perfect for us and now, boom, you're a freaking liar." Her face is a thunderstorm.

"So . . . I can't still be in the band?"

"Are you even kidding? You're so out. You could barely focus on Monday anyway."

I bark out a laugh. "Says the kid who—" I cut off *can only play four chords.*

I walk out of the room, chin up, eyes straight ahead. I'm done with these stupid games. I am who I am. If the world doesn't like it, they can go huff Booper farts.

Griffey's kinda green around the gills at lunch when I sit by him with my tray of rubbery pizza. "You look like you've been put off your tea and crumpets," I tell him.

"Eh, that thing this morning got a little . . . well." He shows me his phone. There are a string of comments under Bella's latest Insta post. They're calling her anti-gay, a bigot, saying she's stuck-up and pretending to be an animal lover when she's really a homophobe, a genderphobe, a jerk.

"Oh." I hand Griff his phone. "That's . . . not what I wanted to happen."

"Me either. A couple of the commenters are in Rainbow Alliance, but most of them aren't. I think they're people she's friends with."

"Or people she *was* friends with." I push my pizza away.

"Yeah." Griffey puts his sandwich back in its bag.

We sit there looking out the window for a while. Then he says something about needing to go to the library to do research for a paper and leaves.

I fail to eat my pizza.

In the photography classroom, Daniel's at our table with his head resting on his crossed arms. Fiona and Braden aren't here yet. I sit next to him. "Hi," I say quietly.

He doesn't look up.

"Are you okay?"

"No."

"What's . . . where's Chewbarka?"

"My basement." He sits up and rubs his face, not looking at me. "Mom's making me take her back to the vet as soon as I get home."

I didn't think my stomach could sink any lower. "Oh."

"Tina left a voice mail saying to call her. But there's no point calling back. Mom said Dr. Snyder . . . well. I guess he's going to make sure Chewbarka's really . . ." He swallows like he's trying not to hurl. "Actually dead this time." His voice is flattened out. He drops his head back onto his arms.

I want to touch his shoulder, to say he did everything he could and at least Chewy lived longer than she would have. But he's so closed off, and I don't know if it even matters that Chewbarka got to live an extra week, since her days were spent in a stinky tent. There's nothing I can say that will unbreak Daniel's heart, or mine. "Maybe . . ." I fold my hands under the table. "Maybe you could call Tina back, though?"

"No point."

He's probably right. He—well, we—did so much to try to save her, and none of it worked. We'll just be disappointed again. "But . . . I don't know. You could try?" I know hope is dangerous. But I can't help feeling it.

I don't think Daniel feels it. He shifts in his chair so he's farther from me.

I touch his shoulder. I don't mean to do it. It just sucks to see him so sad. I want to pull the pain out of him so he doesn't have to feel it.

Fiona comes in and sees us. She gets a weird look on her face that I can't read.

I drop my hand from Daniel's shoulder and hug my stomach since I can't hug him.

26

Heads on a Platter

Daniel

For the first time in my life, I'm too sad to cry.

It's a tight fit in Frankie's crate with Chewbarka. I'm folded up like a pretzel. But I feel 2 percent less bad crammed inside here. I can still smell Frankie in this flattened old dog bed. A little. When the breeze blows through the open basement window and stirs up the air.

My phone rings. I ignore it. I keep my eyes on the door that leads out to the patio under the deck.

I can't go through that door. I've tried everything I can to save Chewbarka, and it came to nothing. Mom will be here in less than ten minutes. We'll get in her car and she'll drive me to Dr. Snyder's office and . . .

Well. Maybe I'll feel Chewbarka's heart stop under my palm too. Like with Frankie.

Or maybe Dr. Snyder won't let me be in the room when he does it. Probably he won't.

Chewbarka licks my neck. It tickles like mad, but I'm so jammed into this cage that there's nothing I can do to stop her. She licks her way up to just under my ear. I can't help the laugh that comes out. It's a tortured laugh, not a happy one.

The sound only encourages her. She wiggles up my shoulder, licking all the way, until her tongue is in my ear.

I twitch and bang my head against the crate bars. "Chewy, stop. Please." I try to get her off me but I'm so tangled up that she steps on my face. Her paw slides off and her claw rakes my nose. My eyes smart at the sting.

I unfold and emerge from the cage like a jacked-up bat waking from hibernation. Chewbarka follows me out with a hopeful expression.

I look at my phone on the floor. The missed call was Tina. There's another voice mail.

I feel the warmth on my shoulder where Ash's hand was. He wanted to make me feel better. Even after I was a jerk at the tent and told him to leave. He still cares about Chewbarka.

About me.

He felt so bad about telling Bella that he let her out him so she wouldn't find out where I was hiding Chewbarka.

I guess . . . the least I can do, maybe, is what Ash suggested and call Tina back.

It won't do any good. But Ash thinks it might.

I listen to Tina's second voice mail: "I'm sorry things happened the way they did. I'd really like to talk to you."

I take a deep breath and hit the callback button. It only rings once before she answers. "Daniel?"

"Yeah." My throat immediately closes up.

"Oh lord, I'm glad you answered!" Her raspy voice is comforting to hear. "Kid, I'm so sorry I left you in that mess. Are you okay?"

"No," I choke. I want to tell her I'm sorry I got her fired, but my voice isn't working.

"I realized a couple hours into the drive that I forgot the dog. I was so focused on getting to my girl, everything else went right out of my head. But I didn't have your number and I was more concerned about what was in front of me than what was behind me."

"I'm sorry," I squeak out. "I got you fired."

"It's not your fault. I'm the one who lied and tried to hide the dog." She clears her throat. "Truth told, I was embarrassed to call you once my daughter got out of ICU and I realized a whole week had gone by. I felt so guilty for leaving you in that mess. You didn't deserve to get stuck with my impulsive choice. You didn't deserve for me to ignore my conscience and not call you. I'm real sorry about that, Daniel."

"I—" I don't know what to say. I think this is the first time an adult has apologized to me and meant it. "Aren't you—you're not mad at me that you don't have a job now?"

She laughs her raspy smoker's laugh. "Truly, it's *not* your fault. Anyway, I been through a lot worse than this and Doc was a crap boss. I'm just glad my daughter's all right."

"How is she?" I cover the speaker on my phone so she won't hear me sniffling.

"They got her set up in a rehab place. She's busted up real good, but she's gonna be okay. Even took a few steps yesterday."

"I'm glad."

"Yeah, me too. It was good to be with her, but I'm sure happy to be back home." There's a pause like she's inhaling a cigarette. "What happened with the dog? I got the idea from Doc that you have her."

"I do. For the next few minutes, anyway. Mom's

gonna . . ." I choke up again. "Bring me back. To the. To the vet office. To . . ."

"Ah, criminy." Tina exhales long. "You've had her all this time?"

"I hid her in a tent."

Tina lets a beat go by. "Bet you fell in love, huh?"

"Yeah." I press my mouth so she won't hear me crying.

"Look, if you can hang tight a few minutes . . . when I realized yesterday she might be alive, I reached out to a lady who runs a medical rescue. I can't take Chewbarka right now, I'm sure Doc would find out and have both our heads on a platter. But my rescue friend said she could maybe help us."

"R-really?"

"She was gonna ask around about a foster home. It was yesterday that we talked, so maybe she's lined something up by now." I hear the cigarette sound again. "Sure wish you woulda called sooner, kid. You not get my voice mails till just now?"

"I did, I just—I thought it was hopeless."

"It's never hopeless. Even when real bad crap happens. You gotta use your grief or your anger or whatever to make things better. Got me?"

"O-k-kay."

"I'll call you back real soon." She hangs up.

I smear my face. Chewbarka cocks her head at me. I hear Mom's car pull into the driveway.

"What am I doing?" I say. "What am I actually freaking doing?" My heart is pounding so hard. If I disappear now with Chewbarka and whatever Tina's doing falls through, I'm toast. Chewbarka will die. Mom will never forgive me. Doc Snyder will probably sue us and put some kind of flag on my name or something so I can never work at a vet or with animals. Everything, *everything* that can go wrong will go wrong.

Mom's car door slams. Her footsteps come toward the house.

I scoop Chewbarka into my arms, slip out the patio door, and close it behind me. There's no time to grab Vlad the Rapid. I'll have to hoof it.

I can't go to the tent. That's the first place Mom will look. There's nowhere to go. I have to keep moving around until Tina calls back. Which could be in five minutes or an hour or—

My phone pings with a message as I'm hurrying away. **The foster spot got filled this afternoon. Working on finding another. Hang in there.**

Thank you, I text Tina back. **Do you know how long it might take?**

Not sure. Rescue org is making calls now.

There's nothing else to say or ask. I'm at the mercy of forces I can't control.

I don't know why I open my messages with Ash. Everything's messed up with us, and it's mostly my fault. But I still feel like he should know what's happening. I tap out a quick message as I speed-walk away from my house:

Maybe there's still a chance.

27

Halfway Through the Crossfade

Ash

Is Daniel talking about Chewbarka? Us? Something else? **What do you mean?** I text.

He doesn't answer. I keep my phone in my hand while I walk Booper around the complex. My eyes are so glued to the screen that I trip three times before I pay attention to where I'm going.

Daniel keeps not answering. I smash down the urge to text him again.

Back upstairs, I curl up on Mom's bed under her ceiling fan. The faint sound of metal scraping plastic is calming. I close my eyes and steady my breathing, letting the soothing static fill my brain.

I don't need to freak out. His text could mean anything. I just have to wait for him to answer.

I open one eye and check my phone. Still nothing.

I sit up fast. I haven't gone on a single run since we moved here. Time to fix that.

I change clothes and jam my feet into my cross-country shoes. They've gotten too small. Or I guess my feet have gotten bigger. But it won't kill me. I grab some headphones and leave.

Running feels *amazing*. I fly along the sidewalks of our complex all pumped up on the music, pouring all my stress about Daniel and Chewbarka and Bella and everything else into my working muscles and pounding feet. It isn't long before I'm winded. I'm *way* out of practice.

I go for longer than feels reasonable anyway, needing to tire my body out so my brain will chill. Then I walk back home, checking my phone every two seconds.

In my room, I open my laptop and set my phone on the desk so I'll know the moment Daniel responds. I look over the song I wrote for Zoey's band. I'm so freaking mad that I cut out all the good stuff so a no-talent buttclown like her could play it. My gender is really all she saw when she looked at me? Come *on*. There are a million more facets to me, to *everyone*, than that.

Bummer that a huge facet of the shiny diamond of Zoey had to be "narrow-minded dipwad." Maybe I should rewrite the lyrics to say *Roses are red, I'm not a girl, I've got five fingers and the middle one's for her.*

Bleh. Stewing's satisfying, but it gets me nowhere. And sometimes I am a girl anyway.

I add in everything I took out of the song, then go through it a gajillion times, changing the lyrics to words that matter to me. All the stuff Mom's been telling me about gender being a whole big colorful spectrum instead of a one-or-the-other binary finally starts to click as I write. I realize I've been trying to categorize every feeling I have as either a guy feeling or a girl feeling, because Dad made me think that's how the world works. Like when I thought "punk-rock songwriter" meant dude and day-dreamer meant girly. Like when it seemed that wanting to fight Daniel's sadness with a lightsaber was boy and cuddling him or blushing was girl. I labeled those feelings with a gender because I wanted it to be easier to know what I am.

But all that's done is make it harder. Life's edges aren't so defined. Like Daniel doing what was right and saving Chewbarka, even though it was technically lying and stealing. Or me wanting to be in Tyrannosaurus Rocks even though I'm not that into their kind of music. Like the Rainbow Alliance kids saving me from being outed and deadnamed, but making a target of Bella.

None of those situations can be jammed into a neatly defined box. Really, *nothing* about how it feels to be alive is strictly a one-or-the-other game: happy or sad, scared or mad, hopeful or despairing. Introvert or extrovert. Boy or girl. Kid or teenager. There's a little of each one in its opposite, and that's what makes life so complex and interesting. More painful, yeah, but also . . . richer. More real.

By the time I'm finished, the song's not punk anymore, but it has punk's best elements: It's stripped down, it's to the point, and it tells the world's social norms to take a flying leap. It's definitely my real voice.

It wasn't that long ago that being between genders felt like being stuck in a bad DJ's crossfade. But for real . . . I'm my own DJ. And *good* DJs know how to layer music. How to fade one song into another so you're riding the wave of both for a few measures and they're working together, instead of against each other. Those moments are complex and interesting and wonderful, the way the sky can be purple and orange at the same time at sunset. How the ocean can be deep and dark and bright and scary and exciting all at once.

It really *can* be beautiful to be complicated and contradictory and in between. To live in that musical and personal space that's halfway through the crossfade.

I giggle with pure, clear happiness. The sound is high-pitched and girly but has some bass to it, and it ends with a goofy squeak—an Ashley shape *and* an Asher one, a laugh I might've found embarrassing or uncomfortable before that's now simply what it is:

Happy.

I scribble the silly shape of it. It comes out looking like Dr. Seuss on an off day, so I add amateur ballerinas in tutus.

I finish tweaking my lyrics, then title the song "Halfway Through the Crossfade." I record myself playing it on the keyboard and singing it. It feels good. It feels *right*. I'm saying my truth, and I'm not afraid people won't like it. In fact, I hope it makes people think. I hope it's a light in the dark for anyone who feels like they have to be one thing or the other when both can be true.

Bummer it can't be used for Girls Who Rock the Future. It's a hella dope song and I'm proud of it.

I open the nightstand drawer that holds my makeup. I pick through the box of nail polish and find a bright blue and an audacious pink Mom bought for me a while ago. It's way too garish for Ashley, but it's perfect now— the perfect pink *and* the perfect color to stripe with the blue on each nail. I paint both hands, slowly and carefully, then admire how it looks: kinda girly, kinda punk, definitely badass. Definitely *me*.

I tuck the makeup I don't use anymore into a plastic bag to give to Esme since her dad chucked hers. It's just drugstore stuff, but it's better than nothing. I smile when I think about how much she and the other Rainbow Alliance kids enjoyed making their flags. Like someone finally gave them permission to be who they are. It was inspiring to see.

Feeling that fire, I open Insta and make a story post

of the first part of the video of me singing my song. I upload the full song to SoundCloud and link it in my Insta bio.

Then I make my account public.

There's a chance Tyler and those kids from Bailey Middle will leave nasty comments.

But I'm not afraid of them anymore.

I navigate to Daniel's profile. I scroll through his images until I find one that resonates, a picture of a pink sunrise fading into a blue sky over a lake. I follow him, then like the image and leave a comment that says, Oh hey, it me!

Mom gets home from work while I'm looking at the top posts tagged #nonbinary, my mind spinning through outfit and makeup ideas to fit every different shade of my stick-it-in-a-blender gender. I was so afraid for so long to follow tags like #nonbinary and #enby and #genderqueer, because Dad made them seem so wrong. But there's a whole huge world out here. And it's *beautiful*.

I hear Mom drop her stuff on the counter, and then she rushes into my room. "I listened to your song five times on the way home," she says, her eyes bright. "Ash, I love you so stinking much!" She grabs me in a huge hug, and even though my nose is jammed into her armpit and she smells like truck grease, I hug her back. "I'm so *proud* of you!" she says.

"Air! Air!" I make a coughing sound.

She lets me go and sits on my bed. "What brought on the change of heart?"

I shrug. "It was more of a pain in the butt to hide who I am than to be who I am."

She laughs. "That's all? It's about expending the least energy possible? Avoiding anything that seems like work?"

"Eh, get off my case. You're a sleepy slug every morning till your coffee kicks in."

She ruffles my hair. "You're wearing running clothes."

"Yeah, I am." I bite my lip. It felt *so good* to run. And I miss being part of a team. My teammates were okay, even if the coach insisted on jamming me into a label that didn't fit. But I'm rethinking this whole "labels" concept. And anyway, like Mom said, things are different at Oakmont. "I might be considering that cross-country thing after all. If it's not too late."

"I'm beyond glad! I'm so proud of you, honey."

"You said that."

"Get used to hearing it. You're awesome times infinity." She kicks off her boots.

"Argh, no! Put 'em back on!" I cover my nose.

"I made a resolution on the way home. I'm gonna quit trying to drive your life for you so much." She stands and picks up the boots. "You're figuring it out on your own. You don't need my help." She smiles, but she looks sad too.

"I'm sure I'll still need advice." Especially about boys. One boy specifically.

"Then I'll try to give it without telling you what to do." She squeezes her stanky boots and does a little happy dance. "What do you want for dinner? There's leftover soup."

I glance at my dark phone screen. "I don't think I'm hungry yet." I'm not so wild in the head about Daniel's mystery text anymore after feeling like I figured out an important part of being human. I don't feel like I *need* Daniel to answer.

But I sure would *like* him to.

My stomach growls. "On second thought . . . can we split a pot of mac and cheese?" It's been my favorite meal since I was old enough to hold a spoon. No matter what gender I am, that salty, gooey, all-natural fluorescent orange goodness hits the spot. Especially after a run.

"With grapes and Goldfish crackers. You got it."

Mom gives me one more hug. "Phew, go take a shower while I cook. You have onion pits."

"You have vinegar foot."

"The family that stinks together sticks together!" She laughs. "That's my next cross-stitch."

I tug a strand of her green hair and follow her out of my room.

28

Doofy Floof

Daniel

Time busts a freaky warp maneuver while I wait for Tina to call me back. Every minute lasts a thousand years. I walk Chewbarka behind the strip mall and gas station, staying out of sight of traffic. Wishing I'd grabbed a coat because good *lord*, it's cold. Mom texts and calls incessantly until I text back, **I'm sorry, I need some time to deal with this**, then temporarily block her. By the time Tina finally calls two hours later, I feel like a grizzled old man, only moving so I don't keel over and die of angst and coldness.

"They finally got hold of Iris, their lady who fosters medical rescues," Tina says. "She's at work and couldn't answer her phone. She can take Chewbarka. But she's not gonna get home till midnight. Can you keep the dog that long and get her to Iris's house over in Greenboro?"

"Yes," I say immediately, even though I have no idea how I'm going to get to Greenboro at midnight. It's on the outskirts of the suburbs, at least a twenty-minute drive—way too far to walk, and there's no way I can go home for the bike and trailer.

"Great," Tina says. "You got something to write with? I'll give you the address."

"I'll put it in my phone." I open my notes and tap in the address Tina gives me. "Got it."

"I'd give you a lift but I told my friend Carla I'd drive her to work at the Ford plant. They might have a third-shift spot till I can find another vet job."

"Good luck. I hope it works out."

"Call me tomorrow and let me know how it goes at Iris's. I've met her a couple times at adoption events. She don't take any crap, but she loves dogs more than anybody I know."

"I will. And thank you. Times a million to the millionth power."

"Don't thank me, kid. I got you stuck in this mess in the first place."

"But you saved Chewbarka. So thanks for that. From her." And me. Even though I'm in the hottest water of my life on this cold night, about to be in even hotter water with Mom and Dr. Snyder, it'll be worth it if I can save this dog.

And I'm so close.

We end our conversation and hang up. "Well, fuzzball, looks like you get to live," I tell Chewbarka. I scoop her into a hug. "You get to live! Living is the *best!*" I laugh and spin in a circle with her. She licks my neck and pees on me. Which makes me remember I forgot to tell Tina that detail, so Iris doesn't know either.

Maybe if Iris fosters medical rescue dogs, she's used to health problems.

I stop spinning. I'm not sure what "medical rescue" means, but it sounds like I'll see some dogs from Very Bad Situations. It might be sadder than the shelter where Dad had them read Chewbarka's microchip.

"It's okay, though," I tell Chewbarka. "They're *rescued*. So they're saved. Like you." I set her on the ground and we keep walking. Her limp gets worse as we traipse past the back of Papa John's for the hundredth time while I rack my brains for a transportation solution.

Maybe Cole's brother could help. He's sixteen and

has an old beater car he's always looking for an excuse to drive.

But I don't have his number. I'd have to get it from Cole.

Well. I suppose now's as good a time as any to test the waters.

Hey, I text Cole as I walk with Chewbarka. **I hope stuff with you is good. Could you give me your brother's number please?**

Three dots appear right away, but then they disappear, and it's a long time before they show back up. Long enough that I figure I'm out of luck. But then a phone number comes in.

Well. I guess I'm not surprised this is all I've gotten. I've thought about patching things up, but haven't actually made a move toward doing it.

Another text comes: **He's grounded. What do you need him for?**

I'm in a situation and could use a ride late tonight, I write. **Long story.**

Oh. There's nothing again, and then three dots. **He's grounded from his car.**

Thanks anyway. I pocket my phone so I won't be tempted to scroll back through our old conversations.

I did that enough right after stuff blew up, and it never once made me feel better.

My phone pings. **What kind of situation? Everything okay?**

I blink at my screen. **Yeah. It's more for someone else.** Chewbarka counts as a someone else. Dogs are people too.

Well. Maybe you could tell me the long story sometime.

I hold my breath for a moment, then smile. **I'd like to apologize. For real this time, the right way. In person. If you're willing to hear it.**

My palm gets so sweaty while I wait that the phone slips out of my hand. I pick it up to find he's replied: **Maybe Sunday we could hang out.**

A bubble of hope rises up. **Thank you.** I look at shivering, limping Chewbarka. "I'll figure this out for you. I will." I pick her up and stuff her under my hoodie with her fuzzy head sticking out the neck. Her fur tickles my nose as I walk, but who cares? She gets to *live*!

My stomach growls at the smell of the pizza. The hunger feels weirdly good. I can't remember the last time I was truly hungry.

It occurs to me as I pace and think that I've been sort

of a jerk to Ash. Maybe more than sort of. I've probably made her—him—think I'm mad, when he was
just trying to help. When he came out to me because he
thought I deserved the truth.

That was probably so hard to do. Because . . . he likes
me. Like a lot, regardless of whether he's a boy or a girl,
and wow, have I been an idiot to not fully see it till just
now.

I don't know what to think about that. But when I
hug Chewbarka inside my hoodie, I remember last night
when I decided it didn't really matter. That the connec-
tion is the important part, not the specifics.

I'll have to freak out about that later. Right now,
I have to figure out how to get to Greenboro. I sit on
the curb behind the nail salon and open my messages.
I realize I never replied to Ash's **What do you mean?**
after I said there might still be a chance. **I'm so sorry I
made stuff weird**, I write. I ask if she knows someone
with a car who'd be willing to drive a dog across town
tonight to save her life.

No answer comes. I maybe made stuff worse with my
rushed apology and sudden request for a favor. Maybe
Ash is angry at me, or hates me for how I responded
when he came out.

I really could have handled it better.

I get up and walk again, avoiding Papa John's. I'm so hungry my bones feel hollow. My phone pings at the back of the gas station: **I texted my mom. She says she can help us.**

I laugh in double relief. They can help, and . . . *us.* Ash said *us!* He doesn't hate me.

Thank you, I write. **Thank you thank you! Thank your mom for me!!!**

Ash sends a happy-face emoji. **She's at book club but she said she'll leave a few minutes early. It's gonna take her a while to get home tho cause book club is by where we used to live.**

No prob, I write, even though it is sort of a prob. I'm really cold and Chewbarka is too.

Where should we pick you up? Guessing you're not at home?

Papa John's, I write. **Let me know when you're on your way.**

Will do. I gotta hurry up and do my homework, oops music distraction. See you in like . . . hopefully less than two hours.

Oh man. How we'll make it that long without freezing, I have no idea. I guess I have to trust that time will keep moving. That it won't stop and leave me stranded in this in-between place, stuck between relief for Chewbarka and dread about facing Mom, between liking Ash and being kinda freaked out. Between holding Chewbarka close and giving her up for good.

That's going to be so hard. Even though I know it's for the best. I *love* this doofy little floof, in equal measure with my sadness at the thought of losing her. The sadness is how I know I love her so much.

I need a distraction that doesn't involve freaking out about however Ash convinced his mom to help. It's more than a small favor to drive out to Greenboro and back in the middle of a freezing night. Especially if she already had to drive far to wherever book club is.

I sit behind the Papa John's, download Instagram, and log in. There's a slew of comments and likes on my old stuff. At the top of the list is a new follow from someone I don't know. I tap to see their story.

It's Ash. Wearing a bright purple hoodie, nails painted pink and blue, playing a song on a keyboard and singing. My phone's tinny speaker doesn't do it justice, and it's only a fifteen-second clip. But I watch it three times. Then I tap his profile photo.

Photos of him—or her, that's definitely a *her* in some of the pics—fill my screen. She's dressed in all different outfits in the photos, stuff I've never seen her in.

Boy-her—or boy-him, I don't know how to think of this so I'll just think of Ash as *they* until they tell me otherwise—boy-Ash has some killer fashion sense too. There are pics in what looks like a dressing room with the tag #IfOnlyIWasRich. They're dressed in a slim jacket and skinny jeans with fancy Italian-looking shoes, or in a punked-out leather jacket with blue jeans and zebra-striped Converse. In one they're wearing a steampunk-style tuxedo with tails and they look so cool I practically get a cramp about it.

I look closer at the photos of Ash wearing dresses and skirts. They're done up like a uniformed schoolgirl in one, with a white shirt, a bow tie, and a short plaid skirt. Their hair is in a wicked-cute anime style, twisted into two buns with a purple curl and a white ribbon under each. In another they're wearing a skirt that looks like autumn, made of draped layers in orange and brown and red and purple, with the purple frilly shirt they wore when we biked to Dad's. In another they're in a lacy pink dress and glasses, looking at the camera with their eyebrows up and the world's sweetest smile. In one they're standing with their mom next to a sign that says *Great Smoky Mountains*, dressed for a hike: baseball hat, sleeveless black T-shirt and khaki shorts, brown hiking boots that look too big. They're flashing the peace sign and grinning like they're ready to hike the whole Appalachian Trail.

I go to Ash's bio screen. There's nothing written, just a link to SoundCloud. I tap it and find the rest of the song Ash was singing in their story.

I hold the phone to my ear. I wish I had headphones so I could listen properly. I can't make out every word, but the lyrics are about how it's not wrong to live in between, that it's what makes life interesting. That two things can seem like opposites, but can both be true at the same time. I love everything about the chorus: *I'm living life my way, a changing spectrum day by day, a challenge to girl/boy clichés, halfway through the cross-fade.*

That's where I am, right now. Halfway through. Waiting for Ash to pick me up. It's cold outside and I'm about to lose Chewbarka.

But I did a *really* good thing for this dog. And she's still here, right now, in my arms. "I love you, you doofy floof!" I tell Chewbarka. I nestle my nose into her neck, trying to savor her stink and her sweetness and the essence of *dog* for a little while longer.

I wish Ash was here to savor it too.

29

Old Soul

Ash

Daniel's shivering on the curb outside Papa John's when we pull up. I suddenly realize that when he told me where he was, he meant outside, not inside. He climbs into the seat behind me with Chewbarka. While the dome light is on, I see a smear of red on his face. "What happened?" I ask, alarmed.

"Huh?"

I point at his face, realizing it's not blood, it's food. I giggle. "Never mind."

He wipes his cheek and sees the sauce on his fingers. "Oops. A lady in there took pity on me shivering and brought me a slice."

"Was it good?"

"Cold and rubbery and it had olives. But I was so hungry it was manna from heaven. Chewbarka liked it too."

"Did you have enough to eat?" Mom asks, ever the mom. "We can stop at McDonald's up the street and grab more food if you're hungry. They're open late."

"I'm fine," Daniel says as he buckles in. "Thanks, though. That's nice of you." His stomach growls audibly.

"I'm hungry again too," I tell Mom. "Let's stop."

In the drive-through line, Daniel tells us about Iris and the medical rescuing and says his mom is going to blow up when he gets home. My mom asks if his mom knows where he is, and he says he sort of didn't tell her.

"Well," Mom says, and I hold my breath. "The only condition of me driving you across town is that you text her right now that you're with a trustworthy adult and you're safe. And that you'll be home by one a.m. and you'll make this up to her. No parent deserves to freak out not knowing where their kid is at night."

I watch in the side-view mirror as Daniel ducks his head. "Yes, ma'am." He starts typing.

I can't stop looking at his reflection. At the way his hair falls across his forehead, at how he purses his lips as he types. How when Chewbarka licks his neck he absently pats her with one hand and hugs her.

Why does he have to be so freaking *cute*? It's entirely unnecessary. I'd still like him even if he looked like a warty old gremlin. The way he's sacrificed so much to save that fuzzy little goof of a mutt . . . my heart can barely take it.

We get burgers and fries. Daniel inhales half of his before we're out of the parking lot. Mom asks for the address. After he gives it to her and she puts it in her phone, he stops eating. In the mirror I see him holding Chewbarka in his lap, his head bent down touching hers. I guess he needs to bond with her before he has to give her up.

The drive is quiet. Mom keeps glancing in her rearview mirror. A couple times she looks like she wants to say something, but then she doesn't. She puts on some Led Zeppelin, too quiet to sing along to but loud enough for the percussion to fill the silence. "Gallows Pole" comes on and traipses through its bouncy chorus, and then the whole song falls apart into a jumbled mess of drums as it reaches its chaotic, cruel end when the hangman kills the dude. Even though the guy's friends and siblings bribed the hangman to save him.

Mom switches the song off. I hear Daniel behind me

getting fidgety. We ride in silence for the last few minutes.

"Can you guys stay in the car?" Daniel blurts as we pull into the driveway.

A stab of hurt goes through me. "Why?" I want to say goodbye to Chewbarka too.

"Because—" His voice is all tight and squeaky. "I, um."

"I've seen you cry before and I'm still your friend," I tell him. "Besides, I'm probably gonna cry too."

"Hell, I might even cry," Mom says. "There's no shame in loving a dog, kid." She gets out and Daniel and I follow.

A sign on the door says DO NOT KNOCK! DOGS WILL WAKE AND S**T WILL GET REAL. TEXT INSTEAD. We stand there awkwardly for a minute. "I'll message Tina and see if she can give me Iris's number." Daniel tries to take his phone out, but Chewbarka thrashes in his arms.

I catch her as she's starting to fall. A dog barks inside the house and the door opens. A tall white lady with a long silver braid waves her arm at us. "Come on, get inside before they all wake up." She's dressed in a brown UPS uniform with dog hair all over the shirt. Another dog barks and suddenly it sounds like fifty of them are going at once in every room of the house. The air smells of pee and dog and disinfectant.

Chewbarka struggles in my arms as we step inside. Daniel takes her and holds on to her like she's a life raft.

"Come on in here," the woman says, ushering us into a living room lined with dog crates instead of furniture. "I'm Iris." She holds out her hand to Mom.

"Kate," Mom says, and shakes it. "This is Daniel and Ash. And Chewbarka."

"Cutie. Can I?" Iris holds out her hands.

Daniel reluctantly hands Chewbarka over. I look down at a fuzzy brown dog barking its head off in a crate near my foot. I squat and hold my hand by the bars so the dog can sniff me. "Hey, little one," I say. "You're okay. I don't bite."

The dog stops barking and its tail wags so hard it whacks the side of the crate. I look in the front corner at a big round bed with a German shepherd laying on it. The dog looks kind of like Zoey's dog Rex, except this one's all deflated. It lifts its head and wags half-heartedly before dropping its head and watching us. Next to it, in a crate with the door open, is a dog with only one front leg and one eye, wagging calmly. Stacked on top of that crate is a smaller one with a chubby Chihuahua barking and coughing.

A small white dog barrels into the room carrying an orange plastic food dish. There's something wrong with its back legs; they stick straight out behind it and it bounce-drags them across the carpet. It's wearing a striped black-and-yellow band around its belly and I can't help laughing. It looks like a fuzzy wingless bumblebee.

"Cool it, Sully," Iris says. "They ain't here to feed you, ya hyperactive little turd." She gives his ears an affectionate scratch as he drops his food dish. "You already had your dinner. Yes, you did. Look here, huh? New friend." She tries to let Chewbarka sniff Sully, but Chewbarka goes bananas, trying to climb up Iris's neck.

"She's scared of dogs." Daniel looks like he wants to take her back.

Iris stands and holds Chewbarka at arm's length to get a good look at her. Chewbarka whips around like a worm when you poke it. A stream of pee comes out of her and runs down Iris's arm.

Iris just laughs. "Oh, you're a leaker! That's all right. We got a solution for that." She hugs Chewbarka close and rubs her ears, then hands her over to Daniel. "Be right back." She leaves the room.

Daniel stands there holding Chewbarka, glancing at the dogs and crates like he's afraid to look at them. His eyes land on the corner where I didn't even notice Mom scratching the nose of a big greyhound in a pen. It's the most ripped dog I've ever seen. Its muscles bulge out all over the place, especially its butt muscles. That dog could run cross-country for days. Its face is all scarred up, dark lines cutting through its graying fur. It watches us with big liquid eyes, one of which is cloudy.

Daniel holds his breath. He stands in the exact center of the room, like if he gets close to any of the crates he's going to cry. Sully hop-scoots over and sniffs his leg.

I squat and pet Sully's incredibly soft ears. "Hi, there," I tell him. "Hello! What happened to you, little guy?"

"Found stuck in a ditch in Kentucky," Iris says as she comes back with a pack of disposable diapers. "Most likely hit by a car while chasing a squirrel. He's a smart little son of a gun, but he ain't got the sense God gave a rock." She takes Chewbarka from Daniel. "C'mere, you fuzzy little cutie." She executes a spectacular dog diapering while standing up with the package tucked under one arm.

I laugh. "You make that look so easy. It took me and Daniel ten minutes to figure out how to put a diaper on her, and we were sitting down."

"That was impressive," Mom says.

"Lots of experience." Iris holds Chewbarka up again and turns her back and forth. "Well-fed, that's good. Tongue doesn't stay in. You missing some teeth?"

"Yeah," Daniel says. "They got pulled a few years ago."

"And cataracts. Gray muzzle. What is she, about twelve? Thirteen?"

"Somewhere around there." Daniel is clenching his fists, looking at the dog missing its front leg and an eye.

"Tiny dogs can live a long time. She might have a good six or seven years left in her."

Daniel's face brightens. "Really?"

"What happened to that one?" I ask Iris, nodding at the dog missing a leg.

"That's Tripod. Found in pieces by some train tracks. Probably got the crazy knocked out of her, 'cause she's the chillest dog you'll ever meet."

"And this one?" I point at the lazy-looking greyhound Mom's still petting.

"Big Dave. Retired racer. Forty-mile-per-hour couch potato." She takes Chewbarka to the German shepherd and squats. Chewbarka is wiggling like a fish out of water again, trying to get away. "All right, come on, you're okay." Iris keeps up a steady, calm patter, petting Chewbarka's ears while she slowly inches closer to the shepherd, who lies watching. "See? Pearl's a quiet girl. No threat here." She blows a strand of hair out of her eyes and looks at Daniel. "Tina says you did a lot to keep this one safe."

"Oh," Daniel says. "Um. I guess." He's looking down at Sully, who's leaning on his leg and panting with a doggy smile. "He was—hit by a car?" He coughs like he's covering a sob.

"Think so. Rescue org down there couldn't afford all the surgery he needed, so they shipped him up here to us. We specialize in medical cases." She reaches a long arm out and rubs Sully's ears. "He had three surgeries and now he's ready for his forever home. Just gotta find somebody willing to squeeze out his pee five times a day and get him a custom wheelchair. And put up with the needy little goober."

Daniel squats and rubs Sully's ears, his eyes moving over the rest of the dogs before stopping on the shepherd.

"What about Pearl?" I ask.

Daniel shoots me a worried look.

"Bred most of the way to death by a backyard breeder, then starved when she stopped producing. Here you go, little one. You're okay." Iris carefully inches closer to Pearl with Chewbarka. Chewy is calmer, as if Iris's

308

voice is soothing. She cautiously sticks out her head and sniffs at Pearl's nose. Pearl wags once, then lies there looking tired.

"I know, baby girl," Tina says, rubbing Pearl's head. "I know. Okay. Here we go. Daniel, hang on to that dingbat's collar, will you?" She nods at Sully.

Daniel holds Sully's collar and Iris eases Chewbarka to the floor next to Pearl. Chewbarka glances at Pearl and then sits, looking up at Iris like she trusts her completely after knowing her for three whole minutes.

"Attagirls," Iris says, petting both dogs at once. "There we go. Polly, cool your jets." She directs this at the Chihuahua, who's coughing her head off.

"Is she sick?" Mom asks.

"Owner couldn't afford her meds, so they dumped her at the vet. Her enlarged heart presses her trachea and it makes her cough. I *know*," she says to Polly. "There's so much going on, you just gotta yell about it!" She touches Polly's chin through the crate. "Take a drink, dingie. You'll last longer."

I doubt Polly speaks English, but she does what Iris says, coughs a few more times and calms. The dogs in the rest of the house are calmer now too, the barking trailed off. Sully hop-drags over to me and noses my hands so I'll pet his ears.

I oblige, glancing at Daniel. He's looking at Pearl and wiping his face. When Chewbarka climbs into his lap, he turns into a faucet, big hiccuping sobs choking out of him. "God, this is embarrassing," he laugh-cries as he hugs Chewbarka with one hand and pets Pearl with the other.

"Don't be embarrassed," Iris says. "I've cried like that plenty times over these mutts. Their stories will break your heart, every time."

"I could never be as strong as you," he chokes. "I don't know how you do it."

"You *are* strong," Mom tells him. "You're here, doing this for Chewbarka."

"Tears don't mean you're weak," Iris says. "They mean you care real hard about what's right and good. That takes balls."

"Guts," I say. "It takes guts. My mom has no balls and she's a world champ at caring about right and good."

Iris and Mom both laugh. "I stand corrected," Iris says.

"Daniel, you're one of the strongest people I know," I tell him. "Everything you did for Chewbarka proves it. It's been the opposite of easy, but you did it anyway."

"You gotta use that passion, though," Iris says. "Find an outlet for it. Channel it. Otherwise it'll just tear you all up."

"Tina said that too," Daniel says. "You're both right. I need to—" He hiccups again, and I love the cute little shape of it. "I need to do something with this."

"Dogs like these need people like you," Iris says. "You're an old soul. Saw it soon as you came in. Old soul with a bright flame." She smiles at him. "You're gonna be all right, kid."

"I hope so," Daniel says.

"I *know* so," I tell him.

30
Human Too

Daniel

I give Chewbarka a last hug. "I'll miss you so much," I whisper in her fuzzy ear. I can't believe how much she's changed my life in a week. How she's helped me see what's important. What matters.

"You know," Iris says as she takes Chewbarka, "we got our Fall in Love Adoptathon coming up next weekend. We can use help getting the animals ready. Bathing 'em, cutting their nails, getting them gussied up so they can find forever homes."

"You won't—I mean, Chewbarka won't be put up for adoption, will she? She has sort of a complicated backstory—"

"Nope. Tina's gonna wait a few weeks till things cool down with that vet guy and then take her home," Iris says. "She told me what she did with the euthanasia. She's a fool, that woman, but I'd likely have done the same."

"Yeah. Me too." I scratch Chewbarka's ears. "Um . . . Iris, would you mind if I just . . . if I snip some fur off her to keep?" It's a weird request and I'm sure she'll laugh or say no—

"Sure." She pulls a bag of stuff from between two cages, roots around, and hands me a scissors. "How about some of this booty floof? She'll never miss it."

Ash quirks an eyebrow at me.

"For the rule-of-thirds assignment," I tell Ash. "A lock of booty floof, and the lock from Vlad the Rapid. Two personally significant locks."

Understanding comes over her face and she smiles. She leans down and snaps a quick photo of Chewbarka with her phone.

Iris snips fur from Chewbarka's tail, then binds it with a rubber band and hands it to me. "Sounds like I'll only have her for a couple weeks before Tina gets her, but come see her sometime."

"Really?"

"Of course. This goob always likes company." She

314

gives Sully an affectionate nudge with her foot and he picks up his food dish again. "Still not dinnertime, dude."

I smile at Iris. "Thanks again. It was great meeting you."

"You too." She walks us to the door. "Be safe getting home."

Once we're in Ash's mom's car, Ash in the back seat with me this time, I can't stop crying. It's not an ugly cry. It's a release of all the tension from the past week. The past two years. The past whole freaking *life*. Tears of gratitude that Chewbarka will be okay, that I think I've finally found people who understand and support me.

I curl up and drop my head into Ash's lap. It's forward of me, but I need human contact, and I hope Ash will be cool with it.

Ash runs their fingers through my hair as I drip tears on their jeans. Their hand feels so nice. As nice as it feels to cry without guilt. Without feeling weak or stupid for it.

After a long time driving in silence, the tears slow. "Why did you decide to tell Bella without asking me?" I say thickly.

Ash's hand stops moving. "I didn't. She was behind me in the hall and saw a photo of Chewy you texted me."

"Oh. So you—" Oops, I feel like a jerk. "You didn't find her and tell her?"

"No. She recognized Chewy right away. She asked if she was hurt and I said no. So then Bella realized Chewy was alive, and that I knew where she was. I didn't tell her you had her."

"Oh god, I'm so sorry. I assumed you told her on purpose."

"It's okay. Everything worked out."

I wrap my arm around Ash's legs. "You're the nicest person I know."

Ash laughs softly. "You're the nicest person *I* know."

"I saw your Instagram."

Ash's hand starts moving through my hair again.

"It's amazing. You're an artist with clothes." Oops. "I mean clothes are your medium. Your palette. Not like you're an artist who wears clothes. Even though you do." Ugh.

Ash makes a *pssht* sound and giggles.

"Should I call you 'they'?" I ask. "Or he, or she? Whatever you want, I'll use."

"They," Ash says like they're trying it out. "They/them. Yeah, I guess I'm they/them. For now. I'll keep you posted." I can hear the smile in their voice. "It'll change, for sure."

"I hope you wear some of those outfits to school. They were great. Especially that skirt with the fall colors."

Ash is quiet, and I think maybe I shouldn't have said that. Maybe it sounded like I preferred when they were a girl.

Which might be true. I don't know.

Not that it matters, because Ash is Ash no matter what I prefer, but still—

"I'll think about it," they say, and I'm glad for the interruption to my thoughts. Ash moves their hand to rest on my arm.

It's comforting.

Ash asks their mom if she'd be willing to take us to see Chewbarka soon.

"Of course," she says. "Maybe we can help Iris out with that adoptathon. She seemed to have her hands full."

"That'd be amazing," I croak. My nose is clogged from crying.

We sink into another comfortable silence. I close my eyes and try to work out what to tell Mom and Dr. Snyder. It takes a while of thinking and sniffling my stuffy nose, but I cobble a plan together: I can tell Dr. Snyder I was keeping her in a tent, which isn't a lie. And I can tell him she got out, and I tried to find her but she's gone.

It'll be hard to lie to his face without crying. But maybe, for once, tears could be useful. Because it'll look like I feel guilty about losing her.

As for Mom . . . well. I'll try a wild new tactic and tell Mom the truth. And hope she'll support me once she gets done being mad.

I really want her support. Need it.

Ash nudges my shoulder and points to Google Maps on her mom's phone stuck in the vent clip. "We're almost to your neighborhood."

I sit up and wipe my face with the back of my arm. "Can you drop me off at the end of the street?" I ask Ash's mom.

"I'd like to see you get safely inside," she says.

"My mom's going to be mad. She might yell."

"She'll be relieved first. Then mad."

That's probably true. "So maybe . . . a couple houses down?" I'm not in a hurry for Ash to see me get yelled at in my front yard.

"I'll park with the lights off and make sure you get in. Then we'll leave."

"Thanks. And thank you so much for doing this. It's great of you."

"Glad to help. But try to keep things tamer, will ya?

All these midnight drives are turning my green hair gray." She pats her head.

I laugh. "Of course. Um, here is good." We're three houses away.

She parks, turns off the lights, and cuts the engine.

"Thank you," I whisper to Ash. "For everything."

"Sure. I'll see you in a few hours at school."

Oof, that's soon. "Okay. Bye." I want to do something else, a hug maybe, I don't know, but Ash's mom is right there. So I get out and close the car door as quietly as I can.

Our living room light is on. I take my key out of my pocket and slide it in the lock. I twist the doorknob, but it's already opening.

Mom slams into me. "Oh my god, Danny! I was *so worried!*" She hugs me hard.

I'm smothered, but I hug her back. Her arms feel good even though she's about to rip my head off. She finally lets go and grips my shoulders, her hands like iron claws. "Don't you ever! Do this! Again!" She hugs me again, spins me, and pushes me into the living room. "Sit."

Mitch is on the couch, his hands pressed together and his mouth grim. "Well, you're not dead. Good job freaking everybody out. Truly A-plus work. Extra-credit points."

"Don't tell me you were actually concerned."

"Of course not." He has the wherewithal to look mad, even through the worry. "Just don't do this crap ever again. Mom's been driving me *nuts*."

Mom makes a *hmph* noise. "You were upset too."

"Sorry to keep you awake so late," I say to Mitch, half sarcastically but half not, because I'm sort of touched that he stayed up. That he was worried.

"*You* didn't keep me awake. She did. And Dad texted me like six thousand times asking if you were home yet." He shows me his screen.

Huh. How about that. "I guess you can tell him I'm home and go to bed."

"Whatever. I still have to finish my homework since I couldn't focus, thanks to you." He shoulder-checks me as he leaves. "Enjoy getting reamed out. You deserve it."

I sit on the couch with Mom and fold my hands. I'm not going to enjoy it, but he's right. I deserve it.

"So," she says.

"I'm sorry I didn't answer your texts and calls. But I need you to please stop making me feel like crap for having emotions."

Her mouth opens and then closes. She wasn't expecting that.

"When you do that, everything gets worse. I feel

320

rejected and alone and like you don't want me around. And then it just feeds on itself and makes me feel like crying even more."

The anger melts from her face. "Honey, I—"

"I'm sorry I hid all this dog stuff from you. It was important to me and I knew you wouldn't understand."

She grimaces like she's mad at herself. "Where's the dog now?"

"I went to drop her off with someone who can take care of her. I'm going to tell Doctor Snyder I was keeping her in our old tent, and that she escaped and I can't find her."

Mom presses her lips together. "I'm not wild about you lying to him. But I see your logic."

"Why does it have to be about logic? Why do emotions never get to play into it?"

She sighs. "I told you, honey. You're so—" She reconsiders. "I just don't want the world to hurt you for being vulnerable."

"Are you trying to hurt me to toughen me up? Because that makes me feel guilty and wrong and bad. I need you to stop project-managing my feelings."

She smiles ruefully. "Believe it or not, parents don't know what to do in every situation the minute they have kids. We're human too. We mess up."

"Dad said that too." I take a deep breath. I don't want to tell her this, but secrets are exhausting and I'm wiped the hell out and don't want to carry it anymore. I tell her about Grace being there when Ash and I biked to his apartment.

"I know about Grace."

I jerk my head back. "What?"

"She worked at that big ad agency where your dad and I met. She's a graphic designer. Really good one, actually. Now she's a single parent of a kid who has medical problems. I'm not . . ." She leans forward with her elbows on her knees, and I see what she was saying about parents being human too. Not having all the answers.

It makes me feel connected to her.

"I'm not thrilled about the situation," she says. "But your dad's a good listener, and she needs a friend." She shrugs. "I like her. Despite everything. She's a good person with too much on her plate."

I don't know what *everything* means. I don't think I want to. But I'm glad Mom knows what's going on. That it's not a big ugly secret Dad expects me to keep for him.

"I love you, kid."

"I love you too, Mom." It comes out rusty, and I

realize I haven't said it in a while. "I'm really freaking tired. Is it okay if I go to bed?"

Her face goes stern. "There's going to be a consequence for this."

"I know."

"I'm not sure what it'll be yet. Something that fits the crime of making me lose my mind with worry."

"We could adopt a dog and you could make me take care of feeding and walking her and everything," I suggest.

"Don't push your luck."

"Just a thought."

"Get to bed. Of course you pulled this on a weeknight." She yawns and rubs her head like she has a headache. "A few hours of sleep is better than none."

We stand up. "I really am sorry. I didn't mean to freak you out. I just wanted to make sure the dog was okay."

"I know. I get it." She hugs me quick and lets go. "Stop growing, will you? You two have been shorter than me your whole lives, and now . . ." She swats at my arm. "I'm not used to this."

"Tell me about it. My feet are so far away it's like they belong to somebody else."

"Go to bed. Off with you." She shoos me down the

hall. "Brush your teeth first. Your breath stinks like hamburgers."

I hope Ash didn't think so. "Sure, Mom. Good night."

She surprises me with a hug-tackle from behind. "I'm so glad you're safe," she says in my ear. Then she kisses my head and pushes me toward the bathroom. "Good night, Danny."

Mitch comes into my room a few minutes after I turn off my light. "I heard what you said about that Grace lady." He sits at the foot of my bed. "What do you think's gonna happen?" His voice is small in the darkness.

"I don't know." I really don't. And I'm way too tired to think about it.

"Do you think we should worry? I mean, I never stop worrying about them getting divorced. But do you think we should like . . . worry harder?"

I laugh, but not in a mean way. "Doesn't matter how hard you worry. Trust me."

He gets up to leave, but stops at my doorway and turns. "I'm sorry I've been a jerk since Cole's party," he blurts. "And that he dumped you as a friend and that I roped you into that thing with Fiona." He starts to step out.

"I'm sorry too."

He turns back but doesn't come in.

"I didn't realize kissing Fiona would be such a big deal," I say. "I didn't want her to think I thought she was gross or something."

"I guess it would've been awkward if you refused," he says stiffly.

"I didn't think about it from your perspective. Same as I didn't realize how much it bothered you when me and Dad did stuff without you. I get it now. I hope you can forgive me for being short-sighted."

We're quiet for a few moments.

"Well," he finally says. "I hope you can work stuff out with Cole. Like if that's a thing you want to do, if you don't hate him for ditching you or whatever."

"Thanks. I hope so too."

"Okay."

"Okay."

He lurks for a few more seconds. "Don't pull that again. I was totally freaked," he says. Then he hightails it out of my room before anything gets touchy-feely.

I fall hard into sleep.

31
Remix

Ash

Thursday morning, even though I've only had a few hours of sleep, I get up early. I want today's outfit to reflect where I am: still at least half dude, but on the way back to girl. A mix. In the crossfade where both are true.

It doesn't feel bad, or like an airport. Or a turtle.

In fact, I *like* it here.

I do about ten wardrobe remixes before settling on a pair of ripped black jeans, the knockoff blue Doc Marten boots I got from Goodwill, a sleeveless pink blouse with a lacy collar, and an unnecessary but cool wallet chain. I thicken my brows with an eyeliner pencil and tie my hair back, then look in my full-length mirror.

I look like five different styles had an argument and nobody won. But it feels fun and quirky and totally me right now.

At school, I head to my locker. Bella is there waiting. My stomach dips when I see her, but I walk over with my head high. I didn't realize till now that I'm taller than her. "Can I help you?"

"I, um." She looks down. One sneaker-clad foot is over the top of the other. She mumbles something I can't catch in the loud hallway.

"What?"

She meets my eyes. "I said I'm sorry. I just wanted to find my dog."

I blink.

"I shouldn't have threatened to out you or whatever." She looks up and down at my outfit and smiles faintly. "One of my friends showed me your Insta last night and . . . well, I listened to your song."

A smile stretches across my face. "You did?"

"Yeah." She seems to relax now that she doesn't think I'm going to yell at her. "It's really good. It made me realize I was, like . . . in tunnel vision, or whatever. Just focused on Chewbarka instead of seeing the big picture." She looks down the hallway.

"Okay. That's cool."

"Yeah, so the big picture, I mean, if Chewbarka's safe, and okay . . . that's what matters. I mean it sucks that—" She bites her lip. "That my dad did what he did. That *sucks* and I'm *so freaking mad* at him. But I'm glad somebody, whoever it was"—she gives me a hard look—"is taking care of her."

"She's in a great place," I say.

"Do you think you could tell me—"

"I can't, really. I'm sorry." I'm not the one who gets to decide this. If Daniel wants to tell her, he can.

She gives a frustrated sigh. "Right. Well." She nods and then starts to walk away.

"Hey, Bella," I call after her. "Thanks."

"For what?"

I shrug and smile. "I needed a kick in the pants."

Zoey watches me walk into our English classroom. She comes over and sits backward in the desk in front of me. "Is that song you posted last night the one you were writing for my band?"

Jeez, has the whole school seen it? "It was. But I guess it wasn't a good fit."

Jordan comes in. "Dude! That song was *fire!*"

I grin at her. "Thanks."

Zoey gives Jordan the stink eye, then turns back to me. "So what are you, then?"

"What do you mean?" I know what she means. I just want to make her say it.

"Are you a girl or a boy?"

I show her my fingernails. "Both. Obviously."

She rolls her eyes. "I mean what's in your pants?"

Jordan looks uncomfortable. "Uh, Zoey, that's kinda—"

"Armageddon," I say, then laugh at Zoey's annoyed face. "I don't ask you about the shape and size of your junk, so keep your questions out of mine. It's super rude."

Jordan covers her mouth to hide a laugh.

"You're a major disappointment." Zoey stalks over to her seat.

Jordan shakes her head as she watches Zoey walk away. "That's the opposite of punk solidarity." She lifts an eyebrow. "What do you think about forming a new band?"

"Not a girl band?"

"A band that dresses however the heck we want and plays good music. Regardless."

"I'm so in."

* * *

329

Toward the end of English, I text Daniel. **Bella apologized. What do you think of telling her where Chewbarka is? I don't think she'll tell her dad. She's super mad at him. But I'll keep a lid on it if you want. It's up to you.**

He texts back just before the bell rings. **If she swears she won't say anything to him, and you trust that she's telling the truth, I'll trust your judgment.**

A bubble of happiness rises in me. **Great! Maybe we can all visit Chewy this weekend.**

I'd like that so much, Daniel says.

In the cafeteria, Bella is eating with a group of kids by the door. I wave at her, then go sit by Griffey.

"Oh, look. You're you out loud." He grins at my outfit.

"I couldn't live with the thought of boring you to death. It weighed on my conscience."

"As it should've."

I do a double take. Bella's coming over with her lunch tray.

She nods at Griff and sits down. "I'm sorry I threatened your friend," she tells him, way more easily than she apologized to me this morning.

Griff shrugs. "Tell Ash that."

"I already did."

I nod to back her up.

"Righteous," Griff says. "I'm sorry people were garbage to you on social yesterday."

Bella sighs. "I kinda deserved it."

"No, you didn't," I say. "Nobody deserves that when they're freaked out about their dog."

She gives me a grateful smile.

"Listen," I say. "If I tell you where your dog is, will you tell your dad?"

"You're kidding, right? He literally tried to *kill* my dog and then *lied* about it. He's at the top of my shi—" She glances at the lunch monitor. "Uh, my crap list."

"I figured. Just had to check. So . . . Chewbarka is with a lady who fosters medical rescue dogs. I think we're going to visit her this weekend. Do you want to come if we do?"

Her whole face brightens. "Are you serious?"

"Serious as a penguin in a tutu. I mean yes, actually. I'm serious."

"Yes! Yes, yes, yes!" It's like beams of light are shooting out her eyes. "Gimme your phone. I'll put in my number. Which day are you going? What time?"

"I don't know yet." I hand over my phone and she types it in. "My mom said she'll drive us."

"Who's us?"

"You know Daniel Sanders?"

"Mitch's twin? The moody photographer kid?"

"Yeah." I think of Mitch as Daniel's twin, not the other way around. "Daniel's . . . well, he saved her life. It's a long story. He should be the one to tell you."

"Then I owe him big-time!"

Bella sits with us for a while. She and Griffey talk about how Bella has trouble in band because she's more focused on showing feeling when she plays than on the sheet music and hitting the exact right notes. Griff says he gets that, but that you can show feeling better if you understand the mechanics of the song. We talk about music and dogs and music again and the school dance and music again, and it's . . . surprisingly nice.

She might even turn out to be a friend.

When Bella gets up to go back to the kids she was sitting with before, I give her a smile and a wave. I love how my life has gotten remixed in the last few weeks. This new song is hella good.

32

Both Can Be True

Daniel

Ash messages me after school Thursday while I'm taking down the tent. They ask if I want to come over for dinner tomorrow.

Heck yes, I write. **But I might be grounded. I'll let you know.**

Before I collapse the ceiling of the tent, I place the lock of Chewbarka's fur and the lock for Vlad the Rapid on its floor. I arrange them diagonally and snap a photo using the grid. I'm sure Braden will make fun of me tomorrow when I present my picture of a dog's butt hair, but who gives a dang? I know what matters to me. And Ash will get it.

That's really all I care about.

That night, I ask Mom if I can go to Ash's for dinner. I expect a no, since she hasn't yet told me my consequence. But she surprises me by saying yes.

"Why?" I ask.

"Because restricting your social life isn't good for you."

"In that case . . . can I meet Cole on Sunday afternoon? He said he was available and I need to tell him I'm sorry."

Mom tilts her head. "I never understood what happened with you two."

"Chalk it up to me being too focused on myself. Plus, well . . . girls."

Her smile is warm. "You've got a busy mind in that head of yours. I'm glad you're making new friends. I'd like to meet Ash sometime. Your dad seemed impressed." Then she tells me that she doesn't want to punish me; she just wants to know she can trust me not to lie to her. My "consequence" is that I have to go to volunteering with her for the next month, and we're going to go to lunch afterward each time. Just us. She says she feels bad that she's been working so much, that she wants to connect better with Mitchell as well and they'll do something together too. She says spending time with the less fortunate helps you know what's important in life.

It's not the worst consequence. In fact . . . I'm kind of looking forward to it. The same way I'm looking forward to meeting with Cole and offering him a real apology.

It won't be easy. I'll probably cry.

But I cry because I care. And I think he understands that.

Before I go to bed, I text Dad my rule-of-thirds assignment with the two locks. **I like how "lock" can mean different things**, I write. **Like you're hiding something away, or like you're keeping it safe and close to your heart.**

Good photo, Dad answers. **Thought-provoking and nice. Nice composition too.** He asks if I'd like to go to a park on Saturday morning and take photos together.

How about we go to Mitch's swim meet? Sitting on metal bleachers for two hours smelling chlorine doesn't thrill me, but this could go a long way toward patching things up. **Then maybe we can go to IHOP. He's always starving after a meet.**

Dad's response is immediate: **I'd like that.**

* * *

I get to photography class a few minutes early on Friday, and I'm surprised to see Ash is already there too. I keep sneaking glances at them while I unzip my bag and get my folder out. I'm pretty sure they're wearing mascara and maybe eyeliner, but they still look boyish in their sleeveless Tony Hawk T-shirt and black pants with cargo pockets. I'm not sure what it means that I can't stop looking at them, if it means anything other than . . . well, than Ash is really nice to look at when they smile. And like . . . every other time. Nice to look at in general, no matter where they might be hanging out on the gender spectrum. They look up from writing something in their study planner and meet my eyes.

I never knew a smile could make me feel so seen. So appreciated and understood.

I hope Ash feels that way too when I smile at them.

The second the bell rings, Ms. Bernstein flips on the projector. "Thank you to everyone who submitted their photo via Google Classroom as instructed," she says. "I'm still waiting on a few of you, so please submit it now so we can get rolling. We'll start with table one. I'll display your photo and you'll come up and tell us why you picked your subject and why you arranged it how you did. Lauren, come on up."

336

My stomach flutters at the thought of standing in front of everyone and explaining my photo. I glance around table four. Fiona tugs at her right earlobe like she does when she's nervous. Braden's chewing a wad of gum like he's trying to pulverize it with his teeth. The only one of us who doesn't seem nervous is Ash.

My nerves ease off as kids take turns. Some of the photos are good—like one that shows a colorful pile of miscellaneous Legos next to an assembled Lego car arranged on a big green Lego board—but some are downright awful, like a picture of a bag of cheese puffs and a can of Coke on a cafeteria table. That kid obviously did his an hour ago.

Fiona is the first to be called at our table. She walks to the front of the room with her chin tilted up and her shoulders back. I recognize her debate persona taking over. She projects self-assurance as she tells us about her mom's baptism gown and her own baptism candle on a swath of altar fabric, and about putting each object at the top intersections to show there's more yet to be written to the story.

Braden goes next. His photo is a pair of torn-up leather gloves and a cracked motorcycle helmet on a street. "These were my mom's," he says in an abrupt tone. "She got killed last year by a dipwad driving drunk. Now we're rich from the insurance but I'd rather have her than the money." He hurries to his seat without waiting for Ms. Bernstein to ask him anything about it.

Ash gives his shoulder a quick squeeze. Braden seems like he's trying not to cry. The room is full of awkward silence.

I stand up quickly. "I'll go next." I walk to the front while Ms. Bernstein opens my photo. I face the class and clear my throat. "The lock on the left is my bike lock. Without my bike, I couldn't have saved a dog's life. The lock of hair on the right is from the dog. The background is the floor of the tent I kept her in while I figured out how to get her to safety." I look at Ash. "I had some help, and I'm proud of what we did, even though it was hard."

"Very good," Ms. Bernstein says. She glances at Braden, who's looking down at a notebook and seems to have regained his composure. "Ash?"

I walk back to our table. My knees are shaky with relief that my turn is over. Ash and I brush our fingers together as we pass.

Ms. Bernstein displays Ash's photo. It's two drawings of figures like you'd see on a bathroom door sign, cut out and set on a plain white fabric. Half of each drawing is guy-shaped and half is girl-shaped, and there are different patterns inside each half. "These two drawings represent my gender and my love of music," Ash says in a steady voice. "I have synesthesia, so when I hear sounds, I see shapes in my mind. I always categorized the shapes of music by male and female. Guy music to me was made of thick, angled shapes, and girl music was made of flowing lines. But I realized recently how limiting it is to categorize sounds, or anything else, as one thing or the other. So I drew what I used to think of as guy music and girl music inside these gendered symbols, and then I mixed them together. I wanted to show that being human comes first, and the parts that make up who you are—your gender, the music you like, what you wear, everything else—is secondary."

For the first time all year, Ms. Bernstein looks impressed. "I'd say you accomplished your goal, Ash. Excellent work." She calls someone at table five, but her eyes linger on Ash's drawings for a moment before she flips to the next kid's photo.

Ash sinks into the seat next to me. "Phew," they say under their breath. "I was freaked out of my noodle up there."

Fiona stifles a giggle. "You did *so* good."

"Yeah, not bad," Braden mutters, his face still aimed down at his notebook.

"Could you tell I rehearsed it like fifty times last night?" Ash whispers to me as the table five kid starts talking.

"Not at all," I say quietly. "You were perfect."

That *smile*.

Dinner at Ash's apartment Friday evening is really good. It's simple, burgers and baked potatoes and salad. But it's fun to watch Ash and their mom constantly switch back and forth between arguing and trying to crack each other up. It's like a sport. Bicker-joking.

After dinner, Ash pulls on a black hoodie with a picture of a wave on it and we walk Booper. The air is cool and fresh and crisp, and the sun is heading into a colorful sunset. Booper is the cutest little dude with his soft, floppy ears and his big front feet that turn outward and his tail that wags as he walks in the golden late-day light. "He looks so happy," I say.

"He always does. I don't know if he actually is or if it just seems like he is because of his whole . . . everything." They wave their hands at Booper like they waved them at me back when they said I looked exhausted and offered to stay with Chewy overnight.

I smile. "Ever wish you were a dog?"

"Yeah. Seems way simpler."

"No lie. Feel what you feel, take a nap, eat food, take a nap. Go for a walk. Take a nap." Booper finds a Highly Interesting Smell by a tree and roots around in the dirt, chuffing and snuffing. We stop walking so he can have a good sniff. "I like that I can be myself with you," I tell Ash. "You've never made me feel bad about being a basket case."

"You're not a basket case. You're a person who feels really hard."

"You know what I mean. How like . . . society says it's not okay for guys to show feelings. So everyone thinks I'm a weirdo when I do it."

"You're not a weirdo either. But yeah, I know what you mean. Guys are supposed to stuff their feelings down. Grunt a lot. Move heavy stuff and be sweaty and manly."

"Hulk smash," I agree. "It's a load of crap."

"Total load. Stoic doesn't mean dude. And emotional doesn't mean girl. I feel dumb for just recently figuring that out."

I guess I had that programmed in my head too. And now Ash is making me reconsider it. "What made you figure it out?"

Ash picks up a red maple leaf, holds it to the lowering sun, and twirls it. "My dad always made me confuse emotions with gender. He'd say stuff like, 'Boys like to act confident and tough. Girls tend to be compassionate and empathetic.' Like everything is always male or female and there's nothing in between. Mom was always arguing with him about it, 'cause she's Mom and she fixes trucks for a living."

"Your mom is basically the coolest."

"She's pretty okay." Ash smiles. "I get angsty that I can't be a strong woman like my mom if I'm a guy part-time."

"You totally can. And you should tell her that. It would make her really happy."

Ash looks down, blushing. "I always wanted her to be right when she'd argue with Dad about gender. But I couldn't believe that she *was* right because . . . I don't know. I guess when you're younger, 'either/or' makes more sense than 'some of both.' But life is complicated. Sometimes two things that seem like opposites are both true. There are a million ways to look at anything."

"That's what I like about photography. You can shoot the same subject a hundred ways and create a unique picture each time." I look at Ash sideways. "I'd love to photograph you. Sometime. If you'd be okay with that."

Ash's blush deepens. It's so pink and lovely in the golden light.

"You're a little of both. I mean a little of a lot of things that are really interesting. I mean you're a *lot* of some interesting things. Some really good things, like funny and cool and smart and you love dogs like I do, which is awesome, and your hair is wicked cool and . . . um, please interrupt me so I quit embarrassing myself."

"You're interesting too." Their hazel eyes focus on my lips. Then they look away.

I clear my throat and we start walking again. "You did such a great job presenting your rule-of-thirds photo today. It made me proud to be your friend."

Tears spring up in Ash's eyes, then quickly spill over. "That . . . might be the nicest thing anyone's ever said to me." They laugh, and it has enough of a sob in it that my eyes water as well. "Thank you," Ash says. "Yours was great too."

"You should give those drawings to somebody in the office. They could use them to label the neutral bathroom, since the girls' and boys' have drawings but that one doesn't."

Ash laughs. "You noticed that?"

I nod. "I'm seeing things differently since you came out to me. Like more clearly."

"Yeah, same."

I want to hug them, but it feels forward. I clear my

throat. "I like that I connect with you on two levels. Like a guy friendship level and a girl—um, a girl romantic level." It's scary to say. "It's confusing, but honestly . . . I like it. It's a good confusion."

Ash wipes their eyes and doesn't say anything. I start to think maybe that was *too* open, that I'm taking this honesty/vulnerability thing too far because that's what I do with emotions and—

"Well. If we're being honest," Ash says. "I like you whether I'm a guy or a girl. And that might make things weird for you, if you don't know if you like . . . you know. What you like."

"I don't think I have that figured out yet." The word *crush* doesn't seem right for what I felt for Ash when I thought they were a girl. It was . . . bigger. Better. More real. Like a crush is a thing you feel from a distance, but what I felt, maybe still feel . . .

Okay, yes, still feel.

Oh my gosh.

What I feel for Ash is right here. Living and breathing and walking around with me. Moving back and forth between us like it has a soul of its own.

I clear my throat. "Well. I'm glad we know each other. No matter what."

Ash smiles. "I'm glad too. It worked out good for

Chewbarka that we do."

"I'd say so."

There's a pause, and it feels a little awkward. Then, at exactly the same time, we both say, "Do you want to—"

Ash laughs. "You first."

"No, you."

"No, you."

"Do you want to go to the dance together?" I blurt. "We could go as friends, or as . . . I don't know. Co–dog rescuers?"

"Oh." Ash's face shows surprise, then disappointment at the word *friends*. "Um."

My stomach sinks. "Oh my gosh, I'm sorry. Rewind thirty seconds and pretend that didn't happen, okay?" I shouldn't have asked and then said *as friends*, way to give a mixed signal Danny, you confused mess of a boy—

"Actually, I was going to ask you . . . if you want to help with that Fall in Love Adoptathon Iris was talking about." Ash tucks a strand of hair back. "It's the same day as the dance. Mom and I are planning to help." They look up at me. "It doesn't have to be a date, or whatever. If you don't want it to be. I just thought—"

"Yes!" I say. "Yes times a million. I'd love to do that with you instead of the dance!"

"Oh—really?" They smile.

"Yeah. Absolutely. One hundred percent."

"Cool." They look at their shoes. "I mean, we could do both. The event during the day and the dance in the evening."

"Oh, you're right. Yeah, that would be amazing. Let's do it!"

"It's a date, then," Ash says brightly. "Or just, you know, two people hanging out. Whichever."

"How about we don't worry what to call it? We could just . . . enjoy the day."

They look relieved. "Yeah. Good call."

"I shouldn't have said 'as friends,'" I tell them. "I want to go as more than friends."

"You do?"

I nod. "But don't, like, feel like you have to dress as a girl if you don't feel it. I still want to be your date if you're, you know, in a suit. Or something guy-ish or whatever." The words feel jumbled and clumsy.

"I think I'm past the point of dressing to meet other people's expectations." Ash smiles. "I'll wear what feels right that day."

"Good. I guess what I'm saying is it doesn't matter what you dress like because it's *you* I like. Your smile, your laugh, your music, your dog, your—um, your everything."

Ash is trying not to smile. "I like your everything too."

We reach a bench by the playground. Ash sits and picks Booper up. They rub his ears and press their forehead to his and tell him what a good doggo he is. Booper laps it up, wagging and ramming Ash's chest. Then he climbs into my lap and rams me with his head.

Ash smiles. "I took Booper to the zoo once," they say. "I wanted to show him all the other animals. But they only had two cats and one small dog."

I tilt my head.

"Yeah, it was a real shih tzu."

It takes me a second. Then I burst out laughing.

Ash scratches Booper's ears. I can't stop watching that beautiful one-dimple smile.

33

Liberated

Ash

The minute we drop Daniel off at his house, Mom asks if he and I are a thing now.

"It's complicated. I have no idea. But at least he knows why I'm Ash now, and doesn't assume I'm a girl all the time." I rub at a smudge on the car window that's blocking my view of the excellent sunset. "I just don't know if . . . you know. If he'll wind up liking boys too."

She gives me a sideways smile. "Pretty sure it's not gonna be an issue. Based on how he was looking at you when we brought the dog to Iris, and tonight at dinner."

I'm glad it's dim in the car, because I can feel my ears going pink. "I think I don't wanna talk about this."

"Fair enough. I didn't want my mom involved in my love life when I was a teenager either. Or still. Even though my love life is currently nonexistent."

"I don't think I wanna talk about yours either."

"Let's play favorite random crap."

I relax into the seat. "You first."

We come up with categories, like roller coasters and Jolly Rancher flavors and daydreams and dog breeds and sunset colors, and tell each other our favorites. It's nice, because we can go as deep or as basic into any answer as we want. "I'm glad you're my kid," Mom says after telling me her favorite band is Green Day, which I know 'cause she listens to them all the time like it's still 1995.

"I am pretty great," I say.

"Don't get a big head about it."

"Too late."

She smacks my arm and tells me I'm lucky I'm cute.

I look out at the sunset. "Can we talk about Dad?"

"Whoa!" She glances at me. "Where'd that come from?"

"I just . . . need to."

She gets a faraway look for a minute, then says, "Okay, shoot."

"Why is he so . . . so *Dad*?"

She smiles ruefully. "I'd ask you to narrow it down, but I think I can guess." She takes a moment to gather her thoughts. "You know how your grandma Rose and grandpa Roger, my parents, went to college? And I did too?"

I nod. "And Dad's parents didn't, and he just went to medical technician training."

"Right. Your dad's always been self-conscious about not having a degree. Notice how he uses bigger words than he needs to? He does *not* like it when people think his lack of education makes him less than them somehow. He's very sensitive about that."

"I . . . did not know that." Though it makes sense, now that I think about it.

"I used to tell him I valued who he was and never thought less of him because of where he came from. But it seemed to rub salt in the wound. He said it was like a rich person telling a poor person, 'You still have value even though you're poor.'" Regret passes over her face. "It hurt him to hear that from me. I didn't understand why then, but I do now, and I wish I'd handled it differently."

Kinda like how Bella and I butted heads over the dog, but now we might be friends. "Seems like a lot of arguments are like that. You don't get where the other person is coming from until you've had time to cool your jets."

Mom nods. "When you were little, Dad thought you were just experimenting. Trying things on, seeing what fit. He kept waiting for you to 'figure it out.' He comes from a family that tends toward reductive thinking. Know what that means?" She stops at a red light.

"Like stripping out complexities? Because it's easier to slap a label on something. So you don't have to think about the whole complicated everything of it."

"Look at you coming in with the big brain." She ruffles my hair. "He rejected his parents' beliefs—that trans folks are looking for attention, that it's wrong to be gay, et cetera. But he didn't go deeper to reject the *way* they thought." The light turns green and she hits the gas.

"Meaning . . . he seems liberal on the surface, but when you scratch that away, you get a conservative?"

"Eh, it's not that cut-and-dried. It can be hard to change the way you learn to think when you're young. The content of your thoughts, you can change by learning new facts. The structure of thoughts is a different ball game. Make sense?"

I nod. "Do you still love him?"

She sigh-laughs. "Ask a harder question next time, will you?"

"Sorry not sorry." I want to know. And I trust her to be honest with me.

"He's a stubborn cuss who's too attached to being right. But also . . . his parents weren't affectionate. Ever. They taught him some screwed-up ways of processing the world. So when I think about little-boy him, learning coping mechanisms for how sad and alone that made him feel . . . yeah, I have sympathy." Her face hardens. "But when it started negatively impacting you, my sympathy dried up. Convincing you that his point of view is the only logical one felt more important to him. He said me disagreeing with him on that and parenting you differently meant I didn't respect his point of view. He already had a hang-up about it because I grew up in a higher income bracket than he did. So it was kind of a perfect storm, and then you got appendicitis and I did the name change and, well, you know the rest of that story."

I mull it over. "Did you ever have to change anything about yourself that was negatively impacting me?"

She laughs. "Let me tell you about the year I learned how to be patient. Your terrible twos were *epic*. Gave me all the gray hairs I cover up with green."

I smile. "So you're saying you're a better person now

because I was stubborn?"

"*Everything* about being your mom makes me a better person."

My smile is so big it hurts my ears.

When we get home, the sky is still flaming orange and purple. Griffey's coming over soon, but I have time to sneak in a quick run. I change my clothes, tie on my too-tight shoes, grab my headphones, and head out.

I trip a couple times because I'm so busy looking at the excellent sunset. As it fades to a dusky purple, I find a running groove and enjoy it for a while before heading back.

Griffey's in my room when I get home. He proudly shows off his brand-new plain white Converse. "They're so pure," he says. "Like two baby bunnies." He takes a bunch of Sharpies out of his bag. "They need a rainbow alien. Or peace signs and hearts and gay symbols. Will you help me decorate them?"

"Sure." I kick off my stinky shoes.

"You should get a white pair too. You could decorate them with the nonbinary colors."

I make a face. "Gender nonbinary sounds so restrictive. Like your gender can either be binary or not binary.

Which . . . is a binary."

"You're more like gender-nonconforming anyway."

"Gender noncompliant. Gender disobedient." I uncap his red Sharpie and pretend I'm gonna stab him.

He holds up his hands. "Held in contempt of gender."

"Busted for smuggling my gender across state lines."

"You're Schrödinger's gender!" He snatches the Sharpie back.

"Did you just compare my gender to a dead cat?"

"And a live one. Simultaneously." He takes a pencil off my desk and starts sketching an alien on one of his shoes. "So is Daniel bi, then, or what?"

I pick up a skirt and T-shirt. "Are you in cahoots with my mom? She's all up in my business about it too."

He shrugs. "You could invite him to the next Rainbow Alliance meeting." He digs in his pocket and comes out with a package of Sour Patch Kids. "Want one?"

I take a green one. "I don't know if it matters what Daniel is. I think labels are more hassle than they're worth. It's easier to just like . . . *be*."

"That's the stinking truth. And anyway, it's about the junk in your heart, not the junk in your pants." He chucks a red Sour Patch Kid at me.

I snatch it out of the air and grin. "Darn right."

Griff and I stay up till almost midnight, playing *Mario Kart* and decorating his shoes and talking about school and music and nothing and everything. He finds karaoke pop songs on Spotify and sings into my hairbrush. It's everything a Friday night should be.

After he leaves, I put on my Ramones shirt with fuzzy unicorn pants and brush my teeth. Above the toilet, a new cross-stitch has been added to the ones that say *Have a nice poop!* and *Buddha would shut the toilet lid.* Along the outside edge of the new one, Mom has stitched a bunch of emojis: the strong arm, the pink flower, the dude with the beard, the lipstick, the one flipping the bird, the nail polish. The unicorn and the you-rock sign and the high-heel shoe. The middle says

This bathroom has been liberated from the artificial construct of a gender binary.

I snap a photo of it and post it to my story. I tag her in it and add #BestMomEver.

After I brush my teeth, I climb into bed and look up the Gatorade video. I've been pushing away the thought that it'll always be out there. That I'll always have a nagging fear that people I know will find it, and see that happening to me, and think less of me for it.

But really . . . it's part of me now. Trying to pretend it never happened feels like denying part of who I am. And boy, am I done with that game. Anyone who thinks less of me because a few jerks teamed up and humiliated me isn't someone whose opinion I care about anyway. Or who I even want in my life.

So maybe it's time to say that. Time to claim *all* of me, including what I went through that made me who I am now.

I was so desperate to hide the Gatorade video when I started at Oakmont. So tied in knots about the gendered signs on the bathroom doors.

Not anymore.

I download the video and post it to my Insta. Being yourself can be a dangerous business, I write. Bullies can make you want to hide who you are, especially if you're unsure who that is. But incidents like this can also show you what really matters.

I look down the hall at the light coming from the living room. Mom's listening to Green Day. I picture her working on a cross-stitch, something subversive and funny and totally Mom.

I know who I am, I write. It took a while, but I've finally found my voice.

Good luck getting me to shut up now.

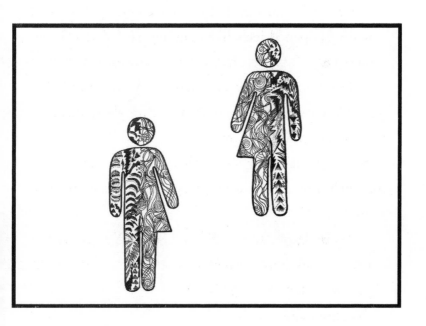

Acknowledgments

SuperAgent John: Thank you for being the first industry pro to believe in my writing. Thank you for continuing to believe in it through every spectacular faceplant, and thank you for aiming my fervent but scattered ambition in a focused direction. Who knew I had a middle grade book in me? You did. You're smart like that.

Editor extraordinaire Alyssa: The kindest, most brilliant kindred-soul editor I could have hoped for. Thank you for shaving off the story's rough edges and tightening up its saggy bits and guiding me through the publishing process with compassion, humor, and wisdom. Your insights made this book so much better, and I am deeply grateful.

Thank you to everyone at HarperCollins who saw the potential in this story and brought it from a draft on my laptop to vivid, breathing life. Thank you to Teo DuVall for a cover that fits the story so beautifully, and thank you to Erin Fitzsimmons for your design expertise in fitting all my silly little sound drawings into the text at just the right spots. Thank you to Jacqueline Hornberger, Veronica Ambrose, and Nicole Moreno for your eagle eyes in catching my typos and inconsistencies

To all the good souls who slogged through early drafts of this book and all the books I wrote before I wrote this one, who encouraged me and pulled me out of the doldrums and provided essential solidarity: Thank you. A special shout-out to Cara Olexa, Sid Birkett, Amy Bearce, Sara Bennett-Wealer, Bruce Hamren, Sarah Archer, Allison Haden, Jean Maskuli, Pat Pujolas, and Georgine Getty.

To my teachers, friends, and fellow parents who provided support, guidance, kindness, and much-needed camaraderie: Karen Anderson, Larissa Howell, Renee Jacobs, Jen Decker-Strainic, Katie Kovach, Sherrie Inness, and Amy Goff: Thank you for being there when I needed you, and thank you for everything you've given me.

To Mom and Pops, who have supported me through every hair color, questionable tattoo, and life stage: Thank you. It's so good to know I always have a home to come home to.

To Matt, thank you for being the bestest co-parent possible to our wild child and our herd of disabled, disheveled, and discount-rack dogs. Nobody can make me laugh in the trenches of four-a.m. kitchen-floor poop cleanups like you can. I love you.

To my wild child, my inspiration: Thanks for letting me write down all the brand-new sentences that come out your mouth; thanks for bouncing off the walls of our house and my heart, drumming a beat everywhere you go; thank you for the songs you sing and the characters you draw and the love that fills you and the hope that drives you. Thank you for answering my questions about day-to-day middle school life and telling me what I'm getting right and being frank when I suck at stuff. Thank you, most of all, for being you out loud. I love and adore you beyond measure.

And finally, thank you to my dogs. Y'all are stinky punks who make a boat-load of messes on the daily, but I sure do love you.